D1557850

The Beckoning Ice

Also by Joan Druett

IN THE WIKI COFFIN SERIES
A Watery Grave
Shark Island
Run Afoul
Deadly Shoals

PROMISE OF GOLD TRILOGY
Judas Island
Calafia's Kingdom
Dearest Enemy

OTHER FICTION
A Love of Adventure

NON FICTION
The Elephant Voyage
Tupaia, Captain Cook's Polynesian Navigator
Island of the Lost
In the Wake of Madness
Rough Medicine
She Captains
Hen Frigates
The Sailing Circle (with Mary Anne Wallace)
Captain's Daughter, Coasterman's Wife
She Was a Sister Sailor
Petticoat Whalers
Fulbright in New Zealand
Exotic Intruders

The Beckoning Ice

A Wiki Coffin Mystery

by

Joan Druett

THE BECKONING ICE

AN OLD SALT PRESS BOOK, published by Old Salt Press, a Limited Liability Company registered in New Jersey, U.S.A..

For more information about our titles go to
www.oldsaltpress.com

First published in 2013

ISBN 978-0-9922588-3-2

Glossary (pages 277-289) compiled by Rick Spilman
and Joan Druett

Antarctic Ocean, February 3, 1839

When the crew of the sealer *Betsey* of Stonington, Connecticut, met their close brush with death, the schooner was steering northeast, heading home after a short but very profitable season far south of Cape Horn.

Just before noon it began to snow hard, but the strong wind was both favorable and constant, and the old schooner was cutting through the water like a racer, so the mate, who was in charge of the deck, didn't feel unduly alarmed. When he called out to a seaman, however, something very strange happened, so he belatedly sent for the captain.

When Captain Noyes came up from the warm fug of the cabin, he stopped short, partly because he couldn't see his hand in front of his face, and partly because the first breath of fresh air cut like a knife. In twelve years of sailing the Antarctic south he had never felt attacked by the cold like this. He could hear the men on watch stamping their numb feet and flapping their arms about their chests. The deckboards were hidden beneath a thick, slippery blanket, while more snow swept down on them in undulating sheets. It was as if the *Betsey* was racing from nowhere to nowhere, trapped in a world of swirling white. God, Noyes thought, he should have been called up long before, and he silently cursed the mate for his idiotic bullheadedness.

Stumbling and sliding in the blinding murk, he finally found the offender. "How long has it been so thick, Mr. Jeffrey?"

"Since before noon," said the mate.

"So what made you finally decide it might be a good idea to send for me?"

Mr. Jeffrey winced at the sarcasm. "It's just that it seemed so strange, sir."

"Strange? What in hell are you babbling about?"

"An echo came back when I shouted out for a hand to heave the log — like there's a nearby ship, or something."

"Echo? What the devil?" Then Noyes abruptly realized the full horror of their situation. "Ice!" he cried, and an echo instantly sounded, *"Ice, ice, ice."*

He shouted, "There's a bloody berg somewhere near!" Desperate to stop the schooner in her headlong course, he screamed out orders — too late. The snow abruptly thinned, revealing a tall ice island on the starboard bow. At the same instant, the sails sagged and flopped. The berg had stolen their wind, and the schooner was moving only by her own momentum.

Seventy-foot cliffs reared over them, blotting out the sky. The *Betsey* surged slowly through the glutinous, near-frozen water, parallel to the shore, just a dozen yards from foaming reefs. The decks were utterly silent, every seaman rigidly still as the schooner glided stealthily on. Noyes was holding his breath,

2

conscious of the heavy thud of his heart in his ears. Then, with a jolt of primitive horror, he stared up into the eyes of a corpse.

The dead man was standing on a high ledge, his back to the cliff. Noyes could see him in detail. It was obvious that the man had been bludgeoned to death. Thick gouts of blood lay frozen on his cheeks and forehead, and clotted his thick, black beard. Yet his expression was so alive with savagery that Noyes felt superstitiously convinced he would become animated, if thawed. Then the scouring of exposed flesh by wind and weather registered. The dead man had been frozen to the cliff for months, if not years.

The *Betsey* reached the extremity of the berg, and the wind seized her sails again. Away she raced towards a clear horizon, leaving the corpse far behind.

One

 *E*ight days later, as the *Betsey* was breasting the first billows of the icy south Atlantic, the lookout raised a sail.

The wind, most unusually, was ahead, so that Noyes was forced to beat his way east, while ships steering for the Pacific were making an easy passage. As a result, by the time the little white blot of canvas on the horizon had divided into three, the *Betsey* had made very little headway. It was as if she were waiting for the oncoming ships.

Another hour, and the trio could be seen from deck—a smart brig and two big ships, making a grand show with their clouds of fully set sail—and the lookout aloft could see the great ensigns billowing over their sterns.

"United States Navy," he hollered.

"Good God," cried Noyes, leaping aloft with his spyglass. "It must be the exploring expedition!"

He couldn't believe it. The United States Surveying and Exploring Expedition had been anticipated for the past ten years, starting out as a grand scheme that was supposed to establish the country's scientific reputation, but which had been turned into a laughing-stock by delays and political shenanigans. For a long time it had looked as if the project would never get underway, but last September, when the *Betsey* had spoken an Atlantic

4

whaler, the captain had told Noyes that the fleet had sailed from Norfolk, Virginia, in August, and was finally on its way to chart the Pacific and render it safe for American commerce. So why the hell hadn't the ships arrived in the Pacific already? In the intervening six months they could have crossed the whole damn ocean—they should be in Australia!

Captain Noyes had no intention of trying to learn the answer. The wind might be ahead, but the weather was fairer than could be expected, and he had his holds packed with furs that he was anxious to get onto the New York market. Even more crucially, he didn't want anyone to know where he'd been. After forging further south than any man had sailed for years, the *Betsey* had blundered over an icy islet crammed with seal-life, one of the very few rookeries that had not been discovered already, and William Noyes was determined to keep the secret to himself.

Accordingly, he ordered a change in course, to give the fleet a wide berth. But, instead of respecting his desire for privacy, the brig broke away from the other two, and tacked to intercept. Again, Noyes ordered the schooner to be put about. However the brig, a dashing little craft with a piratical look about her, was much swifter than the ponderous *Betsey*, easily countering every evasive maneuver.

Then she was alongside. An order to heave-to for boarding was bellowed over the water, Captain Noyes grumbled out instructions, and the *Betsey* doused canvas. He and the sixteen men of his crew lined the rail, watching glumly as the brig stilled with a flourish, and sent over a boat.

"*Betsey* ahoy," said the officer in charge, and stepped on board without waiting for an invitation. He was a tall, well-groomed young man with fluffy blond sideburns, splendidly garbed in a blue uniform with a single gold epaulette—quite a contrast to Noyes who, like his men, was wearing a smelly sealskin suit.

"Lieutenant George Rochester, commanding U.S. brig *Swallow*," the visitor affably said, and held out his hand.

That was something else Noyes had heard—that the exploring expedition was commanded by passed midshipmen and mere lieutenants. Hiding his opinion of this, he introduced himself in the usual manner, giving his name, trade, and last port.

"And you're bound for the States? Excellent—just as we figured," Rochester said heartily when Noyes nodded. "Every manjack who can write is scribbling letters, and we'd be obliged if you'd carry 'em home for us."

So he was to be the mailman for an exploring expedition, Noyes thought with irritation. When he looked over the water he saw that the two large ships had come up with the *Swallow* and were laying to, looking like great fragile birds with the light gleaming on their sails. If he had been the commodore, they would have been making all the speed they could while the weather held, instead of dallying in this treacherous place.

Hiding that opinion, too, he grunted, "Aye, I'll wait for you to bring them on board—unless the weather changes."

"Much obliged." Then Rochester cocked his head to one side, and went on, to Noyes's alarm, "Am I right in saying the sealing season ain't over yet?"

The sealing captain warily nodded.

"And you're homeward bound already? You've been lucky."

Noyes grudgingly confirmed that they had indeed been fortunate.

"We're heading for Hoste Island, where the other four vessels are waiting at Orange Harbour, and will carry out scientific observations there," Rochester confided. "Then we'll sail into deep southern latitudes, to discover Antarctica. What d'you reckon about that, sir?"

Noyes was far too astonished to answer. It was February 1839, and the brief summer was almost over. It was a crazy time to sail far south.

"So I'd be obliged if you'd accompany me to the flagship *Vincennes*—with your logbook, to make an official report," Rochester went on. "Captain Wilkes will want to record your route, and note details of the conditions."

Noyes winced, because this was exactly what he'd dreaded. Then inspiration struck. "What a relief!" he cried.

He saw Rochester blink, no doubt remembering how the *Betsey* had done her utmost to avoid him, and went on with an inappropriate grin, "On account of we have a murder to report."

Rochester listened with deep attention to the story of the near miss and the sighting of the corpse. "You're a lucky man indeed," he marveled. "Quite apart from the cadaver, that iceberg is a hazard for shipping. We should report it at once!"

"I quite agree," said Noyes, and jumped into the boat before Rochester had time to remember the logbook.

An order was given, and the oarsmen shoved away from the side of the *Betsey* — but headed for the smaller of the two big ships. Rochester explained, "Murder being part of the business in hand, we'll drop by the *Peacock* first, to pick up Wiki Coffin."

Startled, Noyes echoed, "Wiki Coffin? Not the son of Captain William Coffin?"

"The famous Captain William Coffin of Salem," Rochester agreed. "You know him?"

"Quite well," said Noyes, still amazed. Captain William Coffin had made a fortune as a privateer in the 1812 war against the British, and then had gone into the China trade, carrying Yankee silver to Canton and returning with fabulous cargoes of tortoiseshell, lacquer wood, silks, and tea. At some stage in this dashing career he had fathered a son in the Bay of Islands, New Zealand — not that anyone in Salem had known about it until Coffin had carried the half-Maori boy home to his middle-aged, childless wife. The rightful Mrs. Coffin, understandably, had been scandalized and mortified. Naturally, too, the gossip had run hot and heavy. At the time, Noyes had had the impression that all New England was talking about it.

But that had been minor, compared to the scandal Wiki himself had caused four years later, when he and his father were visiting Noyes's village. Wiki, by then a broad-shouldered young man of sixteen with warm brown skin, hazel eyes that glinted blue in certain lights, and an infectious humor that creased up his face when he grinned, was handsome enough to catch any girl's eye—and he had caught the eye of a headstrong lass who happened to be the fiancée of one of Stonington's most prominent merchants. And instead of being discreet, they had flaunted their affair.

Noyes, like every other red-blooded male, had been outwardly outraged and inwardly envious. As for Captain Coffin, he'd been so furious with Wiki that the next time he sailed off to the Orient he had left the boy behind. The last Noyes had heard, Mrs. Coffin had packed Wiki off to a missionary college in remotest New Hampshire to learn better manners, and, incidentally, how to convert his savage brethren.

That had been eight years ago. Noyes wondered what had happened in the meantime. He said, "What the devil is a lad like Wiki Coffin doing on the exploring expedition?"

"He's our linguister. In fact," added Rochester broodingly, "he was berthed on the *Swallow* until just over a week ago, when Captain Wilkes shifted him from my brig to the *Peacock*."

Rochester's tone was unmistakably resentful, but Noyes ignored this, exclaiming, "Your *what*?"

"Linguister. And will probably act as our pilot, too, once we get into the tropics. He knows the islands well, including their languages. Speaks Portuguese and Spanish, too, so serves as our translator. He berths with the scientifics," Rochester concluded, while the man in the head of the boat hooked on to a line dangling down the side of the *Peacock*. "So I should find him in the wardroom, eating supper. Wait here," he instructed. "I'll be a minute, no more."

And with that, Rochester sprang up the ladder, which was only five cleats high, the *Peacock* being a flush-decked corvette with just four feet of freeboard. Studying the ship as the young officer disappeared, Noyes thought she was a fine-looking craft, built like a greyhound and obviously a racer, but guaranteed to be uncomfortably wet. A hell of a ship to take into the Antarctic, he thought, then wondered why Wiki Coffin was being summoned to hear the report of the murder.

Rochester, meantime, cast a casual salute in the direction of the squad lined up to pipe him on board before striding aft towards the afterhouse built across the poop. The door to Captain Hudson's quarters was in the front of this house, but he had no intention of wasting time by paying his respects. Captain Wilkes had expressed the wish that every officer should regard every ship of the fleet as his home, and Rochester was happy to comply.

Without hesitation, he opened a door on the starboard side of the helm, which led down a winding companionway. The bottom of the stairs was close to the foot of the mizzenmast, which thrust up through the deck at this spot, hiding the officers' wardroom, which lay between the mast and the stern. It was very dark, the berth deck being below water level, and George paused for his sight to adjust.

He was standing next to the pantry, which was tucked into the curve of the stairs, and could hear voices raised in a quarrel. He had already heard gossip that the morale of the officers of the *Peacock* wasn't good, and it sounded as if the scientifics were unhappy, too. Making a deliberate commotion, he strode around the mast into the officers' wardroom.

He found himself in a gloomy place, very different from the cozy messroom on his own little brig *Swallow*. There was no skylight, as the after house was built over the deck above, so the wardroom was dimly lit with smoky lamps. Measuring twenty feet long, it was like a corridor in a hotel, lined on both sides by doors that led to staterooms. Hats, swords, and guns hung from hooks between the doors. The only furnishing was a long table running down the length of the room, with revolving chairs screwed to the floor on either side, and an unsecured armchair at the sternward end.

Three officers and three scientifics sat about this table with pens in their hands, staring at him. The man in the armchair at the privileged sternward end of the table was the first lieutenant of the *Peacock*, Samuel Lee. Though only about twenty-five, he looked much older, with deep lines bordering his mouth, and bristling eyebrows.

He didn't smile—and George knew exactly why. Like many of the expedition officers, he resented the fact that George had the command of a ship, while he did not. Instead, he asked abruptly, "Come for our letters?"

"We'll be delayed a while yet. They're reporting a murder."

The six men looked at each other, their expressions startled.

"I'm carrying the master to the *Vin*, so he can make his report to Captain Wilkes, and called for Mr. Coffin. Where is he?"

All the faces went blank. No one answered, or even moved. In the odd little hiatus the noises of the ship seemed unnaturally loud. Then one of the scientifics shifted in his chair—a handsome, middle-aged man with a leonine head of russet hair. Still without expression, he jerked his head towards the pantry.

Feeling puzzled, Rochester turned and threw open the door. Inside, Wiki Coffin was perched on a bench next to a black man in a steward's apron. Both were holding dinner plates, and there were mugs of coffee on a sideboard within reach. The steward looked confused, while Wiki's face creased up with pleasure.

Rochester's own smile vanished. "Wiki, what the devil are you doing in here?"

Wiki winced. He'd hoped George would never find out. Eight days ago, after he'd been peremptorily reassigned from his berth on the *Swallow* to the wardroom of the *Peacock*, he had found that he wasn't welcome in these high and mighty quarters. In various ways, the rightful occupants had let him know that they preferred not to share the table with a half-breed, and that the place for him to mess was the pantry.

"Does Captain Hudson know you're eating your meals with the steward?"

Wiki shook his head. He'd seen no reason to make a fuss. No one had asked the steward how he felt about sharing his food with someone who was rumored to be a cannibal, but he'd made the intruder welcome—and the food was better, too. The wardroom steward prepared treats from the officers' private stores— luxuries like tongues, jellied eels, tinned cake, dried fruit, and smoked hams—and he and his companion were the first to taste the results.

"Well, you have to come with me to the *Vin*. There's been a murder."

"On the *Swallow*?" Wiki said, alarmed.

George shook his head. "A sealer we've just spoken told me about it. We're off to see Wilkes so the *Betsey*'s master can report it."

Wiki followed George up the winding stairway to the deck. He headed for the amidships gangway, but halted when he heard his name called. Turning, he saw a man completely clothed in sealskin, with something familiar about him...

The man came close, and memory clicked. Wiki said, "Captain Noyes!"

"You ain't changed a bit, neither," Noyes grunted. Then he lowered his voice. "Tell me about those coves who are taking such a deep interest in my schooner."

He jerked his chin at seven men on the forecastle deck. They stood out from the seamen around them, because they were heavily bearded, in defiance of Captain Wilkes's orders that everyone in the expedition should be clean-shaven. There certainly was an odd intensity about the way they stared at the *Betsey*, Wiki thought, and had a good look at the schooner himself. The reason for their fixed interest was immediately obvious. She was lying low in the water, obviously deep-laden with a valuable cargo of pelts, which made it easy to identify their expressions—blatant greed and envy.

"They're sealers we rescued from their sinking schooner, back in October," he said. "They know you've done well, and are jealous of your luck."

Noyes nodded without surprise. "They joined the expedition?"

"Aye—and wish they hadn't." Captain Wilkes, anxious to take advantage of their knowledge of the southern ocean, had talked them into signing up, but the seven sealers had since regretted it. When the squadron had been lying off Patagonia, surveying the shoals of the Rio Negro, they'd done their damnedest to run away, but had been retaken and flogged. Wiki had been reliably informed that they blamed him for their recapture, and that it would be a good idea to make sure that he didn't find himself alone in their company — advice that he'd heeded.

"Watch out they don't stow away on board of you," he warned. If Captain Wilkes delayed the sealer until after dark the seven men were desperate enough to steal a boat to get to the *Betsey.*

Captain Noyes grimaced, and Wiki added thoughtfully, "I notice you haven't brought your logbook — and Captain Wilkes is coming this way. He's bound to ask questions about your course and the conditions you encountered, you know."

Wiki Coffin was right about Wilkes, because a boat from the *Vincennes* was on the verge of boarding, so close that Noyes could see the gold braid in the stern sheets. He shifted from boot to boot, wondering if the tale of the corpse on the berg was going to distract Wilkes as successfully as it had diverted Rochester, and concluded gloomily that it was very unlikely, if Wiki Coffin didn't keep his mouth shut.

"Why do *you* have to be there when I report finding that corpse?" he muttered.

Wiki blinked. "You *found* it?"

"In the middle of the bloody ocean."

"Not on board of your schooner?"

"Nope. And what's it to you, I wonder?"

"Because I'll be put in charge of the investigation, if there is one."

"*You?*"

"Me," confirmed Wiki. "Before we left Norfolk, the sheriff of Portsmouth, Virginia, deputized me as the agent of law and order on this expedition. Do you want to see my letter of authority?"

"But why the hell would he do something like that?"

"A killer was with the fleet, and the sheriff wanted me to catch him."

"And did you catch him?"

"Aye," said Wiki, adding, "in a manner of speaking."

Captain Wilkes stepped up the gangway, his tall, lean figure tense with impatience. Warned by the whistling of the boatswain's call and the stamp of boots, Captain Hudson hurried out of the afterhouse. As usual, he looked remarkably untidy, his thinning hair blowing about his round, amiable face. His expression, as always, was anxious to please—he was an affable and easygoing man, a necessary trait for someone who had to work closely with the mercurial Wilkes.

Rochester stepped up from his boat, introduced Noyes, and explained.

"*Murder?*" said Hudson.

"So it seems," said George.

Captain Wilkes snapped, "So why the hell didn't you come straight to the *Vincennes*?"

"I thought you'd want Wiki Coffin to hear the report, sir."

Wilkes sniffed, but said, "Well, since we're all here, Captain Noyes can make his report now. If you'd be so kind as to allow us the use of your cabin, Hudson?"

"Of course, of course," said Hudson, and personally opened the door.

Captain Wilkes went in first, and Wiki brought up the rear, looking around curiously, having never visited the afterhouse before. They were in a day cabin, lit with a skylight, and comfortably furnished with a chart desk, table, settee and chairs. Beyond an open door in the sternward partition he could see Hudson's stateroom, which housed two nine-pounder cannon as well as his berth.

Then George cleared his throat, and Wiki realized everyone else was seated. Hurriedly, he took a chair, and Captain Noyes's recital commenced. The story rambled, as if the sealing master was deliberately drawing out the yarn, but at last Noyes ran out of words. Silence fell, punctuated by clicks as Captain Wilkes meditatively tapped a pencil.

Hudson said, "You're sure he was murdered?"

"The blood on his head was as scarlet as the day he was bludgeoned."

"Yet the corpse was standing?"

"If you lie down too long in those regions," Noyes informed him, "your hair sticks to the ice. He was frozen to the cliff he was standing against."

"By his *hair*?"

"By his sealskin suit."

Captain Wilkes interrupted, "And the iceberg's position, Captain Noyes?"

Noyes spread his hands. "I can give you an approximate, but I can't be precise," he said. "There was a snowstorm…"

"What about your logbook?"

"For God's sake, the berg was drifting! My logbook won't help you."

"Let me be the judge of that."

"I don't have it with me."

Captain Wilkes stared. Noyes went red under his weathered tan, but his expression was obstinate. A tense silence reigned.

Hudson looked around and said, "Tea, anyone? Coffee? Madeira?"

"Nothing, thank you," Captain Wilkes snapped. "Mr. Coffin, Captain Noyes, oblige me by coming in my boat to the sealer. Mr. Rochester, bring your boat, too," he added.

Wiki blinked. This was highhanded, even for Wilkes. Captain Noyes's expression, as the two boats proceeded to the *Betsey*, was an eloquent mixture of disbelief, alarm, outrage, and stubbornness.

The stench of half-cured sealskins rose to meet them as they clambered onto the schooner's deck. Even if Wiki hadn't guessed from the heaviness of the *Betsey* that she was full of pelts, the stink would have given it away. Below decks, it was guaranteed to be even smellier, so it was no great surprise when Captain Wilkes ordered him to go down with pen and paper and make a copy of the relevant entries, while he and Mr. Rochester waited on the deck.

The air in the cramped cabin was as disgusting as expected, and Wiki breathed shallowly as he seated himself at the chart desk. He found the logbook without any trouble, as it was a huge affair, measuring two foot by three, bound in great sheets of canvas. The notations were equally large, but difficult to decipher, because they'd been scrawled with a leaky quill pen while the schooner had been jumping about in what had obviously been very rough seas.

Captain Noyes, who smelled almost as bad as his ship, hovered close to Wiki's shoulder as he slowly turned the pages. It took a while to find the entry with the location of the island where the crew had harvested their cargo, and then Wiki paused, conscious that Noyes had gone very still.

He remembered conversations overheard years ago in the sealing village of Stonington, Connecticut— stories of rookeries devastated by rapacious rival gangs after the secret of their location got out. After a long moment he turned another page. Not a word had been said, and not a note had been taken.

Captain Noyes's sigh of relief was gusty. He even became cooperative, pointing out the last position taken before they encountered the corpse-carrying iceberg. As he had said, the location of the berg was approximate, because of the conditions, but Wiki noted it down. Then Noyes watched without protest while Wiki also copied the log entries for the eight days that followed the sighting, which carried the record up to the present date.

As the neat script flowed from his pen, Wiki could hear voices echoing down the skylight from the deck. George was trying to persuade Captain Wilkes to reverse his decision about shifting Wiki from the *Swallow* to the *Peacock*, but without giving any reason, though his voice was tense with outrage. He was still arguing as Wiki finished, and only silenced when he arrived back on deck.

Night had fallen, and the three expedition ships were indistinct shapes in the gathering dark. Wiki gave the copied log entries to Captain Wilkes, who merely glanced at the pages before ordering Rochester to leave Mr. Coffin at the *Peacock* on the way back to the *Swallow*. Then Wilkes dropped into his boat, and with a single snapped command was on his way to the *Vincennes*.

Noyes could hardly wait for them to go. Wiki had hardly joined Rochester in his boat before orders were barked to get underway. The rattle of ropes and canvas followed, and by the time the boat arrived at the *Peacock* the *Betsey* was under full sail and bearing away.

Wiki stood up and put his foot on the gunwale, ready to climb up the side, but George stopped him by gripping his arm.

"Wilkes wouldn't listen, damn him!" he said in a low, shaking voice. "I should have told him exactly how they're treating you on the *Peacock*."

"No," said Wiki. George didn't know the half of it—there was a great deal more than bigotry that was wrong on board the *Peacock*.

"I feel responsible. You only joined the expedition because I talked you into it."

That was true, but Wiki said, "You can't blame yourself."

"But damn it, Wiki, I do!"

Wiki bit back a sigh. Above, on the decks of the *Peacock*, it was very dark and quiet. Lanterns hadn't yet been hoisted in the rigging. To end the pointless discussion he climbed the gangway, and stood watching as George's boat pulled away. Then he turned and strode aft.

The decks seemed strangely deserted, he thought with a frown. Then he glimpsed a bulky shape—

barging out at him from the deep shadows of the stacked exploring boats amidships.

Wiki dodged away, to find that more attackers were coming from behind. Ducking, he darted sideways—just in time, because the belaying pin aimed at his head landed numbingly on his shoulder. He almost fell, but caught his balance. Then he backed against the mainmast and sank into a defensive crouch, while seven brutal men moved in for the kill.

Two

*L*ieutenant Christian Forsythe was growing bloody impatient.

Overhauling the sealer and forcing the captain to haul aback for boarding had been first-rate sport, granted. Then, when Rochester's boat had failed to come back from the schooner, mysteriously heading for the *Peacock* instead, he had seized the chance to ferret out a bottle he'd kept hidden, and get drunk. But the bottle had been emptied, and dusk had descended, and still the captain of the *Swallow* had failed to return.

The last Forsythe had seen of the *Swallow* boat, it had been heading back to the sealer. What the hell was up? After eight days of rain, mist, and heavy seas as the three expedition ships had steered from the Rio Negro towards the Straits of Le Maire, the weather had cleared and the wind was fair. But, instead of taking full advantage of the lull, Captain Wilkes had chosen to hang about gamming with that damned Stonington sealer, and Rochester, for unknown reasons, was with him. The lieutenant prowled the decks of the *Swallow* in a growing temper, snarling at the lookouts and helmsman as he passed, wondering what was up with their bloody captain.

Captain. Captain George Rochester, skipper of this here brig. Forsythe snorted with self-derision. Just six months ago he would have split his sides at the very idea of being second-in-command to twenty-four-year-old Rochester. Technically, Forsythe outranked George, as he had passed his lieutenant's examinations ten years ago, and bloody hard, they were, too. Indeed, he had even been master of the *Swallow* for an interesting three-week spell.

But Rochester's record was astounding. Not only was he the young fellow who had topped the class in his examinations — which was the reason he had been given command of the *Swallow* in the first place — but Rochester had enjoyed the fastest promotion to the rank of lieutenant in history. It was a feat that outshone every other officer in the expedition fleet, including the commander, for, incredibly, Wilkes was still only a lieutenant, outranked by several of his officers just because of vicious enmity in Washington. Rochester could owe a lot to his rich, influential grandfather, lawyer to the mightiest, but Forsythe had to admit that there must be some natural brilliance there. In fact, Forsythe reckoned that Rochester would be an admiral before the next decade was out. So he also figured that it was only diplomatic to address him as captain.

For the same reason, when he finally heard the swish and clunk of oars that heralded Rochester's return, he didn't say, "*Where the hell have you been?*" — which were the words that came naturally to his lips. Instead, he inquired, though in dangerous tones, "Somethin' up, cap'n?"

George clambered up the side, leaving the oarsmen to hoist the boat. "The sealer captain reported a murder, so I called at the *Peacock* to collect Wiki."

"*Murder?*" Constant Keith echoed. When the junior midshipman arrived at Forsythe's shoulder, his round face was rapt in the flickering light of the cressets.

"The *Betsey* almost run afoul of an iceberg in a snowstorm, and as they were getting clear of it, they spied the corpse of a man who'd been bludgeoned to death."

"On an *iceberg?*"

"It must've been quite a sight," George meditated. "Dead as last week's mutton, but still standing, stuck to the ice by the frozen hairs of his sealskin suit."

Young Keith looked suitably impressed. "And they want Wiki to find the killer, sir?"

"Doubt if he can," Rochester said. "It's a very old crime. The corpse could have been stuck to the ice for months, if not years."

"And the answer's obvious," said Forsythe.

"It is?"

"A gang of sealers got into a fight, and the dead man come off the worst."

"That does sound likely," said Rochester. "But do seals live on icebergs?"

"Bound to," said Forsythe, though he didn't feel all that certain.

Rochester hesitated, then said, "I didn't like the look of things on the *Peacock.*"

"Wa'al, it's common knowledge that the morale ain't good," Forsythe said. "Did you know the crew mutinied the very same day we sailed from Norfolk — refused duty before they were even down the bloody river? Lieutenant Lee sorted it out with a few floggings, and they sent a message back that it was only a little dissatisfaction over the grub, but it ain't surprisin' if

23

trouble still simmers. Captain Hudson's too easy-goin', and Lee's a disciplinarian to make up for it."

Rochester nodded. Samuel Lee, first lieutenant of the *Peacock*, had the reputation of a martinet—and Forsythe was right, a mild captain and a lash-happy second-in-command made a bad combination.

He said, "Did you know that those seven sealers we rescued from the wreck of their ship are all on the *Peacock*?"

"Those mutinous bastards? I thought they was spread all about the fleet so they could pass on their special knowledge to as many men as possible."

"Well, now we're getting close to their old hunting grounds, they're assembled on the *Peacock*. I saw them there when I dropped by to pick up Wiki—still led by that great hairy brute of a man, Frank Folger, and looking uncommon curious at the sealing schooner, too."

"She was low in the water," Forsythe reflected.

"Aye, heavy laden—and stank to high heaven. Wiki told me they'd give a lot to lay their hands on the location of her big haul of pelts."

"So where was the sealing beach?"

Rochester shrugged. "Wiki went down and copied the entries in the log, and gave the copy to Captain Wilkes."

"So the sealers know that Mr. Coffin saw the log?" exclaimed Keith.

Rochester frowned. "It would be easy enough to guess."

"But that means Mr. Coffin is in danger, sir!"

Dead silence, filled only by the ripple of water, and the creak of the rigging. The sky was overcast, so the

24

only lights that specked the dusk were the cressets that hung in the rigging of the *Vincennes*. The *Peacock* was almost lost in the dimness.

Then Forsythe shrugged. "Wiki's a big boy. He can look after himself."

"Against *seven*, sir?"

"He's one of the scientifics, so messes in the bloody wardroom, doesn't he? They wouldn't dare."

"But that ain't the case," said Rochester, troubled. "The officers refuse to share the wardroom with a colored man, so Wiki is messing with the steward."

Forsythe roared, "*What?*"

He was as outraged as if he'd never called Wiki Coffin a half-breed bastard a dozen times or more, and was just drunk enough to want to do something about it. However, he also sane enough to cast a look at the *Vincennes*. The flagship was lying still, most of her sails brailed up, so that it was obvious that Wilkes was taking his sweet time about ordering a cannon fired to get the fleet underway again.

The Virginian swung round, and said, "Cap'n, I would like to take the boat."

"Why?"

"So I can go over to the *Peacock* and sort things out."

Horrified, Rochester protested, "You can't interfere in the affairs of another ship!"

"Can't I? You just watch me. He's one of ours, and an insult to him is an insult to us."

"Dear God," muttered Rochester. He shifted from one boot to another in an agony of indecision. There were plenty of conflicts with Forsythe ahead — not only was the Virginian higher than he was on the Navy List, but Forsythe had very strong views about how the

Swallow should be sailed — and he didn't fancy a battle of wills when he was so angry about Wiki's treatment, too.

Finally, he prevaricated, saying, "Captain Wilkes did instruct us to regard every ship of the fleet as our own. But I do insist that I come with you."

"Better not, cap'n, not if you don't want a blot on your record," said Forsythe, who had fatally blotted his own record a long time ago.

Rochester hesitated again, but then gave in. "If Captain Wilkes gives the signal to get underway, I'll wait fifteen minutes, but no more," he finally said. Forsythe simply nodded, and was down in the boat and hollering for five oarsmen before Rochester could think up another argument.

The boat was halfway across the black and shimmering gap between the two vessels when Forsythe heard muffled grunts from the deck of the *Peacock*, along with some warlike Maori chanting, and the thump of fists on flesh. "Pull!" he hollered, and his oarsmen hauled like demons, as keen to join the battle as he was. Hooking onto boat falls in a hurry, they tumbled up the low side of the ship and over the gangway in a mass.

Forsythe arrived first. He stopped, his arms spread to hold the boat's crew back while he summed up the situation. Wiki and another man were cornered up against the mainmast, and, to Forsythe's stupefaction, the second man was tattooed. The light from the cresset above flickered over the whorls that darkened his face. He must be the man the sailors had nicknamed Jack Sac, the expedition's Maori passenger — and yet Jack belonged to the Ngati Porou tribe, who were mortal

26

enemies of Wiki's tribe, which was Ngapuhi. How the hell, Forsythe wondered, had Wiki managed to turn this traditional foe into an ally?

It was fortunate that age-old grievances had been sorted out, as it was obvious that without Jack at his side Wiki would have been senseless long ago, and probably dead by now. Both Maori men were fighting for their lives, whirling capstan bars about their shoulders to fend off assailants who wielded belaying pins like sealing clubs. Wiki's face was a mask of blood—but not his own, it seemed, because one of the thugs was huddled in the scuppers cradling his head-butted nose. Forsythe was delighted to find that Wiki could fight so dirty—but he was very much the worse for wear, favoring one arm, and swinging his staff one-handed. So where the devil was the officer of the watch?

Then Forsythe recognized the attackers. By damn—young Keith had been right. The men trying to kill Wiki and his unlikely friend were the sealers they had rescued from their sinking ship, and who had been nothing but trouble since. "Goddammit, you bastards!" Forsythe bellowed, stalking forward. "Seven against two? I always knew that sealers were bloody cowards!"

The six whipped around, and the seventh scrambled to his feet to join them. They shifted until they were shoulder-to-shoulder, and Forsythe could see their slitted eyes. He growled with pleasure, hauling his sleeves up his snake-tattooed forearms, and then advanced in a crouch with his fists spread to each side. When he saw the sealers glance at each other, and waver, and begin to back away, he knew his oarsmen had adopted the same stance—but then, to his utter disgust, one of the sealers shouted to the quarterdeck for help.

The shrill pipe of a boatswain's call responded immediately, as if the petty officer had been watching from the shadows. Boatswain's mates materialized out of the gloom, and arrowed in on Wiki and Jack, who gave up the capstan bars immediately. Once they had them disarmed, however, the mates began to pummel them, lashing out with their canes as well as their fists, while the sealers, held lightly by other petty officers, watched with open enjoyment.

Forsythe roared, "Belay that!"

The bo'sun's mates all turned to stare at him, looking confused, their mouths hanging open. The officer of the watch hurried up, his speaking trumpet in his hand, and said, "What the hell is going on?" Then his eyes widened as he recognized Forsythe. Much more politely, he said, "What are you doing here, lieutenant?"

"Good to see you, too, Pilson," said Forsythe. "You could say I've come to collect the two hundred dollars you lost to me the last time we were at table, but I was delayed by a nasty little battle I discovered when I come on board. These bastards," he went on, waving a broad hand at the seven sealers, "were trying to make mincemeat of our linguister."

"It's not two hundred," Pilson said indignantly. "You have my chit for exactly eighty-seven — and as for the fracas you interrupted, I promise you that it will all be sorted out in the morning, and proper justice will be done. In the meantime *all* the miscreants will be locked into the brig, until Lieutenant Lee decides what to do with them."

Wiki said urgently, "Lieutenant Forsythe, that's…" but Forsythe ignored him, saying with contempt to Pilson, "Leave all nine to battle it out behind bars, huh, and clean up the bloody mess in the morning? Because it *will* be a bloody mess, and we'll be stalled in our passage yet again, to haul aback for a double burial. Believe me, mister, I've seen that way of gettin' rid of troublemakers before, but you sure as goddammit don't do that with Wiki Coffin. Or his tattooed friend," Forsythe added, just for the hell of it.

"But Lieutenant Lee's orders…"

"Wa'al, for Christ's sake send for Lieutenant Lee, and let's hear his orders from his own lips—or do you want me to rouse up Cap'n Hudson?"

Pilson's eyes flickered. Forsythe took a decisive stride towards the afterhouse, and the lieutenant said sulkily to a bos'un's mate, "Give Lieutenant Lee my apologies, and say his presence is required on the amidships deck."

The petty officer disappeared into the darkness. In the taut silence that followed, Forsythe eased up to Wiki and said, "So what the hell was that about?"

Wiki worked his stiff jaw, and tried to scrub blood off his face with the hand that had escaped the most damage. "They jumped me as I came on board after copying the sealer's log for Captain Wilkes. They knew damn well that I'd read the location of the beach where the *Betsey* collected her bumper cargo of skins, and were set on beating it out of me."

So Keith had been right, Forsythe meditated. And what would have happened after they had extracted the information from Wiki was obvious—he would have been knocked on the head and tipped over the rail, and no one would have done a thing about it.

He gestured at Jack Sac and said, "And him?"

"Te Aute?" said Wiki, giving the Maori his proper name. "He arrived out of nowhere, tossed me a capstan bar, and stood alongside me."

Forsythe's brows were very high. He said to Jack Sac, "You're Ngati Porou?"

"Yes, boss."

"And you ain't even *tried* to murder this Ngapuhi fellow?"

Wiki winced.

"Mebbe one day," said Te Aute, and grinned.

Forsythe said to Wiki, "How the hell did you get him on your side?"

Wiki shrugged, though it obviously hurt to lift his left shoulder. Te Aute answered for him, saying, "I been ten years in America, boss. Makes a big difference, eh? Lotsa things that were important back home get forgotten."

Forsythe grinned evilly at Wiki."You reckon you can rely on that?"

Then he was distracted by the sight of Lieutnenant Lee emerging from the afterdeck companionway. The first lieutenant of the *Peacock* was looking highly irritated, smacking his short cane against the side of his leg as he came.

Forsythe turned back to Te Aute, and said, "You've signed up with the navy?"

Te Aute shook his head. "Not me, boss."

"You're sure you didn't touch the pen?"

Te Aute shook his head again, and Forsythe faced Lee as he came to a halt.

"Sam," he said, and the two officers shook hands. They knew each other well, and not just because of the navy. Neighbors at home, they were equals socially, though Lee's family was a great deal more wealthy and influential than Forsythe's branch of his clan. Lee sent Pilson to his station on the quarterdeck, turned back to Forsythe, and said, "This is a hell of a time, Kit. What's up?"

"Wiki Coffin and his tattooed friend here are in a spot of bother."

A pause. Samuel Lee's gimlet eyes thoughtfully studied Forsythe's broad face, and then he said, "My information was that they were creating mayhem on my deck."

"Mayhem there was," Forsythe agreed. "But if your informants reckon they know who started the fight, they've chosen the wrong men. It was those bloody mutinous pirates of sealers, who shouldn't be trusted a single goddamned inch."

"We can work that out for ourselves — after a proper investigation in the morning."

"Uh-uh." Forsythe shook his head. "You don't treat supernumeraries like miserable little swabs of seamen."

"Supernumeraries, Kit?"

"They're *civilians*, for God's sake! Check the muster book — before I ask the folks on the *Vin* to check it for you. Jack Sac hasn't touched the pen, he says, which means he ain't on the crewlist. Leave him be — and as for our linguister, start acting like the civilized gentleman you pretend to be, back home."

Lee bridled, and said, "That's fighting talk, Kit."

"I'm talking about the way you're treating Wiki Coffin. He's not just any ordinary bloody nuisance of a

31

scientific, but the deputy of the sheriff of Portsmouth, Virginia! Or didn't you know that, when you banned him from the wardroom? It ain't goin' to look good on your record, Sam."

"What the hell do you know about my record?"

"No more than the Navy Department is goin' to find out. Deputy Coffin sends regular reports back to Virginia, which I happen to know because I delivered one of 'em to a homebound whaler, myself. And, what's more, if those reports stop comin' because of the writer's unfortunate demise during a brawl in the brig of the *Peacock*, there's goin' to be official questions asked."

Another pause, while the two senior officers stared aggressively at each other, and then with an angrily abrupt movement Lieutenant Lee swerved and barked to the bos'un's mates, "Drop all charges and dismiss."

There was a pause as everyone looked at each other, confused, and he shouted, "Get to your duty, and if I hear of any trouble like this again, I won't be asking any questions or listening to any excuses. I'll string up the offenders and flog them till their bones are chalk! *Do you hear me?*"

Without another word, the mates and the sealers scattered, disappearing rapidly into the darkness. After a glance from Forsythe, his men dropped down into the *Swallow* boat, and abruptly the deck was almost deserted. Only Wiki and Te Aute remained, both looking very cautious.

Lee drew Forsythe aside, and said, "You're making a bad mistake, Kit."

"I don't think so, Sam."

"Your pet linguister is a spy."

"He's a … *what?*"

"All the officers are convinced of it. It's uncanny, the way Wilkes knows everything that goes on, and what people say in private. You can't open a bottle or start a game of cards without him hearing about it. There has to be a spy, and your linguister fits the description. You know yourself that he's closeted with Wilkes far too damn often—he's even worked as his clerk. And his crony Rochester was given a ship when he was just a passed midshipman and only just passed, at that."

"Garbage," said Forsythe with deep disgust. "I'm disappointed in you, Sam. Rochester was given the *Swallow* weeks before Wiki Coffin joined the expedition, and Coffin did that clerking for Wilkes because he can read and write Portuguese—and I know that because I was there when Wilkes ordered him to do it."

"But I've heard…" Then Lee broke off, as the report of a cannon sounded from the *Vincennes*. "Damn," he said, and turned to shout in the direction of the quarterdeck, "All hands, to get underway!"

"I'm off," said Forsythe. And, after barking at Wiki, "You take better care of yourself than you appear to have done so far," he joined his men into the boat. Within seconds, they were gone.

Three

$\mathcal{W}$iki waited until the rush of seamen getting to their stations had passed, and then he lowered himself stiffly down the main hatch ladder, wincing at every step.

The shoulder where Folger's club had got him in the initial attack was stiff and swollen, and when he'd rolled away he had taken a nasty kick in the ribs. His forehead hurt where he'd head-butted one of the sealers, and his left eye was swelling shut from a flying fist. After Te Aute had arrived to stand at his side, and they had set to whirling the capstan bars *taiaha* style, the sealers had attacked with far more caution, but still he was sore all over.

Te Aute had vanished, as was usual with him. Wiki often thought the Ngati Porou man moved about the ship as invisibly as a lizard, or a *kehua* — ghost. It was a survival trait that he had learned on forest warpaths as a boy, and honed over ten years of living on his wits in America. Having not taken nearly as much punishment as Wiki, he still moved smoothly, with silent agility.

Accordingly, when a form materialized from the cluttered dimness, Wiki expected it to be the Maori. Instead, it was one of the midshipmen, a bookish sort of fellow with rounded shoulders, lank hair that hung over one eyebrow, and horn-rimmed spectacles. Wiki had noticed him during his explorations of the ship, because he was so much older than the other junior midshipmen, being about twenty-one or two, and appeared so unsuited to a life at sea. White-faced, and soft in physique, he looked much more like a scholar than a seaman.

His face was just three feet away, a pale blob floating in the gloom, with a stray gleam from the eyeglasses. He said, "Mr. Coffin, sir, I do apologize. I wasn't looking where I was going..." Then his mouth fell open as he registered Wiki's battered and bloodied state, and he said in a high, shocked voice, "My God, sir, what happened to you?"

Wiki pushed his good hand over his sore, blood-smeared face, winced, and said, "I'm sorry, but I can't remember your name."

"Dove—Midshipman Valentine Dove—but you must see a surgeon, Mr. Coffin. Come, sir, permit me to assist you to your berth."

"There's no need for that," Wiki said, rather grumpily, but felt a hand grip his upper right arm to support him as he limped along the narrow aisle. "And there's no need to call me *sir*, either."

The voice in his ear sounded scandalized. "But you're a *sheriff*, Mr. Coffin, and I would certainly call a sheriff *sir*, back home in Pennsylvania."

Unexpectedly, Wiki felt amused. He said, "I'm only a deputy."

"But I hear you never fail to find the killer, sir—that you have a kind of sixth sense about men's motives for committing crimes, which leads you to the identity of the murderer."

Wiki grimaced. It was true, but he didn't want to talk about it. Instead, he limped along in the dimness, bumping painfully against projecting dunnage every now and then, but steadied by the midshipman's hand.

Undeterred, Mr. Dove said, "What a wonderful feeling it must be, sir, to be a force for good, when there is so little that's good in this world."

Good lord, Wiki thought. Dove had an impossibly elevated idea of the part played in society by the agents of law, order, and the collection of taxes. He said wryly, "Don't underestimate the career you have chosen—an officer of the navy is vastly superior to a mere officer of the law, believe me."

"But I never chose to be a navy officer, sir!"

Wiki bit back a sigh. He felt in no kind of condition to listen to confidences, but said, "So why are you here?"

"It was not my choice, Mr. Coffin—I had a career I loved, but there was a problem, and my family... My father was a commodore, and his father before that, and his *grandfather* before that, and—and they were all *ashamed* of the choice I had made, and said it wasn't *respectable*, and they prophesied nothing but loss of character. They assured me that I would find sea-life to my liking, but I hate it, sir! The lieutenants treat me like a dog, and the seamen think I'm the lieutenants' spy. What kind of character is that, I ask?"

Wiki, thinking of what his friend George Rochester had confided in the past, said, "All midshipmen think they are treated like spies and dogs. As time goes by, they get over it. And this is your first voyage, right?"

"Yes, it is, sir. And it should be my last, Mr. Coffin!"

Wiki agreed with him, but only silently, because he thought that the midshipman was doomed. Since Mr.

Dove hailed from a proud seafaring tribe, it would be impossible for him to avoid his fate.

"My family is wrong, I know it—and now that I am far away from their persuasions and arguments, sir, I think about doing something that's so much more to my liking. And I swear that my character would not be harmed by it! That I wouldn't bring shame to them all!" Then Dove clicked his tongue, and said, "But I'm chattering on about myself, sir, while you're in pain, Mr. Coffin, and who knows what bones might be broken? Come, I'll get you to your berth, and then fetch Dr. Holmes."

The gloom ahead had become broken by halos of light from hanging lanterns, barred by the massive shadow of the foot of the mizzen mast. When they rounded the mast and the companionway, it was to find that the wardroom beyond was empty, with all the varnished doors shut. The officers were all on deck, presumably, and the scientific residents in their berths.

Wiki led the way, hobbling to his stateroom, which was the lowliest one, right next to the pantry. It was just six feet by eight, furnished with just a bank of lockers with a lip on top to hold a thin mattress, and a small desk with a chair, but since he had arrived on the *Peacock* he had turned it into a haven. The bunk was neatly made up with blankets he had purloined from the purser's store, and above it a makeshift shelf held the books that had been his solace during this period of isolation. Two favorite volumes were lying on the desk—books by Edmund Fanning and Amasa Delano, two wily old sea-dogs who had left lively narratives of their adventures. One of the lamps, filched from the table, also stood on the desk, glowing brightly, the wick having been regularly trimmed and the chimney cleaned.

"Now, sir, you sit down while I find the surgeon," said Dove.

Wiki's head was throbbing, and he knew that if he collapsed onto his berth, he would never get up again, so he followed orders, and sat on the chair. As he heard Mr. Dove turn into the pantry and ask the steward to point out the door to Dr. Holmes's room, he wondered distractedly who the midshipman reminded him of. Then, as he listened to him arguing with the surgeon, he suddenly pinned it down—Mr. Puffin, the law clerk in the office of George Rochester's grandfather. Mr. Puffin, who took care of Wiki's investments, was a great deal older than Midshipman Dove, but had exactly his manner. Deferential, but determined.

"Rouse up Dr. Sickles, if it's so urgent," Dr. Holmes was saying. Dr. Sickles was the surgeon who treated the crew.

"But it's Deputy *Coffin* who is in need of medical attention, Dr. Holmes, sir," Midshipman Dove insisted. "The expedition's *linguister*, sir. A *scientific*."

Silence, and then an audible sigh. Footsteps, and then the surgeon came through the open door, followed by Midshipman Dove. Suddenly the little room was very crowded.

Dr. Holmes said, "My God, you look a mess. Take a tumble?"

"In a manner of speaking," said Wiki.

"Warm vinegar, I think."

"I beg your pardon?"

"*Fomento vinegar*. For your bruises." The surgeon pushed his way out, and when he came back he was carrying a bottle and a small spirit lamp that he set on the desk and lit. Then, after closing the door, he looked at Wiki, and said, "If you would take off your shirt?"

"Here?" said Wiki.

"Where else?" said Dr. Holmes dryly. "My hole of a cabin is no larger than this, I assure you."

Very conscious of them both watching, Wiki stood up and removed his woolen Guernsey frock and the dungaree shirt underneath. "Sit, sit," said Dr. Holmes irritably. "You're too damn tall for me to treat from down here."

Wiki sat, and bore the surgeon's inspection as stoically as he could, though every now and then a hard probe hurt. Because he was deep-chested and low-waisted, like his mother's people, his torso was where he had taken most of the punishment. Bruises were swelling the muscles of his arms, with one particularly large one spreading down from his left shoulder, where Folger's club had landed. Nothing seemed to be broken, though, and apart from the blackened eye and the graze on his forehead, his face was intact.

Pronouncing himself satisfied, Dr. Holmes wiped warmed vinegar over the bruises, and stood back, and Wiki dressed again. "Plenty of rest," said the surgeon. "A day in bed, and you'll be much better by supper tomorrow."

"Aye, sir," said Wiki, though he had no intention of complying. From past experience he knew that stiffness was best worked off with exercise — though avoiding the sealers was also a priority, just as it had been for the past eight days. And with that, to his relief, the two of them prepared to leave.

Impelled by a sense of gratitude as well as courtesy—for Midshipman Dove had been very kind, and Dr. Holmes, after his initial reluctance, had been professional—Wiki struggled to his feet to see them to the door. He opened it, they progressed through—and a harsh voice with a southern accent exclaimed, "Mr. Dove, what the *hell* are you doing in the wardroom?"

The lieutenant who confronted them was a blond, lean, sinewy man in his early thirties. Wiki, who had only glimpsed him in the distance before, thought he must have been good-looking—right up to the moment that his left cheek, half-severed by a sword stroke, had been sewn back by a rushed surgeon. The scar affected the lid of the left eye, which drooped almost shut, but the other was fixed like a needle. He had a lethal, pantherlike look about him, as if he had taken part in real warfare before joining the expedition.

"I was helping Mr. Coffin, sir," Midshipman Dove said, unshaken.

"When you were supposed to be on deck on duty?"

"Mr. Coffin was greatly in need of assistance, Mr. Matthews."

"That's true," Wiki said. "And I am most grateful to the midshipman."

The lieutenant turned, and looked him up and down. He didn't seem at all surprised at Wiki's bruised appearance, evidently knowing already about the battle and its outcome. Instead of bothering to reply, he turned back to the unfortunate junior officer, and said in icily dangerous tones, "Do your duties involve any dealings with civilians, Mr. Dove?"

"Mr. Coffin is an officer of the law, sir. He's the accredited representative of the sheriff's department of Portsmouth, Virginia, sir. Everybody knows it."

"Well, if everyone knows it, it must be so," Mr. Matthews silkily agreed. "But I'm certain Mr. Coffin will oblige me by confirming that even the most illustrious officer of the law is a civilian, not a member of the crew, and therefore none of your business. So get it into your head," he went on, his voice rising dangerously, "that your job does not involve nursemaiding the strays who are attached to the wardroom! Get the hell out of here, Mr. Dove, and do not come back!"

"Sir," said Midshipman Dove, and left the wardroom—but not before Wiki glimpsed the brief look he cast over his shoulder as he rounded the foot of the mizzen mast.

If ever murder was written plain, it was in Valentine Dove's expression. So intense was the hatred that a chill lifted the hairs of Wiki's neck. Then the midshipman was gone.

Four

$\mathcal{N}$ext evening, when Wiki put down the book he was reading, and stood up to go into the pantry for supper, he became sensible of a change in the ship's motion.

The weather that day had been moderate, with watery sun filtering through the clouds, a calm sea, and light winds, and he had spent most of the time aloft, where he could stretch his stiffened limbs without being bothered by the sealers. He and Te Aute had met up in their usual place, the mizzen top, where they perched on a folded sail and gossiped about America, and so the day had passed pleasantly enough. But now the weather was kicking up, which augured badly for the night ahead.

A squall hit. Wiki could hear the distant rattle of hail on the deck above. The ship executed a sharp pitch to leeward, and he had to brace a hand against the bulkhead to save himself from falling. When the ship steadied he straightened with a wince, opened his door, and looked into the wardroom, where there were men about the table already. The lanterns hanging from the deckhead were swinging madly on their chains, sending dizzy haloes of light about the gloomy space. Another pitch. The door at the top of the stairway slammed open, and a wave thudded down the stairs. Wiki hung onto the doorframe, listening to orders being bawled on deck. The vast amount of sail was now a danger instead of an asset, and all hands were being called to take in canvas in a hurry.

Evidently, the hail had turned to rain. Lieutenant Pilson came stumbling down the stairs to grab an oilskin coat from the rack at the foot of the mizzenmast. At the same time, he shouted out for the first lieutenant. Lee emerged from his stateroom — the privileged one, nearest to the stern on the starboard side — pulling on his jacket. The other officer ran back up the stairs, and the door at the top crashed shut.

Another stiff roll, the door swung open, and a second wave washed down the stairs, accompanied by the sounds of crockery smashing in the pantry. Lee swore, and grabbed his balance by clutching at the back of the armchair at his end of the table. Timing his movements to the jerk of the ship, he staggered the length of the wardroom to the foot of the companionway, snatched an oilskin, and headed up. A moment later he reappeared, coming halfway down the companionway to yell for Matthews. The lieutenant came out of his room, snapping braces over his shoulders and struggling into his jacket. He followed Lee's example by grabbing one of the oiled coats. As Matthews opened the door to the deck at the top of the companionway, Wiki could distinctly hear the hiss of the torrential downpour.

The three scientifics who lived on the *Peacock* — Horatio Hale, Titian Peale, and James Dana — were sitting at the table with Dr. Holmes. They had tumblers half-full of Madeira firmly gripped in their fists, while one of them had the bottle safely secured. Before anyone could speak there was another great lurch, and more water thudded down the companionway. Everyone at the table lifted his feet to keep his boots clear of the flood, and Wiki hung onto the back of a chair. Then, when the *Peacock* finally settled, they all lifted their glasses and drank, studying Wiki at the same time.

"What happened to you?" said James Dana.

"He got into a brawl with some seamen," said Titian Peale.

Wiki looked at the speaker, feeling surprised. Peale was a commanding, handsome, middle-aged man with a thick head of waving hair that was titian-red in color to match his name, and, as Wiki knew from their altercations on the Rio Negro, an irritable temper to match the red hair, too.

"And only just escaped being slung in the brig," the naturalist went on.

Good lord, thought Wiki. How did Peale know that? Did he gossip with the seamen?

"Then thank God it was stopped," said Holmes. "It's *unthinkable* that a scientific should be incarcerated like a common sailor."

Wiki stayed where he was, holding onto the back of the chair, and wondering about the change in their attitude. The thawing of the atmosphere was palpable, he thought. Peale gestured at the table, which was another surprise. Wiki diplomatically chose a seat near the foot, and shook his head when the naturalist made another gesture, this time at the bottle.

"That's a really spectacular black eye," Peale remarked.

"I know," said Wiki. Quite apart from the discomfort and being able to see out of only one eye, he had not been allowed to forget it, because so many seamen had made jocular comments.

Dr. Holmes said, "There are some spectacular bruises, too. Another application of *vinegar fomento* is in order, I think." He stood up and then, timing his movements to the jump of the ship, he headed for his stateroom.

"I recommend leeches," said Titian Peale to Wiki.

"I beg your pardon?"

"For your black eye. *Hirudo medicinalis.* I have great faith in bloodsuckers."

"*Bloodsuckers?*" echoed Wiki, appalled.

"I used bloodsuckers to fix my black eye, when I had one."

"*You?*"

"Yes, me," said Peale, smiling for the first time. "It happened during a fracas with the passengers of a sordid little sloop, up a miserable creek in Florida, back in January 1818."

"Florida!" Wiki was impressed. Florida was a remote, exotic territory, populated by hostile Indians and savage wildlife, barely colonized by its Spanish possessors.

"I was just eighteen years old, and it was a remarkable experience. We camped in the marshes, and dined on the blackbirds and parakeets I shot, and visited a house in the wilderness that was constructed of oyster-shells rudely cemented together, and furnished in the finest Parisian mode."

"And you got into a fight?"

"On account of an eight-foot alligator. I'd shot it twice in the head, so had good reason to believe that life was extinct. But after we boarded the sloop it suddenly started lunging around, and the passengers objected. Violently. It was after that," Titian Peale added, "I learned that leeches are wonderful for mending a black eye. Don't you have leeches in New Zealand?"

Wiki did not have a notion, but he'd never come across any personally, so had no trouble exclaiming, "Dear God, no."

"Well, there are plenty in Florida. After we'd landed and made camp, my companions went to a pond with torches, and caught bloodsuckers around the banks. They put a bunch of 'em under the affected eye, and applied more as they fell off sated with my blood, and by morning all the blackness was gone. Thank God," Peale added. "It was important to look respectable, you see, because we were headed for St. Augustine to present our credentials to the governor."

While Wiki was mulling this over, the ship made another lurch to leeward. Dr. Holmes, coming back into the wardroom with the vinegar and a spirit lamp, was forced to lean on the frame of his doorway to keep his balance. Then, with the weather roll, he staggered over to Wiki and said, "Off with your upper garments."

"Here?"

"It's a damn sight warmer than either of our cabins."

Wiki supposed he was right. The stove that was set at the foot of the mizzen mast was working hard to produce some heat, and while the generally dank atmosphere of the wardroom prevailed, it was certainly warmer than his own berth.

So again he removed his Guernsey and then his shirt, and sat still while Dr. Holmes wiped warm vinegar over his bruises, and the scientifics watched. His body might have been more supple with the exercise he'd had that day, but the bruises were even blacker.

Horatio Hale broke the silence. "Is any form of medicine practiced in your native land?"

Hale was the pale, bookish, twenty-one-year-old expedition philologist. His expression as he eyed Wiki's smooth, muscled torso was unmistakably envious, despite the bruising. Wiki said, "*Karakia* — prayers — and lots of cold water."

Holmes exclaimed, "You call cold water a *cure*?"

As it happened, Wiki had very little experience of Maori medicine, as he'd spent very little of his adult life in the Bay of Islands, and was blessed with splendid health, anyway. But he said with perfect confidence, "The patient always gets better, if he doesn't die first."

"I'm surprised *anyone* survives."

"You'd be even more surprised to see how many get well," said Wiki. "With the coming of the white man, though, there are new diseases and new treatments. A lot more people seem to die, or so I've noticed." The vinegar-dabbing had stopped, and the surgeon seemed to have finished, so he pulled on his shirt and jumper.

James Dana, with such a disconcerting change of topic that it was obvious he hadn't been listening, said, "When Captain Rochester came for you the day before yesterday, he told us there was a murder on the sealer."

Wiki looked at him. The geologist was an impressive-looking man with a Roman nose and a head of waving hair. Though he was very young, he already had a formidable reputation.

"They *reported* a murder," he said, and pointed out, "There's a difference."

"So why were you summoned?"

"Because I'm a sheriff's deputy—what passes as the agent of U.S. law and order on this expedition."

"*You?* But you're our translator—and Captain Wilkes's clerk, at times, or so we hear."

"Before I left Norfolk, I was deputized by the sheriff of the Town of Portsmouth."

"But why?"

"The sheriff strongly suspected a killer was sailing with the expedition."

"And you brought him to justice?"

"Aye. In a manner of speaking."

"But surely your job finished then?"

"No, as a matter of fact, it did not," said Wiki. The voyage had been marked by a string of crimes, both on board ship and on shore, and he wondered if it would ever end.

"He's got a certificate," said Horatio Hale, who had seen it.

"A letter of authority?"

"Aye," said Wiki. The letter of authority was in an inside pocket of his Guernsey, so he hauled it out, unfolded it, and spread it out on the table. It was a grand parchment affair, highly embellished with a seal, a red ribbon, the coat of arms of the Town of Portsmouth, Virginia, and a number of significant looking signatures. The ribbon had faded with much exposure to officials all along the eastern coast of South America, and the seal was sadly cracked, but still it looked imposing.

48

"And that was why you were asking all those questions up the Rio Negro," said Hale. "Particularly," he added importantly, "after I discovered that body."

As Wiki remembered, it was only one of several bodies, but he didn't comment.

"And was there a body on the sealer?" asked Peale.

Wiki shook his head. "They simply reported it."

"So where the devil was it?"

"The sealer nearly run afoul of a drifting iceberg, and as the schooner passed the crew all saw a dead man on the ice."

"A sealing man?"

"It's very likely."

"What made them think he was murdered?" said Dr. Holmes. "It could have been from natural causes, considering their dangerous way of life."

"According to their captain, his head was beaten in."

"And the iceberg floats on?"

"A hazard to navigation," Wiki agreed.

Then he was distracted by a shout of, "Ready about!" followed by the piping of the boatswain's mates on deck. The gale was moderating, he thought, because the ship was about to be brought round on the other tack. The planks overhead echoed to the thump of feet as men hurried to their stations. "Helm's alee!" came the distant cry. More shrilling of pipes as the jib-sheets and fore-sheet were let go and overhauled, and then, "Mains'l ha-a-a-ul!" Wiki sensed the thump as the mainyard brought up against the backstays, and then the stiffening of the ship as the weather mainbrace was hove taut. The deck sloped the other way as the *Peacock* leaned into the wind, and their motion smoothed as she

49

settled to the new heading. At last, he thought, the bow was pointed at the straits again, and the chances of passing through were improving.

They all looked up as first one step and then others sounded on the companionway. Lee, Pilson, and Matthews came down the stairs, followed by two other officers whose names Wiki didn't know. Evidently the rain had stopped, because they had taken off their dripping, cumbersome oilskins. After the coats were slung onto the rack, everyone except Matthews returned to deck.

Matthews came to the table, and filled a tumbler with wine. Everyone looked at him, but no one said a word. Suddenly there was a loud cry from above, followed by a tumult of shouting. It sounded like an emergency. Matthews leapt out of his seat, and was halfway up the companion when he was met by Lieutenant Lee, coming down.

"What's up?" Matthews asked.

Lee's face was grim. "We need a surgeon."

Dr. Holmes stood up, sending his chair clattering. "An accident?"

"Aye, if you can call it that. Midshipman Dove has cut his throat."

Five

Wiki was appalled, because it didn't seem possible.

Dove, that kindly, sensitive young man, had taken his own life? The clerkish type, Midshipman Dove was completely unsuited the life of an officer, and had told him that he hated life on board—but there was no way Wiki could have guessed that he loathed the sea with such passion that he was likely to take the way out by cutting his throat. Surely he had hinted that he had big plans for his future, now that he was free of his family?

"Where is he?" he demanded.

Lieutenant Lee said, "The body's in the maintop."

Wiki saw Holmes wince. The maintop, the platform on the top of the lower part of the mainmast, was seventy feet above the swaying deck.

Lee added, "Better take oilskins—it's raining hard again."

Wincing, Dr. Holmes took down one of the wet oilskin coats from the cluster on the rack. When Wiki did the same, the surgeon simply nodded, and Wiki realized that producing his letter of authority had been very well timed. Completely forgetting his battered state, he pursued Dr. Holmes up the companionway and out onto the night-shrouded deck.

The rain hissed down on the planks, bouncing up to splash on coamings and bulwarks before seething into the scuppers. The cresset lanterns, which were now hanging in the rigging, had haloes around them. Wiki saw a muddled crowd of sailors gathered about the foot of the mainmast, all looking up to where two men were bent over the nettings and calling down to them. The ruckus silenced as Lee arrived. With a snap, he bid the men to get about their duty, and then nodded at Holmes to lead the way.

It was Wiki, however, who jumped onto the bulwarks first. His stiff muscles protested, but he ignored the discomfort, scrambling up the ladderlike shrouds, hand over fist, surefooted despite his stiffness. The tablelike platform of the maintop loomed high overhead, braced by the steeply backward-leaning futtock shrouds. Taking a bracing breath, Wiki swung out onto these, clambered upward and outward, and then, timing his move with a roll of the ship, threw himself over the rim of the maintop with a thump on his sore stomach, and scrambled to his feet.

Two men gaped at him from the pitching darkness. One said uncertainly, "You're not the surgeon. What's your business here?"

"I'm the sheriff's deputy," Wiki said.

"Ah," said the seaman. There was unexpected understanding in the grunt. He nodded, observing to his mate, "So he be Mr. Coffin."

Which meant that the sailors were better informed than the educated scientifics, Wiki thought ironically, but then forgot it, all his attention focused on the huddled form at the base of the topmast. Even if he hadn't been warned, he would have known that Dove's spirit was gone. There was a primitive, instinctive feeling of something vital fled, leaving an empty shell behind.

Moving slowly and cautiously, Dr. Holmes arrived up the lubber hole—the gap by the mast where spars and furled sails were lowered during maintenance of the rigging. Then he crawled out onto the maintop, assisted by a sailor who held a fizzing lantern high. A shaft of light fell onto the corpse, exposing a deep, black, dripping chasm under Dove's jutting chin.

"Dear Jesus," Dr. Holmes whispered.

Midshipman Dove has cut his throat. He had done more than that—he had cut so deeply that it was as if he had been trying to cut off his own head. The rain poured down, rattling on Wiki's oilskins, washing water ... and blood ... and blood ... all over the platform of the maintop.

"That poor young fellow sure weren't muckin' around when he calculated to put an end to 'imself, were he, sir," said the seaman to Wiki.

Wiki didn't answer. He couldn't. Something bitter had risen up in his throat, and he had to keep on swallowing.

Dr. Holmes picked up the bloodied right fist, and held it in the lantern light. The long, curving blade of a razor glinted, still gripped tightly in the dead fingers.

He said, "He was truly desperate—even more desperate than most."

"Why? What do you mean?"

"Usually there are two or three preliminary cuts, as if the victim had to force himself to carry on with the dreadful act—as if he teetered on the verge of changing his mind. Here, we have one decisive slash."

Wiki looked down at the corpse. Dr. Holmes was stating the obvious. But Valentine Dove had not seemed the desperate kind of person, he thought then.

Everything about him seemed deliberate, as if he weighed up the situation before deciding what to do. And, according to what the lad had said, he had made an important decision already...

Lieutenant Lee arrived over the maintop, and issued orders. Wiki watched the two seamen truss the body and sway it down to the deck, to be carried to the sailmaker for sewing into a shroud. Then he followed by sliding down a backstay, taking most of his weight on his good right hand, while Dr. Holmes cautiously descended the shrouds.

"We will signalize the *Vincennes* in the morning," Lee said when they arrived at the bottom. "I expect written reports from you both by the first bell of the morning watch."

The need for a medical report was obvious. Wiki could see Dr. Holmes's lips moving as he calculated that he would have to get the report finished by four-thirty in the morning, which left little time for sleep. But a legal one, too? Puzzled, he said to Lee, "You want one from me?"

"Don't you have a fancy document testifying that you're the agent of American law on the expedition?" The words were sarcastic, and didn't need an answer. Lee nodded curtly before heading for the afterhouse to inform Captain Hudson.

Dr. Holmes made straight for the door of the companionway, obviously eager to get the horrid clerking job done before he headed for his berth. Wiki followed at a slower pace, abruptly aware of his stiffness and soreness again, though he was anxious to get rid of the oilskin coat he had taken off the rack at random. It had been wet when he put it on, and had absorbed even more moisture in the rain. Like everything else issued by the Navy Department back in Norfolk, Virginia, the garment was so shoddy that it was scarcely worth the trouble of wearing.

He stopped in the open doorway, taking a long time to pull his arms out of the sodden, clinging sleeves, because of his swollen left arm. A lantern hung directly above him. Wiki blinked, his attention caught by a blotch that showed up in the lamplight, on his forearm above his right wrist. Not rainwater—or not just rainwater. The moisture was red—the scarlet of recently shed blood. He recognized it at once, though the rain washed it away, leaving his wrist clean.

Blood—from where? Had he been cut in the fight with the sealers, and not noticed it all day? Wiki pulled up the sleeve of his woolen smock to check, but there were no cuts in his skin, just a couple of darkening bruises. The blood had come from somewhere else.

From the inside of the sleeve of the oiled coat.

He turned back the sodden oilskin sleeve. Too late—any blood had been washed away. The splotch on his wrist had stayed there only because his Guernsey had covered it. Then, as he ran his hand down the rail of the companionway on the way down, he felt a trace of stickiness. When he arrived in the doorway of the pantry, he inspected his palm under the light of the hanging lantern.

More blood. Not much, but recognizably blood.

He could hear the scientifics directing a stream of questions at Dr. Holmes, and the doctor asking them to be quiet so he could concentrate on what he was writing. Still holding the dripping coat, Wiki stepped into the pantry, and turned it inside out. However, there was nothing to be seen. Because the coat was so porous, the rain had washed it inside as well as out. Wiki replaced the coat on the rack, and headed for the midshipmen's quarters.

The seven young men who huddled about the hanging table were shocked and white. Their eyes widened as they took in the true splendor of Wiki's black eye, and one pursed his lips in a soundless whistle, but no one said a word.

Wiki said, "When was the last time you saw Midshipman Dove?"

They looked at each other. One, who looked about fourteen, muttered, "Not since breakfast, me. We was in different watches."

"I went on watch with him," another, slightly older, boy volunteered. "But I was assigned to a different mast."

"Did he seem any different than usual? Moody? Worried?"

They all shook their heads.

"He hadn't had a shock—bad news, run afoul of a bullyragging officer?" Wiki was thinking of Lieutenant Matthews.

Again, they all shook their heads. "Wouldn't know, if he did," said one.

"His sea-chest?"

They all looked at each other, and a silent message seemed to pass between them. Then one said, "Ain't here. We sent it right away to the purser."

If their intention was to forestall accusations of thieving the dead boy's duds, this was understandable, but there was a puzzling undercurrent in their manner.

Frowning, Wiki said, "You managed to rouse up the purser at this time of night?"

"Aye, sir. He berths right next to his office, and we hammered a lot on his door."

"I see," said Wiki, though he didn't see at all, and was willing to wager that the purser didn't, either. But that could be left till later, while an inspection of the body could not. If he didn't hurry, Valentine Dove would be sewn into his shroud, along with all the clues his body might betray. He asked for the whereabouts of the sailmaker's room, and they gave him directions.

The little room was easily found, because the door was open, which was surprising, considering the task being carried out within. Wiki knocked on the doorframe, and the sailmaker turned from where he was working at a bench. He was one of the older men of the expedition, meaning he was in his late thirties. His face was weathered from hundreds of hours spent aloft and on deck mending sails, and set as hard as the leather palm he used to push through the needle.

His bristling brows lowered when he saw the state of Wiki's face, but the only sound he made was a grunt—which was a presage of what was to come, because he was uncommunicative in the extreme. Over the years, Wiki had found that sailmakers came in two types. There were the friendly, garrulous ones who seized the slightest chance to embark on tortuous seafaring yarns, and there were the arrogant specimens who despised ordinary seamen, being convinced it was their sailmaking art alone that kept the ship going. This fellow swiftly proved himself to be one of the latter.

When Wiki described his business the sailmaker's expression became even more hostile. "Sheriff's deputy? What the devil is that supposed to mean?"

"I'm the official representative of the sheriff's department of the Town of Portsmouth, Virginia."

"Well, sure as hell you don't look like anything official to me."

"I have a letter of authority to prove it—and orders from Lieutenant Lee to write up an official report."

"Report of what?"

"Of Midshipman Dove's sudden end."

Firmly, Wiki stepped inside, knowing that he was never going to get an invitation. The small workroom smelled like all the other sailmakers' rooms Wiki knew, of tar, hempen dust, rope, beeswax, and canvas. In this case, however, the air was also thick with the rusty stench of fresh blood. Dove's naked corpse was lying on a rectangle of gray canvas, and was white—dead white. In shocking contrast, the deep gash across the throat was black, the gouts of blood hardening fast. The sailmaker had closed his lips and the staring eyes, but the mouth of the wound still gaped.

"Where are his clothes?"

"Sent 'em to his mess, as was right."

Wiki frowned, thinking that the midshipmen hadn't mentioned that, then put it aside for the moment, saying, "If you don't mind?"

The sailmaker reluctantly shifted away from the bench, his eyes suspicious in their webs of wrinkles. Wiki moved close, and studied the severed throat, noting again what Dr. Holmes had pointed out, that there were no hesitation cuts, the gash being swift, deep, and decisive. Steeling himself, he lifted first the left hand, and then the right, inspecting them. They were stiffening, the whiteness giving away to iron-gray at the fingertips. There were no cuts on the palms.

"The razor?"

"What?"

"When I saw Mr. Dove's body on the maintop, there was a razor gripped in the right hand."

"You mean this?"

The sailmaker was holding up a razor. Its cleaned blade shone in the lamplight. Wiki started to set down the dead right hand, but as he turned the wrist, something caught his attention.

He said, "What's this?"

"What?" The sailmaker moved forward, and Wiki showed him. There were dark marks on the backs of the wrist and clenched fingers, like bruises, only dark claret in color, not blue.

"The buttocks will be the same," said the sailmaker, more cooperative now that he felt important, having expert information to share. "And the heels," he added.

"What do you mean?"

"I've sewn up a dozen corpses or more in my time, and have noticed it often. The body goes white and then gray, except where it leans on something hard. All the blood sinks to the bottom, and goes wine-colored, like that. It's as if the veins and arterials what carry the blood have been squashed, or summat."

"Compressed by the weight of the corpse?"

"Aye, you could put it like that."

It sounded likely, Wiki thought—except that he distinctly remembered that Valentine Dove had been huddled on his side with his right arm thrown out, the razor gripped in his hand.

"So how did those marks get onto the wrist and hand? And when?"

"Mebbe when they was lowering him from the maintop to the deck."

Maybe so—but Wiki could think of another reason for the bruises. He said, "I would like to be present while a surgeon inspects this body."

"Dr. Holmes has already looked at this here corpse."

"That's true," Wiki allowed, though the inspection in the maintop had been perfunctory in the extreme. "Nevertheless, I shall request Dr. Holmes to inspect the body again, in the morning—so I'd be obliged if you wouldn't sew him up."

"Too late," the other said. With an air of grim satisfaction, he drew the canvas over the dead face, and picked up needle and thread. "Which is I've already had orders that the corpse is to be ready for burial at dawn, and it takes more than an Injun what calls himself a deputy to countermand Lieutenant Lee's instructions."

Six

$\mathcal{A}$fter the squally night the day dawned serenely, with a fair topgallant breeze. Incredibly, though the rugged coast they were passing was uninviting in the extreme, the weather was sunny and mild. It was as if the weather wished to laugh in the face of death.

Wiki, sitting in a sheltered spot on the starboard side of the amidships deck, basked gratefully, feeling his stiffened muscles relax as his battered body absorbed the unexpected warmth. The *Peacock* was sailing very slowly, and as he sensed the changing tug of the sea, Wiki realized that Wilkes was waiting for the turn of the tide that would carry the three ships through the Straits of Le Maire. With this pause in their course, it was a convenient time to hold a funeral.

Accordingly, it came as no surprise when orders were given to heave the ship aback, and all hands were called. Then the end of a box appeared as Mr. Dove's body was brought up the main hatch. Wiki was startled to see that a junior midshipman merited a coffin, instead of just a shroud like a common seaman. He had just time to see the plain deal box had holes bored in the bottom — to make certain it sank, no doubt — before it was set on trestles, and the Stars and Stripes spread over it.

A half-mile away the *Vincennes* and the *Swallow* were lying at a standstill, also hauled aback as they waited for the tide to turn. Obviously, a stream of signals had been exchanged, because their ensigns, like that of the *Peacock*, were at half-mast. The flagship was lowering a boat—to send over the fleet chaplain, Mr. Elliott, Wiki assumed.

Then he saw that there was also an officer in the stern sheets, arrayed in cocked hat and boat cloak, and he wondered if Captain Wilkes was attending. Though Dove had been a mere junior midshipman, he had belonged to a prominent navy family, so this seemed a reasonable guess, but as the boat bobbed closer Wiki realized to his disgust that the visitor was one of the most despised officers in the expedition fleet, the smug and pompous Lawrence J. Smith. At the Rio Negro, Smith had been appointed flag lieutenant of the fleet, replacing Lieutenant Craven, who had been summarily dismissed on the most trivial of grounds just because Captain Wilkes was in a temper. Now, Wiki deduced, the new flag lieutenant couldn't resist a chance to flaunt his rank.

Formal hails echoed from the quarterdeck and the boat, and a boatswain's mate twittered on his call, piping the signal for "*Alongside*," as the boat touched the hull of the *Peacock*, and then "*Up the side*," as Smith ceremoniously mounted the ladder, followed by the reverend. Then came the somber call "*All hands to bury the dead*," which echoed back and forth about the ship, accompanied by massed shuffling as every seaman rose to his feet. A single drum rattled, and the ship's marines marshaled into a line with their Navy-issue Hall rifles reversed.

Captain Hudson and seven officers emerged from the afterhouse door, resplendent in dress uniform. In strict order of rank, they marched to the starboard side of the amidships deck, with the surviving midshipmen, the three scientifics, the purser, and Dr. Holmes bringing up the rear. As they arrived they took off their hats and bowed to Lieutenant Smith and the reverend, who both bowed back, and then they assembled behind the coffin.

The fleet chaplain, the Reverend Mr. Elliott, stood at a lectern, his vestments flapping in the breeze. A bandy-legged little fellow, he was a familiar figure, having delivered Bibles to every mess. The seamen laughed at him behind his back, partly because of his openly expressed fears that his charges would be corrupted by carnal scenes in foreign ports, but mostly for his struggle to stop everyone from working on Sunday, even when God had sent a storm.

"I am the resurrection and the life, saith the Lord," he recited, but Wiki wasn't listening. Instead, he was studying the officers, wondering which one of them had gripped Dove's hand about the razor, and then dragged it by force across his exposed gullet ... wondering if the murderer was still unaware that in the moment of violence blood had run inside the sleeve of his oilskin coat.

Matthews and Lee were standing next to each other, the sun twinkling on their left-shoulder epaulettes and the lines of gold buttons that swooped down their jacket fronts and adorned their cuffs and pockets. Like the other officers, they were holding their cocked hats, their faces exposed to the sun. Lee, though only about twenty-five, was deeply weathered, his face creased with two deep lines on either side of a wide mouth that was set like a trap. He was clean-shaven, according to the specifications laid down by Captain Wilkes, but his thick, straight hair had been allowed to grow over his ears, emphasizing his piercing eyes, which were deep-set under bristling eyebrows.

Matthews's face, by contrast, was as smooth as if stitched flat by his scar—yet Wiki was suddenly touched by a sense of familiarity. Matthews was taller, older, and slimmer than Lee, and his hair was a paler brown, but abruptly Wiki knew beyond doubt that the two men were related. In the Pacific, people distinguished each other by bone structure, stance and mannerisms, developing a sixth sense for identifying different families and tribes, and he was sure the instinct was serving him well now. Lee and Matthews were close kin—cousins, probably, maybe even half-brothers.

Did this have any bearing on Dove's murder? "Out of the deep have I called to thee, O Lord," declaimed the reverend, but still Wiki paid no attention, turning implications over in his mind. *Ko nga take whawhai, he whenua, he wahine,* he thought—*for the reason for trouble, look at property, look at women.* Jealousy and greed were the two usual motives for murder, in his experience, but, if one close relative was looking after the interests of another, could there be a third?

He knew already, from what he had overheard from the pantry, that Lee was the focus of mutinous talk among the officers who were hostile to Captain Wilkes. Was Matthews another rebel? And what about the rest? Wiki transferred his gaze to the other lieutenants. He knew one of them slightly—Oliver Hazard Perry, the son of a naval hero, because Perry had been one of a party he had once accompanied on shore. A second man, William Walker, had been reasonably polite, introducing himself when Wiki had first come on board, and distancing himself from the unpleasant discrimination that had followed. And then there was Pilson, the officer of the watch who had remained aloof while the sealers were beating Wiki up.

The last two officers were strangers. While Wiki had glimpsed them, and undoubtedly heard their voices, he didn't know their names. One had dissolute eyes, shadowed as if he seldom slept, while the other had a long, pockmarked face. What were their names? And what kind of men were they? Wiki thought he would give a great deal for a private chat with George Rochester.

At long last the chaplain cried out, "We now commit this body to the deep." Everyone shifted from one foot to the other, deeply relieved that the discomfort of standing rigidly still on an unsteady deck was coming to an end. Two boatswain's mates lifted the end of the plank, and the box containing poor Valentine Dove slid out from under the flag and down the slope with a harsh grating noise, followed by a dull splash.

After the first ripple, there was nothing to betray that it was gone. So there went the corpse, thought Wiki, carrying the only evidence that Dove had been murdered. The marines marched to the gangway, lifted their rifles, fired a salute, and the ceremony was over.

The boatswain shrilled on his call, sending the watch to their various posts. Wiki stayed where he was, surrounded by off-duty seamen. Then, over their heads, he saw a comical near-accident unfold.

Lawrence J. Smith, at the gangway, was bidding a formal farewell to Captain Hudson and a bevy of lieutenants, when he abruptly staggered. For the space of a heartbeat he was on the verge of toppling overboard, but then he caught his balance by snatching at Hudson's arm. Hudson, taken unawares, stumbled a pace, and had to grab at one of his officers, who sidestepped, knocking against one of his fellow lieutenants, who tottered drunkenly too, setting another officer off-kilter.

Then, to the veiled disappointment of the watching seamen, the complement managed to straighten up. Wiki heard polite mirth from the officers as they tried to laugh away embarrassment. When Lieutenant Smith turned to descend the ladder, however, he was red in the face with temper, his mouth tightly pursed.

Perhaps, Wiki thought later, that was the reason he stumbled again. This time, there was no arm to snatch, so over Smith went. One minute he was there, and the next, he was not. Instead, there was the echo of a splash.

Consternated shouts. Wiki, like many others, rushed to the rail. The tubby lieutenant was thrashing around in the water seven feet below, his overcoat streaming about him. He was sinking lower with every struggle, trying to scream but only managing to produce muffled gurgles. The officers wavered, hampered by their tight dress uniforms, so it was Wiki who kicked off his boots, though his sore body winced. He was pre-empted, however, by Lieutenant Matthews, who jumped over the gangway and into the water.

He was only just in time, because Smith was drowning fast. Matthews ducked deep, and they surged up together. Matthews caught hold of the bottom cleat of the gangway ladder. Smith threshed in panic, tore himself free, and almost sank again. The scar-faced lieutenant reached out for the hem of his coat, and dragged him back, but still Smith persisted in blindly trying to fight him off.

Matthews needed assistance, that was obvious. Again, however, Wiki was forestalled, this time by Smith's boat, which arrived from around the stern quarter. Brawny arms reached out to haul in the half-drowned man, and then Lieutenant Matthews slid over the gunwale into the boat. Wiki could hear the boat's crew congratulating him on the rescue.

There was a pause while the boat was hooked on, then it was hauled up with its two sodden occupants inside. Mr. Matthews was standing up, supporting Mr. Smith, and the flag lieutenant's expression was hysterically furious. Hands were extended to help Smith out of the boat, and the moment he was on the deck he twisted around, searching the crowd with his wild stare.

His arm shot out, the extended finger pointing directly at Wiki, and he shouted, "Wiremu!"

Wiki flinched. Not only was everyone staring at him, but he hated being called by the Maori version of his American name, William. Lieutenant Smith, a neighbor back in Salem, had considered Wiki an interesting curiosity since the day Captain Coffin had brought him home, and calling him Wiremu was a condescending affectation.

Reluctantly, Wiki walked forward to join the crowd at the rail, and contemplated the dripping, furious little fellow.

"Lieutenant?" he said.

"Wiremu, are you the sheriff on this ship, or not?"

Wiki blinked, even more taken aback. He couldn't help a sideways glance at Captain Hudson, who was looking equally baffled.

Then he said to Lieutenant Smith, "Why do you ask?"

"Because you have to start an investigation!"

"Into what, sir?"

"I was shoved, sir! Someone pushed me!"

Dead silence all about the decks. Then Captain Hudson said, "My dear fellow, what are you saying?"

"I would have *drowned* without Mr. Matthews's timely rescue!" Smith's stare, still focused on Wiki, became accusing, and Wiki, already feeling guilty about being so slow to jump into the water, knew he was in for a lengthy chiding the next time the new flag lieutenant found him alone.

"Certainly, you owe him your life," Captain Hudson agreed benignly.

He wasn't paying Mr. Smith his full attention, though, because he was studying Wiki's black eye with his brows raised instead, while the tubby flag lieutenant's voice rose querulously. "But I insist, most *emphatically*, Captain Hudson, that I felt a hand shove me over—and I want Deputy Coffin to find the culprit and bring charges!"

"Captain Hudson," said Wiki, feeling desperate.

"Yes, Mr. Coffin?" But before Wiki could think of anything to say, the commander of the *Peacock* muttered with a badly concealed grin, "Have trouble arresting a suspect?"

Wiki quenched a sigh, thinking that this was a most inappropriate time to be jocular about his black eye.

He said, "A tumble, sir. But as for Mr. Smith's charge, I honestly don't see how I — "

Lieutenant Matthews said, "Captain Hudson, sir, Mr. Smith definitely stumbled. We all saw it distinctly. And the earlier bout of dizziness, too."

"Exactly," said Captain Hudson, and turned with an air of relief to the flag lieutenant. "You simply lost your balance, my dear Smith. You were overcome by the sad occasion, assuredly It's an emotion that does you credit, but you really should consult a surgeon about your lightheadedness."

"But both times, I swear — "

"Tut, my good fellow." Hudson's voice became brisk. "You're in a natural state of shock, and will remember things different when you get over it. And I see signals a-flying from the *Vin*."

"I protest — "

"Signals of the utmost urgency," Captain Hudson assured him. "The tide is on the turn."

And, with that, he issued directions to Lieutenant Lee. A stream of orders followed, one of which was to get the flag lieutenant back onto his ship. Smith, swathed in a borrowed boat cloak and supported by the reverend's arm, was hurried down the side, this time without accident. The last glimpse Wiki had of him was his furiously frustrated expression

Seven

The flagship fired a cannon. It was the signal to get underway, and steer through the Straits of Le Maire.

Boatswains' calls shrilled, orders were shouted, and seamen dashed to their stations. Wiki pushed through the crush to get to the amidships hatchway, and then headed down ladders to the orlop deck, in the bowels of the ship, in search of the man who looked after the ship's accounts and stores.

This was William Spieden, the purser, whose office was in the most logical place possible, in the stern of the hold, close to where the provisions were stored. It had been a trek to find it, though, and to Wiki's relief when he knocked, a voice called, "Come."

He opened the door, to find a room smelling of ink, silverfish, mice, dusty books and damp paper. Because the office was well below the waterline, it was lit with hanging lamps. A counter divided it into two, with Mr. Spieden on the other side. Shelves packed with account books were secured on the wall behind him, while manifest boxes and an iron strongbox stood on the floor. A sea-chest was stowed beside them. The only other furnishings were the tall stool where the purser was perched, and a lantern, which hung right above his head, casting a circle of light onto the ledger he was consulting.

Despite the dank chill, the purser was in shirtsleeves, his double-breasted swallowtail coat and cocked hat hanging from hooks on the after bulkhead. He straightened his back, pushed his rimless spectacles up his nose, and said, "Mr. Coffin."

Amazed, but thanking God that his name was known here, Wiki said, "Good morning."

"That's a really impressive black eye."

"So everyone tells me."

"I recommend the application of a cloth well-soaked in tea."

"*Tea?*"

"Strong, cold tea. Left on all night is best."

"I'll remember that," said Wiki. Then he firmly changed the subject, pointing at the chest that had been stored next to the strongbox. "I believe it was delivered last night?"

"The dead of night, when two midshipmen came hammering at my door." Spieden's stateroom, as Wiki gathered from the complaint that followed, was too confoundedly accessible to young men with no consideration for their elders. It hadn't taken much effort to open the door, shove in the chest, and lock the door again, but being roused at that hour had been highly irritating. While Spieden regretted the tragedy of the young man's suicide, surely his messmates could have kept the chest until after the burial was over?

When Spieden ran to a stop, Wiki said, "I need to examine the contents."

"Why?"

"Perhaps you've already made a list of Mr. Dove's belongings?"

71

Spieden sighed. "I really would like to know what you think gives you the right to open that chest and look inside."

Once again, Wiki described his appointment as a sheriff's deputy, going on to point out that it gave him the legal right to appraise property, especially of those deceased.

"*You*? A United States *official*?"

"Aye," said Wiki. Ignoring the implied insult with the ease of long experience, he produced his certificate of authority.

Spieden unfolded it, and spread it out on the counter. Then, to Wiki's surprise, he produced a sheet of paper and proceeded to copy the flourishing words. The scratching of his pen went on for a long time, but at last it was done, down to the last signature.

The purser looked at him over the tops of his spectacles, and observed, "This is quite imposing."

Wiki smiled. "That's what it's meant to be. But I wish it was in better order."

It had been folded into a tight wad when handed over to Wiki, and had been unfolded, displayed to captains and foreign officials and refolded many times since. Wiki had contemplated pasting another sheet of parchment onto the back, and rolling up like a scroll, but that would have made it difficult to carry around.

Spieden turned it over, looked the back, and turned it over again. "Perhaps a sheet of very fine lawn would help?"

"Lawn?" In that context, it was a new word for Wiki.

"Lawn is a delicate but strong fabric. Pasted to the back of the document, it would allow you to keep it folded, but without breaking at the creases."

That seemed a good idea, so Wiki asked, "Do you have any here?"

"I think so." The purser pulled out a drawer at the back of the counter, and produced a large piece of delicate fabric, so fine that the lamplight shone through its whiteness, turning it translucent. It was stitched along the edges, so evidently had been intended as a gentleman's handkerchief, or maybe even a lady's neck scarf. Why would any sailor buy such a thing? As a present?

Wiki picked it up. It felt soft in his rough fingers. "This is lawn?"

The purser nodded. Then he said briskly, "Two dollars."

Wiki lifted a disbelieving brow, even though it hurt. "For a handkerchief?"

"You do have the money?"

"Of course I have the money!" Wiki was paid a salary of two thousand, five hundred dollars a year, just like the other scientifics. Most of the first advance had been invested on his behalf by George Rochester's grandfather, of the famous Boston law firm—though the paperwork had been done by his clerk, the highly efficient Mr. Puffin—but Wiki had funds in the strongbox on the *Swallow*, as well as cash in his pocket.

He said, "Throw in the paste, and it's a deal."

"Young man, you drive a hard bargain," said Spieden. He was smiling so broadly it was obvious it was a joke. Wiki handed over the coins, and the purser rang a little bell. A tousle-headed boy arrived at the run, was handed a scribbled chit, and then dashed off again. Within a surprisingly short time he was back, bearing a contraption made of two large rectangles of light wood braced with narrow oak slats and with two leather straps screwed to the lowermost board.

After setting the contraption on the counter, the lad produced a small flask of water from one pocket, and an envelope of white powder from another. Then he proceeded to combine the powder and the water by pouring the contents of the envelope into the flask and shaking it vigorously, all the time studying Wiki with round blue eyes. He was red-haired and freckled and looked about ten. Wiki wondered how he'd managed to join the expedition, and if his mother worried about him.

However, he was mostly curious about the contraption. "What's that?" he asked.

Apparently the boy was too lowly to be allowed to speak, because the purser answered, saying, "A botanical press."

"Used by the scientifics?"

"The naturalists carry these presses with them when they go on shore," Spieden agreed. "With a few sheets of paper and a little gum tragacanth to secure flowers and foliage in place, they press and preserve all manner of botanical specimens. I don't see why we shouldn't have the same success with your certificate, once we've pasted the lawn to the back."

He fossicked around in the drawer again, coming up with a brush. This, he handed to Wiki, who, discerning that the word "we" was rhetorical and he was the one to do the actual work, brushed paste onto the fabric. Both the purser and the boy watched intently, and Wiki could hear the boy's noisy breathing.

Seven bells rang—eleven thirty. On the deck above, the boatswain shrilled the order for stations, and feet stamped as men hurried to lines and sheets. Wiki distinctly heard the thwack of a cane and a squeal as some slow-moving sailor was surprised into faster action. Then he sensed the thump as the mainyard came against the backstays. By the time he had finished, the deck was sloping the other way.

The purser said, "Now, leave the fabric to half-dry before applying it to the parchment."

Wiki obediently set the sticky sheet of lawn onto a sheet of paper, with the certificate face-up beside it. Then he said firmly, "Mr. Dove's sea-chest?"

"Mr. Dove committed suicide. There's no crime to investigate."

"It *was* a violent death, Mr. Spieden."

Silence. Then Spieden reluctantly lifted a flap in the counter, allowing Wiki to the privileged side of his sanctum.

Wiki felt about in his Guernsey for the notebook he kept in an inner pocket, found a pencil, and hunkered down. When he lifted the lid of the chest, it became apparent why the midshipmen had been so shocked and white-faced when he had questioned them, and why they had got rid of the chest so quickly—blood-soaked clothes were piled in a messy heap on the top. The garments were stiffened and black, and a rancid smell filled Wiki's nostrils as he gingerly searched the pockets.

For a while it seemed there was nothing to find—no watch, and no cash. Then he felt a wadded-up paper in an inside jacket pocket. When he drew it out it was blackened with blood, which didn't seem promising, but prying the folds apart revealed two sheets of paper, one much larger and stiffer than the other. The small one was a note that was so stained it was impossible to read, but the other hadn't soaked up as much blood, because it was heavier. While the back of the document was smeared and spotted, the front was perfectly legible.

Wiki looked at the crest, read the cursive words, and whispered, "My God."

Spieden said, "What is it?"

It was a draft on a bank in Rio de Janeiro, Brazil, for the sum of five thousand dollars. Wiki handed it over, and watched Spieden's mouth purse up in a silent whistle.

He asked, "Was Midshipman Dove rich?"

"It seems evident that he didn't kill himself because he was poor," the purser said dryly. Fishing about in his drawer yet again, he found an envelope, slid the draft inside, and wrote on the outside. Wax was heated, and after the envelope was securely sealed, a second key was produced, this time from a chain attached to his belt. This proved to be for the iron strongbox, which squealed in protest as the key was turned, and groaned as the weighty lid was lifted. Wiki had just a glimpse of money bags and bundled papers before the envelope was stowed inside, and the safe was locked again.

But was the draft the only one? Putting the blood-soaked garments in a heap on the floor, Wiki went through the clean clothes, searching the pockets carefully, then folding them again after finding nothing, and piling them to one side, away from the bloody ones. As he neared the bottom of the chest, it became increasingly obvious to him that the chest had been searched already, but when he looked up to cross-examine the purser some more, it was to find that the office had suddenly become busy. A dozen men were pushing up to the counter—the cook's mates for the daily requisition of flour, fresh water and hard bread, a servant sent by the captain's clerk for paper and ink, the sailmaker for rope and canvas. The bell was rung repeatedly, and the messenger boy came at the run. Off he went with scribbled chits, sometimes with the applicant trailing after him, while other men waited for goods to come back.

Then three lieutenants and a senior midshipman arrived to beg for powder for a ceremonial salute of cannon when the *Peacock* arrived at Orange Harbor. Two of the lieutenants and the midshipman were strangers to Wiki, but the fourth was Pilson. He ignored Wiki, instead taking part in the argument with Spieden, who insisted that he would need a letter from Captain Hudson. It took a while, but the officers finally left in quest of their letter, to be replaced by a delegation of seamen wishing to register a complaint on behalf of their messes. Apparently the mess bill, which included such items as tea, sugar, tobacco, mustard, pepper, thread, soap, tinware and cutlery, had included a surcharge for tea—"Which has doubled in price," they said, and wanted to know why.

"Because we're short of said item," said the purser, while Wiki listened with interest. He knew that the officers had to provide private stores to augment their basic ration of fresh water, salt meat, hard bread, and flour, but he'd had no idea that ordinary navy seamen had to pay for such things.

"But it's never been extra quality, sir, considering what we was charged," the leader of the group argued. "And what you're demandin' now is jest plain robbery."

"Call it what you like, I don't have any choice. We've plenty of coffee, on account of those bags of good Brazilian we bought from a Salem trader out of Rio, but as for tea we've almost run out, and won't get any more until we stock up from the storeship *Relief* when we meet up in Orange Harbor—and that might not be for days yet, Captain Wilkes not making me cognizant of his plans. So you can call it a scarcity price, and you just have to lump it or go without."

"Well, we ain't goin' to sign for it, not at that price," the seaman said stubbornly. The purser shrugged, indicating he couldn't care less if they chose to give up their tea, and the delegation took themselves off, muttering darkly as they went.

It was Wiki's chance. He stood up, gestured at the neat pile of unbloodied clothes he had sorted through and placed on the floor at the side of the chest, and said, "Have you already made a list of all this, Mr. Spieden?"

"I've already told you that I haven't."

"But you have searched through these things?"

"Mr. Coffin, you are the first man to open that chest since it was stowed in this room."

So it must have been the midshipmen, Wiki thought. They hadn't stolen any of the kit, though, because the wardrobe was so complete. While most officers were able to afford only one change, Valentine

Dove had owned two spare sets of undress uniform, with flat peaked caps to match. There were extras for full dress, too—two pairs of white satin breeches, two pairs of white trousers, and two white vests to go with the magnificent swallow-tailed single-breasted jacket with its standup collar embroidered with acorns and oak leaves in gold thread.

Wiki was impressed—George Rochester's grandfather, who had raised George after he'd been orphaned as a child, was wealthy and generous, but even George didn't own as many changes as this, and Forsythe, who was constantly in debt because of his addiction to gambling, had a wardrobe that was not only much more scanty, but hardworn, as well. Yet, though it seemed evident that Dove's wardrobe was intact, all the pockets were empty. He must have carried money, but there wasn't a single coin. Nor were there any mementoes—no miniatures, no letters, no reminders of his family.

Then Wiki was interrupted by the redheaded boy, who nudged him on the upper arm. The boy had a gold-hilted dress sword in one grubby paw, and a cocked hat in the other, both the property of the deceased. The splendid cocked hat was the same as Spieden's, bound with one-and-a-half-inch lace with tassels at either end. A cockade was held in place with more gold lace. After adding these to his list, Wiki looked again at the big pile of folded uniform garments, wondering what would become of them all. On whaleships a dead man's duds were auctioned at the foremast, a ritual presided over by the captain, who traditionally claimed that the proceeds were sent to the family. Though the whaling crew didn't believe this for an instant, being convinced the captain pocketed the cash, they bought up the poor remnants, pretending it was out of sentiment, but usually because they were short of such things themselves.

It would take a rich man to buy this wardrobe. Wiki said curiously to the purser, "What happens to all this?"

Spieden pursed his lips, looking at the blood-drenched garments that had been set aside. "Soaked for a few hours in cold fresh water, they should wash up clean enough for shipboard use."

Wiki grimaced. "What about the good clothes?"

"The chest, complete with its contents, will be sent back to the deceased's family at the next civilized port we touch."

So, Wiki deduced, it was only because the ship was heading for Cape Horn, well away from civilized ports, that he'd had the chance to appraise Dove's belongings. He turned back to his task, and soon after that was down to the bottom of the chest, where two mahogany boxes were chocked into place with books on seafaring and navigational practice. The books were new, and when he riffled through them it was evident they'd never been opened. Dove's rich and ambitious family had provided everything possible for the lad's first navy voyage, but he hadn't had the aptitude or the liking.

Wiki took out the boxes, levered up the little gold catches, and opened their polished lids. One held a fine sextant, and the other an equally expensive telescoping spyglass. Afterwards, he wasn't sure why he took the sextant out—perhaps to weigh the beautiful instrument in his hands, and admire the fine workmanship. It was when he started to put it back that he noticed that a felt-covered triangular block in the righthand upper corner of the box, designed to hold the sextant securely in place, had come loose.

Carefully setting the sextant aside, he wriggled the large wedge out of the corner. It was very light, and when he turned it to expose the side that had originally been glued to the case, he saw that it was hollow. Inside was a roll of little papers.

"What's that?" the purser said.

Wiki shook his head, and stood up to unroll the cylinder. It broke up into fourteen slips, which scattered on the counter. He picked up one and Spieden took another, and there was a moment's silence while they read the scrawled name and the sum of money noted on each one. Then they looked at each other in stunned speculation.

"This is an IOU!" Spieden exclaimed.

"And so is mine," said Wiki.

Together, they went through the lot. All were receipts for money borrowed from Dove, each signed with initials at the bottom, and with a name printed at the top of each slip, evidently by Dove himself. There were five names altogether. One man—Jerkin—owed just one sum, while Plison had signed two IOUs. Lusser and Clamber had signed three chits each, and a man by the name of Sweetman owed the dead Dove the enormous sum of one thousand, three hundred dollars, spread over four chits. When the purser added all fourteen up, the total was impressive.

Jerkin, Sweetman, Plison, Lusser, Clamber. All the names were unfamiliar to Wiki. He said, "Do you know who they are?"

81

The purser shook his head, looking puzzled. "They must be from other ships."

Wiki said, "Do you have any ideas about why they borrowed it?"

"Of course I do! Euchre! Four card monté! They borrowed from the innocent to satisfy their depraved craving for cards!"

"There's a lot of card play on the *Peacock*?"

"Mr. Coffin, you've no idea! They play in the wardroom and the midshipmen's mess—even in the afterhouse, if Captain Hudson is away from the ship. It's a scandal—midshipmen toying with the devil's tickets when they should be applying themselves to their books, and lieutenants providing the worst of examples!"

Yet there were no names from the *Peacock* complement on any of the chits. Wiki sorted through them again, but the writing, though childish, was clear. *Jerkin, Sweetman, Plison, Lusser, Clamber*. Only the scribbled initials were indecipherable.

It was surprising, he thought then, that Forsythe was not one of them. The Virginian had an infamous gambling habit, but though he seemed to owe money to just about everyone, he had apparently not borrowed from Mr. Dove.

He said, "What are you going to do with the chits? Show them to Captain Hudson?"

Spieden paused to think, and then said with decision, "I'll put them in the strongbox, to be returned to Mr. Dove's family. The unhappy and difficult job of getting them honored is their problem, not ours." And the purser took out another envelope, ready to seal and store the chits, just as he had the bank draft.

Wiki said hastily, "I must make a list of the names and amounts first."

"Why?"

Wiki's mind was racing. It was impossible to say that the men named on the chits were all murder suspects, because he had no evidence that the razor had been forced across Midshipman Dove's throat. Finally, he said, "It's part of the official appraisal. And Captain Wilkes is bound to ask me for the details of this gambling business, if the news ever gets to his ears."

There was another long pause as Mr. Spieden debated with himself, and Wiki got ready for more argument. However, the purser nodded, so he picked up his notebook again. It had fallen shut, which meant he had to riffle past the pages of notes he had taken on the Rio Negro and then the only entry he had made since leaving Patagonia — the name of the sealer *Betsey* and the position of the corpse-carrying iceberg that Captain Noyes had reported. Turning to the next blank page following the list of chest contents, he copied down the names Dove had printed on the tops of the chits, along with the sums of money. Again, he was startled by the amount involved — and yet, he thought, feeling very puzzled, the boy had had no coins in his pockets. Where had the money come from?

Jerkin, Sweetman, Plison, Lusser, Clamber. He said to the purser, "You're sure none of the names are familiar to you?"

Spieden was silent a long moment, his lips pursed and his head tilted a little. "I did wonder about this one," he said, and sorted out the two chits that were headed with the name of the unknown Plison. "Do you think the lad may have confused the letters L and I, or that they have become smudged so that one looks like the other?"

Plison ... Pilson. Wiki remembered much about Pilson, including that he had been so conveniently absent when the sealers were trying to beat the position of the *Betsey*'s sealing beach out of him. "That's very likely," he said slowly. "But why is he the only one from the *Peacock*?"

"Perhaps he borrowed money on behalf of others."

The two chits were for $60 and $50, respectively, which added up to the not insignificant sum of one hundred and ten dollars, a lot of money for a man to indebt himself on behalf of his friends. Then Wiki wondered if the others had reasons to wish to be anonymous, and the power to force Pilson to sign the chit—Lieutenant Lee, for instance. Judging from what Spieden had said, Captain Hudson, if he had known, would have forbidden the practice—just like George Rochester, back on the *Swallow*—and Lee would have been in serious trouble if evidence of gambling had surfaced.

Then Wiki thought that even if Rochester had been lenient, there wouldn't have been any opportunity for card-play on the *Swallow*, with its much smaller complement. Remembering an adage his stepmother often quoted about Satan loving idle hands, he remarked, "They seem to have a lot of leisure time here—too much, perhaps."

"There's *plenty* to do on board this ship—in the way of assisting the scientifics!" Spieden exclaimed. "Why can't they consider the aims of the exploring expedition, instead of frittering away their time in base habits? There's nothing too high or too low *I* wouldn't be prepared to do myself, in the interests of the enterprise — I'd black the boots of Captain Wilkes, if it would help!"

At that highly inappropriate moment the door burst open, the three lieutenants having returned with the letter from Captain Hudson. Wiki hurriedly pushed the chits under a ledger, and hunkered down to repack Dove's belongings in the chest.

Every now and then he paused, to covertly study the officers. How rich — or poor — were these three men? He felt certain now that Pilson was an inveterate gambler, but how about the other two?

Ko nga take whawhai, he whenua. For the source of trouble, look for money.

Eight

Wiki didn't have a chance to retrieve the chits and inspect them again. Before he could take them from under the ledger Titian Peale arrived, looking busy and important. As the naturalist immediately announced, he'd decided to educate the ordinary seamen in the mysteries of his discipline.

"So many of the officers are ignorant of science and disinclined to help out with observations that I have made up my mind they should be shamed by those they consider their inferiors," he declared. He would begin with a lecture on ornithology in general and the common wheatear, *Oenanthe oenanthe*, in particular. This was because he had noticed much interest taken when a specimen had landed on the *Peacock* in an exhausted condition a few weeks earlier. The poor creature had been seeking a haven, but instead had been captured by the naturalist, to the great excitement of all on deck.

"What a splendid idea! We should all learn to do what we can to further the aims of the expedition," Spieden said, adding rather tactlessly, "no matter how humble that contribution might be." Then he busied himself writing down details of the gear Peale wanted for his demonstration, including the preserved body of the famous wheatear itself, while Peale stared at the botanical press with a frown.

"Who requisitioned this?"

"I did," Wiki confessed.

"Well, I hope you're not going to monopolize it, as this expedition is confoundedly short of such stuff. It's a valuable piece of equipment."

"Only for a little while," said Wiki. "Mr. Spieden has kindly loaned it so I can fix my letter of authority."

"Fix it? What do you mean?"

"And it's about time to attach the fabric to it, and put the machine into operation," said Spieden, saving Wiki from a reply.

They all looked at the certificate. The seal and gilded crest of the Town of Portsmouth managed to glint importantly in the lantern light, despite the document's battered state. Wiki touched the lawn, and found the glue tacky, so he turned over the document, and spread the fabric onto the back. It clung at once. He smoothed it out with great care, while the purser and the red-haired boy watched with interest, and Peale gave a lot of advice. Then the naturalist became tired of the clumsiness of Wiki's rough seaman's hands, and elbowed him to one side so he could take over the job himself. Wiki watched as he placed a sheet of paper on the bottom half of the press, set the document face-down on this, set a second sheet of paper on top of the lawn backing, put the other board on top of it, and closed the wood-and-paper sandwich by securing the two leather straps.

As Peale buckled the second strap, eight bells rang—dinnertime. There was a thunder of feet as hungry sailors rushed to collect their buckets of coffee and wooden kids of food from the galley. Wiki, who felt hungry himself, wondered what delicacies the steward might have waiting in the officers' pantry, but was forestalled by Mr. Peale.

Picking up the botanical frame as if he was determined not to let the valuable gadget out of his sight, the naturalist said, "It's time you displayed a little courage and spirit, Mr. Coffin."

Wiki's mouth fell open. "I *beg* your pardon?"

"Get off your high horse, and condescend to dine with us at the wardroom table."

"*What?*"

Ignoring this, Peale marched out of the office, and headed for the series of ladders that led up to the main hatch, while Wiki pursued him furiously. It was still sunny on the weather deck, which was bustling as rations were handed out and the watch was changed. The lieutenants and midshipmen were lined up along the quarterdeck rail with their sextants, taking their noon sights.

The naturalist had finally stopped, to contemplate the scene. Arriving beside him, Wiki snapped, "It wasn't my choice to eat in the pantry."

"What do you mean?"

"I was made to understand that the wardroom refused to share the table with a colored man."

Titian Peale stared at him. "And how, exactly, did this come about?"

Wiki paused. That first afternoon on the *Peacock*, he had arrived in the wardroom with his sea-chest on his shoulder, to find it empty except for the Brava steward, who had shown him to his berth. No sooner had the steward gone than an officer had materialized at his stateroom door with a message from the rest. *The wardroom, as we all agree, is supposed to be reserved for*

88

officers and gentlemen ... So after some discussion we've decided that the best solution is for you to mess in the pantry with the steward.

Wiki had simply stared, unable to believe what he was hearing, because nothing in his past seafaring existence had prepared him for it. While many of the whaling masters he had sailed under had been rough and ignorant, a surprising number had been well-read gentlemen who had gladly walked the deck with him, discussing politics and history—and none of them, whether ignorant or educated, had cared in the slightest whether a seaman was black, white, or brindle, just as long he had strong shoulders and could heave an accurate harpoon. Good men were promoted on merit, not their social standing or color, so that Wiki had learned his seamanship from extremely competent mates who were Fayal Portuguese, black men from the Cape Verde Islands, and Gayhead Indians. But, it seemed, the sky would fall before a man of color would be given rank in the navy—or allowed to eat at the wardroom table, apparently.

Then had come the warning—that if he made any trouble, he would find himself swinging in a hammock on the berth deck. *Before you know what hits you, you'll be standing watches as a common seaman before the mast.*

Normally, shifting to the berth deck would have been an appealing alternative, as Wiki had always managed well in the foc'sle, but on that first afternoon he'd had eight good reasons for not wanting to live with the ordinary seamen. Seven were the sealers, who certainly had planned a vicious revenge for their recapture and flogging on the Rio Negro. And the last was Jack Sac—Te Aute—who at the time was considered hostile. So, the threat had been a potent one.

Grimacing at the memory, he said to Peale, " I don't want to repeat it, but it was a strong message, believe me. And it came with a warning of what would happen if I didn't buckle under."

"Am I allowed to ask the name of the man who delivered the message?"

It had been Lieutenant Pilson. Wiki looked away without answering.

As the silence drew on, Peale drew out a pipe from a pocket, which he filled and lit with deliberate care, having tucked the botanical frame under one arm. Then he said, "Well, Mr. Coffin, I think I'll get onto my high horse, too."

"What do you mean?"

"I've decided to join you and our steward in the pantry for dinner."

Wiki stared at the older man's smoke-wreathed face, then laughed, and said, "You remind me of my stepmother."

For the first time, Peale looked startled. He echoed, "Stepmother?"

"My father's legal wife. Perhaps you don't know I'm only half-Maori?"

"I believe your father is Captain William Coffin— that flamboyant fellow we've come to know quite well since colliding with his ship in Rio. In fact, we put our specimens on board of his brig, so I hope he's safely on the way to Philadelphia."

Wiki hoped so, too. "Well," he said, "until I turned eleven or twelve—I'm not sure which—I stayed with my *whanau*—my family—in the Bay of Islands, mostly with my grandparents, who live very much in the traditional way. Then one day my father dropped anchor in the bay, marched ashore, and announced he'd had a great idea. He didn't have any other children, so he'd decided to carry me home and recognize me as his son and heir."

"Interesting notion. How did you feel about it?"

"Crossing the great ocean and visiting America sounded like a first-rate adventure, and it wasn't as if my father was a stranger. My mother had married another man not long after I was born, but my father and Koro—my grandfather—were still great friends, so he called quite often. My father approved of me— highly, as a matter of fact—so in my innocence I thought that all of Salem would feel the same way."

"And when you weren't accepted with open arms?"

"It did come as a bit of a surprise," Wiki admitted.

"But I imagine it didn't take long for the truth to dawn?"

"Oh, it happened right away, when my father introduced me to his legal wife. Until the moment I arrived at her kitchen door, you see, she hadn't a notion that I existed." Wiki grinned, and said, "She threw a most impressive fit of hysterics—screaming, kicking, fainting, the lot."

"And this is the woman you call your stepmother?"

"Aye."

The naturalist paused, thinking about this. "And you said I remind you of her?"

"Well, not the hysterics," Wiki allowed. "But you do remind me of the first time she took me to church."

"*Church?*" Again, he saw, he had startled the apparently unshakable naturalist.

"Aye." Wiki remembered the clutch of Mrs. Coffin's gloved hand on his skinny wrist as she had dragged him along, determined that if she was to be burdened with her husband's little, brown, ill-begotten son, she would make sure he was turned into a civilized Christian.

"She hassled me down the aisle to her usual pew at the front, and shoved me down in the seat, but the church elders immediately made me stand up again, and sit with the other colored folks in the rear of the church. So my stepmother tossed her head, stalked to the back, and planted herself down right next to me." He laughed and said, "I was very embarrassed. I don't know who I hated most, my new stepmother for taking her strong stand, or the narrow-minded elders who caused it."

Titian Peale studied him, puffing meditatively. Then he said, "So that's why you jumped to the conclusion that the scientists are a bigoted bunch, and didn't even bother to check with us to see if you were right."

"But that isn't the reason at all," Wiki exclaimed. He remembered the camp on the Rio Negro, where the scientists had appropriated an empty pilot house; he remembered how silence had fallen every time he walked inside—a silence that had told him he wasn't welcome. The scientifics had made it plain that he was to sleep with the gauchos outside, and though Wiki, quite frankly, had preferred the company of the *rastreadors*, he remembered the insult well. Was it any wonder that he had jumped to the conclusion that Peale and his friends would agree with the officers' stance?

"If you'd bothered to talk," Titan Peale went on, "you might have found out that we weren't like the Salem folks—that, in fact, we felt rather insulted that you should take such obvious and deliberate pains to avoid us. If you'd revealed the true situation, you might even have found out that we would be happy to side with you against the officers. But you didn't even try to talk about it, did you?"

With total unexpectedness, Wiki's eyes stung. To hide it, he turned and stared at the quarterdeck, where the officers were putting away their sextants, having finished taking their sights. Just this time yesterday, Midshipman Valentine Dove would have been one of their number. At this moment the thought seemed unbearably poignant.

"You should get to know the officers, anyway," Titian Peale said. "One or two of *them* might not be terribly happy with the stand the others have taken, either."

"I certainly agree that I should get to know them better," snapped Wiki—though for a very different reason. And, with that, he turned away, and headed for the stairs to the wardroom.

Nine

"*Do* you remember making up words as a child?"
asked Mr. Hale.

Wiki took a long moment to realize he'd been asked
a question. The day before, when he had taken his seat
at the table, the reaction from the officers who were
present had been surprisingly muted. Titian Peale had
been close behind as he came down the wardroom
stairs, and when the naturalist had urged him to a chair
between himself and Mr. Hale, the lieutenants had
simply looked at each other, shrugged, and made no
objection. Since then, however, he had been virtually
ignored. If he asked for the salt or the bread, it was
passed to him, but it was almost as if he was back in the
pantry, able to hear the conversation, but unable to take
part.

Wiki had not even learned the names of the two
unknown officers. No one had attempted to make
introductions, so he had been forced to try to find out
for himself, by following the conversations. And today
he had been watching the lieutenants particularly
closely, because there was a strange undercurrent of
excitement in the room. It was as if they were
celebrating something. But what? That no one owed
Midshipman Dove money any more? The deeply
unpleasant Lieutenant Pilson certainly had reason for

94

rejoicing, if indeed he was Plison—but what about the others? *Jerkin, Sweetman, Lusser, Clamber...*

So, when Hale asked his question, Wiki was lost in thought. When he jerked to attention, it was to find the philologist looking at him earnestly, waiting for an answer. What the devil had he said? Something about making up words as a child?

"No, I don't remember," Wiki said. "Why do you ask?"

"I was meditating about your facility for languages. I've observed that babies make up words using every known syllable—and strongly believe, in fact, that this is how the first languages evolved." Then he took a breath, looked soulfully at the ceiling, and recited, "In the gurglings of infants, the springs of ancient tongues were nursed."

Wiki was too astonished to find a reply to this last, which he supposed was a quotation from someone he had never read. Then one of the two unknown officers said with a derisive grin, "Hale writes poetry."

It was the man with the bloodshot eyes and dissolute face. Hale glanced at him, and said, "That is certainly so, Mr. Russell. Do you have an objection?"

Russell ignored this, going on as if Hale wasn't there, "His mother's Sarah Josepha Hale, the editor of *Godey's Lady's Book*, you know—not that I'd expect a person like you to have heard of it."

As it happened, Wiki had a couple of issues of *Godey's Lady's Book* in his sea-chest. His aunts loved the hand-tinted fashion plates of demure women in bell-like skirts, and listened raptly as he translated the improving stories, which were always received with gales of laughter. He also already knew that the philologist's mother was the famous arbiter of female morals, and thought that it was embarrassing enough for him, without having to withstand barbed comments, too.

However, Hale paid no attention to Russell's malice, going on as if he hadn't spoken, "Though babes are born with every syllable and sound, most small children retain only those they hear every day, soon forgetting the rest. Indeed, they forget the unused ones so completely that when they come across them again the sounds seem alien. I wonder, though, whether there are some who do not forget. If you were one of those, it could account for your ease in foreign tongues."

Wiki shrugged. He'd never thought about it.

"When you first learned English, was it easy?"

"I always spoke both English and *te reo Maori*. I don't remember having to learn either of them."

"An illiterate Indian like *you* spoke English as a child?" exclaimed Pilson.

Wiki looked at him, thinking *Pilson ... Plison*. Keeping his face blank, he said, "Of course I did. European and American vessels dropped anchor in the Bay of Islands all the time. There were plenty of English and American seamen to talk to."

Though not in the winter, he remembered. Winter was the time when the people worked in the plantations, planting the crops of potatoes that were going to be in huge demand by ship captains in the refreshment season, and hopefully bring a tremendous profit. Winter was the time of privation.

"Just sailor talk, then," Pilson sneered. Wiki had the impression that if he was on deck, he would have spat over the rail.

"Deputy Sheriff Coffin has an excellent command of English," said Lieutenant Lee without expression, adding meaningfully, "Including being able to read and write."

Wiki saw Pilson flush. For once, he didn't have a rejoinder.

Horatio Hale said to Wiki, "And your Portuguese and Spanish?"

"Portuguese came first. At the age of seventeen I shipped on a Nantucket whaler with the idea of getting back to New Zealand. We recruited some seamen in the Azores, so I learned Portuguese from them. Then I learned some Spanish in Valparaiso, and became fluent in the South China Sea."

Hale blinked, surprised. "South China Sea?"

"Aye. I jumped ship from an English whaler at Ternate."

"Jumped ship?" exclaimed Pilson, who didn't seem to be able to keep his mouth shut for long. All the lieutenants at the table looked at each other with eyebrows lifted.

"But you're some kind of sheriff, ain't you?" the officer with the pitted face said to Wiki. His wide, froglike mouth was pulled down with what seemed to be habitual contempt. "How did a confounded ship-jumper get the job of investigating crimes?"

"I just happened to be in the right spot at the right time."

"And I saw you fossicking in Dove's sea-chest! What the hell were you up to? The boy put an end to himself, God save his soul, so there ain't no crime to solve."

"But there *is* a report to write," said Wiki. "And it won't be complete until I can find a likely reason for doing something so desperate."

"Was you looking for a suicide note?" said Pilson. For no obvious reason, his smirk widened into a grin.

Wiki paused, feeling puzzled, but decided to ignore it. Instead of probing, he took a deliberate risk, saying, "The reason for suicide—for any crime at all—is usually women or money, or so I've found in the past."

The unknown lieutenant laughed. "Women? Young Dove?"

"Then it must have been money. Was Dove deeply in debt?" Wiki watched the officers glance at each other, while silence descended. Calls echoed from aloft as more sail was set, but no-one paid attention.

Then the nameless lieutenant said, "But it's obvious why Dove cut his throat."

"It is?"

"He couldn't take it any more."

"Take what?"

"Life at sea—the expedition—Wilkes!"

"I didn't know that he was unhappy with Captain Wilkes."

Pilson said in a knowing tone, "A suicide note would've told you different."

Wiki paused, studying him, and then said, "This is the second time you've mentioned a suicide note."

"Well, don't suicides usually try to explain why they're putting an end to it all? Ain't it logical? I mean, they have to give a reason, or none of it makes sense."

"So you feel certain that Mr. Dove wrote something?"

"Suiciders usually write a letter to explain what they're doing, don't they? That's all I'm saying."

Wiki pounced. "A letter, not a note?"

"Ain't they the same?"

"A letter is usually mailed. Do you think it was put on the sealer *Betsey*?"

"That's impossible," Lieutenant Russell snapped. "The letters have to be read before they are put in the bag, and we certainly didn't see one from Mr. Dove in the bag that went on the *Betsey*."

Wiki exclaimed, "You censor the midshipmen's letters?"

Lieutenant Lee said, "It was a directive issued by Captain Wilkes."

"But why?"

"Surely it's obvious? It's to make sure that sensitive information about our movements doesn't get out to the general public. We're not allowed to say where we have been, let alone speculate where we might be going."

The words were bitter, Wiki thought, but before he could comment Horatio Hale spoke up. Displaying his remarkable ability to ignore anything that didn't directly involve his pet subject, he said, "And that is how you learned Polynesian dialects like Samoan and Tahitian? By jumping from your ship at Polynesian islands?"

"I had *kanaka* shipmates, of course."

"*Kanaka*?"

"Pacific Islanders."

"You know the origin of the word?"

"It's Hawaiian. *Kanaka* is the Hawaiian word for *man*. I suppose Hawaii was the first place where

American captains asked islanders what they called themselves, because Yankee seamen now use that word to describe all men from the Pacific."

"You have a different word in your language?"

"*Tangata*," said Wiki. "Though it really means *people*."

Hale hauled out a notebook, and wrote it down.

"And do many *kanaka*—or *tangata*—join American ships?" he asked.

"Hundreds," said Wiki. He had never joined a crew in the Pacific without finding another New Zealand Maori or a Samoan or a Tahitian.

"But why do they do it?"

Wiki shrugged, thinking of men who had been born under coconut palms pulling whaleboat oars in icy seas around Greenland and Alaska, and living off salt beef and ship's biscuit. New Zealand Maori had a long and illustrious seafaring tradition, their ancestors having made immense voyages from the heartland of Polynesia that were talked and sung about at home, but he was not sure of the rest.

"Just for the hell of it, I suppose," he said. "For the adventure."

The dissipated-looking Russell laughed and said, "Our idle bastard of a New Zealander don't look very adventurous to me. He begged a ride home, but he ain't even working his passage."

For once paying heed to what one of the officers said, Horatio Hale elaborated to Wiki, saying, "Jack Sac, if you remember, is the other New Zealander with the expedition."

"I know," said Wiki.

He was biting down anger. Te Aute had spent ten years that were adventurous enough, traveling with circuses and entertainers, using his wits to keep body and soul together. He had been put on board the *Vincennes* by an influential Philadelphia selectman who was anxious to see him back home with his people, and had paid for his passage. But somehow, in the throes of one of Captain Wilkes's shifting of men, Te Aute had been moved to the *Peacock*.

"Tell me," said Hale, "have you made his acquaintance yet?"

"Once or twice," Wiki lied. Again, he thought of the ghostlike way Te Aute moved about the ship, and how he materialized only when and where he wished. The first time he had materialized like that, it had been in the dimness of the between decks, and Wiki had nearly perished of fright. But Te Aute had quickly made his friendly intentions known. Was his ally safe from retaliation from the sealers? Wiki hoped so.

"What a joy it must be for the two of you to talk over the endearing scenes of home! And in your native language, too."

Wiki arched an eyebrow, which tugged where it was cut. The Ngati Porou Maori had been recruited by a passing Yankee whaleship at about the age of fifteen, and within a day of docking at New Bedford had wandered off to have a look at America. In the intervening ten years his native language had become very rusty, except for the war chants and dances he'd performed on stage and at side-shows. But, with practice, it was rapidly coming back.

Then Hale's questioning was interrupted by the redheaded lad who worked for Mr. Spieden, who nudged Wiki's arm, and whispered in his ear that the purser wanted to see him.

Urgently.

Ten

*W*hen Wiki arrived at the purser's office, it was to find Mr. Spieden rummaging about behind his counter, seeming very agitated.

The purser straightened, and said, "What did you do with the chits?"

"Chits?"

"The IOUs you found in Midshipman Dove's sea-chest. Where are they?"

"You said you were going to lock them in the strongbox, so I left them sitting on the counter," Wiki said. He was feeling guilty, because he had completely forgotten the chits when he stormed out of the office after Titian Peale.

Spieden pushed his spectacles higher on his nose. "That's what I thought happened, but I can't find them anywhere, so I assumed that you must have them. Are you sure you didn't pocket them by mistake?"

Wiki felt about in his inside pocket, but only the notebook was there. "They were under a ledger," he said.

Spieden lifted all the books and ledgers on the counter, with no result. "I've already looked in all the places I can think of, most of them twice."

"The officers must have taken them—the three lieutenants who came to collect their gunpowder. I hid the chits under a ledger when they came in, but they arrived so suddenly that I don't think I was quick enough. Someone must have come back after I left, and stolen the chits while you were distracted."

He saw the purser grimace ruefully. "All three came back after you had gone, with some ludicrous and trivial complaint about the gunpowder I'd issued."

"Who were they, do you remember?"

"Russell, Blackmer, and Pilson. Russell and Blackmer were very loud."

"So it must have been Pilson who stole the chits," said Wiki, and sighed. "They will have been destroyed by now." He remembered the air of jubilation at the wardroom table. The disappearance of the IOUs, he thought, meant that there was no record of the debts. No wonder they had been happy.

Russell. Blackmer. Pilson. He said, "What does Blackmer look like?"

"He has a pockmarked face — smallpox as a child, I believe. Comes from a prominent Alabama family."

Blackmer. Wiki knew who he was, now. But his name hadn't been on any of the chits. *Plison. Jerkin. Sweetman. Lusser. Clamber.*

Then Spieden distracted him, saying, "Captain Hudson's clerk delivered Midshipman Dove's journal. All the officers have to keep one, you know."

And hand it in for inspection every Saturday, as Wiki knew well. Back on the *Swallow*, Friday nights were marked by a sudden burst of energy from George Rochester, his lanky figure hunched over his desk as his pen scratched away.

He said, "Can I see it?"

The purser took a tall book with marbled covers from the shelf behind him and pushed it across the counter. Wiki opened it, and then he paused, puzzled. The columns for daily positions and wind and current measurements were filled in with streams of confident numbers, but the notations of wind and weather, sails and sightings were unreadable. Though in the same clear, childish hand as the names at the tops of the chits, the words made no sense.

"They're in code!" Wiki exclaimed. *Pilson – Plison*, he thought. The names on the chits must be in some language known only to Valentine Dove.

Spieden turned the book around and had a look himself, but his expression remained unconvinced. "Perhaps he was just a shocking bad speller," he said. "He couldn't even spell his own name."

Wiki looked at the place where the purser's fingertip pointed. "Midsh. Valt. Dov," it read. But that didn't mean anything, he thought—he had once voyaged with a New Bedforder who couldn't decide whether he should spell his name Sherman or Shearman.

He said, "I believe that even Shakespeare had trouble spelling his name."

"But surely it's easy enough to spell *Dove*."

That was true. "And he would have had a good education."

"A private tutor, most probably."

So it must be code, Wiki decided. And yet the journals were inspected on a weekly basis. How had Dove gotten away with it?

He said, "Who is Captain Hudson's clerk?"

"Frederick Stuart—a fine man, one of the best. He is dedicated to his duty and the aims of the expedition, and is a good draftsman, besides. Captain Wilkes finds him most useful."

Wiki picked up the journal, and said, "Would you mind if I took this along to his office, so I can ask him about it?"

Spieden frowned at him over his spectacles, but finally said, "If you bring it straight back."

"Thirty minutes," Wiki promised, and went.

He was back within twenty, and yet he'd had quite a conversation with the clerk, who had said many good things about the purser. Indeed, William Spieden and Frederick Stuart seemed to belong to a mutual admiration society. Mr. Stuart had declared that the purser was a whole-souled man, one who clung faithfully to the aims of the expedition. Like Stuart himself, he was a staunch admirer of Captain Wilkes, which seemed to be the opinion of shamefully few — didn't Mr. Coffin agree? Wiki had had no trouble admitting that he had great respect for Captain Wilkes's science and dedication, because it was nothing but the truth. And so Wiki and the clerk got along famously, becoming so amicable that Mr. Stuart was perfectly happy to discuss Midshipman Dove and the journal — which, as he described, was definitely not in code.

"The plain fact of the matter is that the poor boy was unable to write proper English," he said. "All he could produce was gibberish. It was due to a congenital idiosyncrasy — or so the Dove family conveyed in a communication to Captain Hudson. An influential family, very powerful in navy circles, and so paying no

106

mind to the unintelligible state of his journal was not a difficult matter, you understand."

"Mr. Dove didn't send letters home, then?"

"Letters?" Mr. Stuart looked startled. "I suppose it's possible. The family might be able to understand their son's writing style—or maybe he got a messmate to write down what he dictated."

"So he might have put a letter on the *Betsey*?"

Stuart frowned, "What makes you think that?"

"Lieutenant Pilson seemed to think that a letter was written—but there wasn't one in Mr. Dove's chest, so I wondered about the *Betsey*."

"If the lieutenant believed that there was a letter, then it certainly does indicate that poor Dove found someone to write letters for him—or that his folks could work out what he was trying to say," the clerk allowed. "So your guess that it's in the bag that went onto the sealer could be right on the mark."

"On the other hand, Lieutenant Russell assured me that he checked mail before it went into the bag, and there was no letter from Mr. Dove—so I wondered if perhaps it wasn't delivered in time. Is there a mailbag kept ready for the next homeward-bound ship we speak?"

Mr. Stuart didn't know. Looking after the mail was not part of his job. He said, "Perhaps a bag was carried to the *Vin* after the boy's burial? Ask Mr. Spieden," he advised, and Wiki, after thanking him, took his leave.

"So you were right," Wiki said to Mr. Spieden. "Midshipman Dove wasn't writing in code."

"Well, well," said the purser, looking gratified that his guess was correct. "I knew it wasn't code, because there's no regularity. So why did he write such gibberish?"

"He had a congenital idiosyncrasy — or so his family reported to Captain Hudson."

"Congenital idiosyncrasy? That's one way of describing a complete inability to write intelligible English," said the purser, his tone dry. And with that, to Wiki's surprise, he sent off the boy for a pot of coffee and mugs, and when the steaming pot arrived he shut and locked the door, and invited Wiki to sit.

Wiki perched on a stool on the customer side of the counter, while the purser sat on his stool on his side, all set for a cozy chat. Mr. Spieden, it seemed, was enjoying himself, as if he considered this a first-rate guessing game. Perhaps, Wiki thought, he was like Forsythe, and fancied himself as a sleuth.

Wiki said, "Lieutenant Pilson seemed to believe that Midshipman Dove wrote a letter before he died, explaining why he was about to do something so drastic. Do you think it's possible?"

The purser frowned. "All letters came to me for sorting into the mailbag that was put on board the sealer, but I don't recollect one from Midshipman Dove."

"That's what Lieutenant Russell said, too."

"And, in view of that congenital problem, that he wrote one at all seems highly unlikely."

"Mr. Stuart wondered if Mr. Dove had a messmate who was willing to write to dictation."

Mr. Spieden looked aghast. "Surely not, considering his state of mind! He committed suicide, Mr. Coffin! In one of the most violent ways possible!"

Wiki said dryly, "As Lieutenant Pilson assured me, people do leave suicide notes."

"But they don't dictate them, Mr. Coffin! And if they did, the listener is hardly likely to write the words down! He'd be trying to prevent the dreadful act!"

"You're absolutely right," said Wiki. "Which leaves us quite a puzzle." He sipped coffee thoughtfully, and then said, "Lieutenant Lee gave me to understand that all letters are vetted before they are put in the mailbag, to make sure that nothing is let out that Captain Wilkes would prefer to be kept secret."

Mr. Spieden paused, staring into his mug of coffee. "I hadn't heard that before, but the letters are delivered to me by the officers, not by the men who wrote them, and it does seem likely enough that the officers have already checked them, under orders."

"I was also given to believe that if Midshipman Dove *had* written a letter, he would have complained about Captain Wilkes's leadership."

"Well, that's news to me! And, if so, I'm glad the letters are vetted!" Mr. Spieden said with vigor. "There has been too much criticism of the expedition already — do you know that the papers dubbed it *the deplorable expedition*, even before we left?"

Wiki did know it, but didn't say so. Instead, he asked, "If any letters were delivered too late to be put on board the *Betsey*, where would they be now?"

"There's another mailbag ready for the next ship we speak," said the purser. "But it's not here. It was sent to the *Vin*."

"So, if Midshipman Dove did write a suicide letter, and it missed the bag that was put on the sealer, that's where it would be?"

The purser contemplated Wiki over the top of his spectacles for a very long moment, and then said dryly, "Is this how the great sleuth works?"

Wiki blinked. "I beg your pardon?"

"Half of me argues that the letter doesn't exist and that it would be gibberish, if it did, but the other half tells me that I should remember your record, and pay close attention to what you say."

Wiki smiled, in appreciation of Mr. Spieden's shrewdness. "Well," he said, "when it's considered how damaging the letter might be, it seems wise to make sure that it truly doesn't exist."

Mr. Spieden said nothing, but looked more thoughtful than ever, so Wiki finished his coffee, put down his mug, hauled his notebook out of the pocket in his Guernsey, and said, "Would you be kind enough to repeat the names of the officers who were here in the office at the same time I was copying the chits?"

As the purser recited them, Wiki noted them down. *Passed Midshipman Jenkins, Lieutenant Russell, Lieutenant Blackmer, Lieutenant Pilson.* Then he compared them to the names he had copied from the chits. *Plison, Jerkin, Lusser, Clamber, Sweetman.*

He said, "Is there any chance that Jerkin is actually Jenkins?"

"I was thinking exactly the same thing."

"If Dove's problem meant that he spelled some words backwards, perhaps we should wonder about Lusser, too."

"Lusser read backwards is Russell?"

"It seems possible," said Wiki, and checked his notebook again. Lieutenant Russell, if he was indeed

Lusser, had initialed three chits, with a total of one hundred and eighty dollars.

"But what about the other two?"

Wiki shook his head. Sweetman and Clamber were as enigmatic as ever, but he now had the names of three men who had benefited from Midshipman Dove's death.

Men who were suspects in his murder.

Eleven

It was Saturday—which, for both junior and senior officers, meant a day to be celebrated with a midday feast, often with invited guests.

To Wiki's astonishment, he was one of those invited guests, his company having been craved by the midshipmen's mess. The card had been delivered to him the evening before by a boy who looked about the same age as the purser's lad, and was apparently the midshipmen's steward. Though Wiki had no idea why he should be so honored, he had accepted with alacrity, seeing it as a chance to get to know Valentine Dove's messmates.

Two of the seven surviving midshipmen were on deck, on watch, so Wiki didn't know about their emotional state, but the other five certainly seemed to have got over the shock of Dove's violent demise. Not only was he buried and out of sight, but they had the easy recovery of youth—apart from Jenkins, none of them looked more than sixteen.

Now, they were talking animatedly among themselves, eyeing Wiki surreptitiously over the tops of their wine glasses but not engaging him in conversation yet, so he took the chance to look about the room.

The only other occasion when Wiki had been a guest at a Saturday midshipmen's feast had been on the *Vincennes*, near the beginning of the voyage. The mids of the *Vin* had been an affluent lot, with lavish tastes in decoration. Their messroom had been draped in red-striped curtaining, and hung with mirrors and brass candlesticks, with a fearsome collection of cutlasses, swords and pistols displayed on one wall. Long couches had been draped with damask, and the floor had been covered with rugs.

By contrast, the surroundings here were spartan in the extreme. The long plank table, hanging from the deckhead by ropes threaded through holes in the corners, had no cloth, and the only illumination came from a couple of lamps. The midshipmen's sea-chests were their dining chairs, and it was obvious that the young officers slept in hammocks, because of the hooks on the bulkheads. It reminded Wiki of a time, years ago, when he had visited George Rochester on the ship of war *Potomac*. George had been a junior mid, and like these young fellows, he had lived in the bowels of the ship. His quarters, like this messroom on the *Peacock*, had been dark, dank, and had smelled of clammy bilge.

At the time, George hadn't seemed to notice it, and neither did these young men now, who chattered as happily as if their shipmate had not been dropped into the sea. Wiki turned his contemplation to Jenkins, who looked about his own age, twenty-four, and as if he had as many seafaring years under his belt, too. Jenkins was a passed midshipman, which meant he had passed the examinations, but had not been promoted to the rank of lieutenant. Lacking patronage and a rich family, he could remain at this intermediate level for years, an experience that embittered some men. Wiki wondered if Jenkins felt cheated, but found it difficult to tell anything about him from his averted face.

Then all at once he realized that the chatter had stopped, and the boys were looking at him expectantly. Lifting his brows, he waited to find out why he was here.

A youngster with an ingenuous face was the first to pipe up. "Could you tell us about that gruesome murder up the Rio Negro, sir?"

Aha, thought Wiki, the mystery was solved. The boys were after bloodcurdling yarns from his crime-solving career with the expedition, which undoubtedly would be highly embroidered when they passed them on to their shipmates.

He said, "Which murder?"

"Scuttlebutt has it that the body was up a tree and the head was rolling around on the dirt underneath."

Wiki smiled. "I'd really rather talk about Mr. Dove's death."

"But that's just a suicide, sir!"

"I was told he might have left a letter."

"A letter?" The boys stared at each other, puzzled.

"There wasn't one in his sea-chest—but I had the strong impression that someone looked through the chest before it was delivered to the purser's office that night, so I wondered if it had been taken out."

Silence. The young lads looked at Jenkins, who flushed and said, "That was me, but I didn't find no letters, nothing like that."

"Did you remove anything?"

Emphatically, Jenkins shook his head. "And if you reckon you don't believe me, then these boys here will set you right, because they was watching all the time." He reached out for a bottle and filled his glass, spilling only a few drops. "I put everything back after I'd done searching, all neat and tidy the way it had been before, and then put the blood-soaked clothes on top, and shut the chest. And then we carried it along to the purser's office."

"What were you looking for?"

"An IOU. I didn't want it to get to my family."

"You owed Dove money?"

One of the boys burst out, "Everyone owed him money, Mr. Coffin!"

Wiki stared. "*Everyone?*"

"Well, not absolutely everyone. But lots of men, from all over the ship. Anyone who was short of the ready knew they could go to Dove for something to tide them over. He charged interest, but who cared?"

"He was a *moneylender?*"

"Aye, sir. If you knew him, sir, you would understand it better, because he looked just like a fellow who spends all his time in an office, crouched over ledgers and money-boxes. He had the soul of a banker, sir—if it hadn't been for his family, he would've been happily at work in some kind of commercial money-managing place, and everyone would've been much better off."

Good lord, thought Wiki. Mr. Dove's ambition had been to work in the world of finance? No wonder his highly traditional navy family had questioned its respectability!

He said, "But why would the men go to him to borrow money, rather than go to the purser for an advance?"

The boys all looked at each other, and then one by one they shrugged. Wiki thought he knew exactly what was going through their minds. Though he liked Mr.

Spieden, he knew that pursers had a bad reputation for gouging the seamen, and also remembered that the seamen had grumbled about what they were being charged for tea. Also, being straitlaced, Spieden would certainly have asked why the applicant wanted an advance on his pay, and it would have been hard to convince him that it wasn't for gambling, or a drinking spree in port.

Wiki loaded his fork with pie and then chewed slowly as he thought over this new development. The hash, he noted with a corner of his mind, was on the dry side, but tasted well. Then he shifted on the chest where he was seated, turning to face Jenkins, who sat alongside him.

"How many IOUs were you looking for?"

"Just one."

"One particular one?"

"Aye. The one with my initials on it."

"How many did you expect to find?"

Jenkins shrugged. "I was only interested in one, but there might have been a couple of others. But it made no difference, because I found none."

"Just a couple of others? When so many men owed him money?"

"He only made officers sign his chits."

Wiki sat very still, riveted by this. Then he said, "Why just officers?"

"Dove reckoned that when it came to repayment, they would laugh at him instead of handing over the money."

It was more than that, Wiki thought, and he remembered the flash of open loathing he had surprised on Dove's face when the boy glanced back at

Lieutenant Matthews. Humiliating the officers by making them sign his chits was a very subtle and eloquent kind of revenge.

"Did the lieutenants know he was deliberately insulting them?"

Jenkins didn't look surprised, shaking his head instead. "No, of course not. I don't believe they knew that he was lending money to anyone else but them."

Wiki studied Jenkins again, wondering if he had been affronted by being treated with the same lack of trust. Finally, he said, "How much do you owe?"

"One hundred and ten dollars," Jenkins answered promptly. "And I will pay it back to the family, once I get home—if I get home. But I don't want my father to find out about it—which he will, if that chit is sent to Dove's parents."

"And you gambled with the money?"

"No!" Jenkins looked at the other boys rather resentfully, and then muttered, "I needed it to pay my share of the mess bill."

That made sense. Officers clubbed together to buy little luxuries like wine and fancy pickles, and as Wiki knew from Forsythe's parlous financial state, the bill could amount to several hundred dollars.

He said, "But you still don't know where your IOU is?"

"Unfortunately, no. And I don't like to think who might have it."

So, when the lieutenants had destroyed the chits, they hadn't bothered to inform Jenkins. Wiki said, "When you went through his chest, you didn't expect to find some kind of ledger with all these financial transactions?"

Jenkins merely shrugged. "I wasn't looking for anything like that."

"Dove kept it all in his head," one of the other boys said.

Wiki exclaimed, "In his *head*?"

"It was there in his brain—every single sum of money, along with names."

"The entire list of debtors and what they owed?"

"He was hopeless with words, sir. I know it, because I tried to help him, and just ended up tearing my hair. Whatever he wrote down was so madly confused it was impossible to make sense of it. I offered to write his journal for him, but he told me it didn't signify—that it was fixed. I didn't really understand what he meant, sir, but I reckon he got away with it because he was so good with figures that his navigational columns were a model for the rest of us. He truly was a genius, sir."

"Did he work out the positions on paper, or just in his head?"

"Oh, he could write figures down, just like any of us," said another boy. "We all got him to help us with our exercises, but though he could calculate on paper like a master, Mr. Coffin, he did all his own figuring in his head."

"And his memory was incredible, truly," the first one added. "Show him a long list of equations, and two days later he'd recite them off without a hitch."

Wiki was frowning deeply, thinking that this was a very ominous development. If Dove kept all his accounts in his head, the slate had been wiped completely clean when he was killed. Apart from the chits—and he didn't expect that the IOUs still existed—

the evidence of hundreds of dollars' worth of debt had vanished for ever, never to be retrieved.

Then he had another thought. "He must have kept a bag of coins, ready for lending out. So where did he stow it?"

Silence. The eyes that had been focused so raptly on Wiki's face slid away. The air of guilt in the room was almost palpable. Jenkins might have been looking for the chit when he went through the dead boy's belongings, but the boys who were watching him had certainly been hoping that he would turn up a fat purse. Had it been found? And shared out, on the understanding that no one talked about it?

Wiki gave up, knowing he would never get an answer, and said, "And something else. He must have had a system."

"Sir?" said one of the boys.

"How did everyone know that he was operating as a moneylender? And how did the men who wanted to borrow money approach him? It wasn't as if he had an office!"

"The news just got around," the boy said uncomfortably, and Wiki was aware of their group evasiveness, again.

Then they were interrupted. One of the two midshipmen on watch rushed into the room, crying, "Cape Horn, we're off Cape Horn! You must come and see! Any moment now, and we'll be in the Pacific Ocean!"

It was an historic moment. Six months to the day since the fleet left Norfolk, Virginia, the *Peacock*, *Vincennes* and *Swallow* were breasting the first swells of the

Pacific, and now they were passing the infamous landmark. The boys left their seats in a rush, and fought to be first up the ladders to deck. This was something they would talk about for many years, and describe to their grandchildren.

Wiki arrived more slowly, partly because he had trouble believing that they were off the icy tip of South America. For the past two days the temperatures had been so mild that he, like the seamen, had been going about in shirtsleeves, and when he arrived on deck it was still very warm, and the sky above was a misty, limpid blue. The sea was so placid that it was as if the *Peacock* was floating on a gentle alpine lake, and when Wiki looked aloft, the hamper was a magnificent sight, with every inch of canvas set, studding sails stretched out from the ends of the yards like great butterfly wings. Yet, there was Cape Horn. It was there, just two miles away. Cape Stiff, the dread of every mariner.

He remembered the first time his ship had struggled west about this hated promontory. He had been aloft on the Nantucket whaleship *Paths of Duty*, hauling out the earring of a topsail in a snow squall. He had been seventeen, it had been his first voyage as a seaman, and the *Paths of Duty* had been fighting to beat nor'west after having been driven by a tempest to the fringes of the Antarctic Ocean. Wiki remembered battling frozen canvas with torn nails and mangled fingers, his hands bare because it was impossible to get a grip with ice-slicked gloves; he remembered looking down at the deck seventy feet below, to see shipmates struggling through neck-deep waves; he remembered the shrill orchestra of the rigging in the heavy swell and screaming wind — the groan of timbers and whine of

120

ropes, with every backstay thrumming its own personal chord. And he remembered the friend who had tumbled from the ice-sheathed yard to perish at once in the desperately cold sea, and how he and the other men aloft hadn't even paused in their fight with the recalcitrant sail, because it would be death for them all if they did.

He hadn't even *seen* Cape Horn before. Cape Horn had simply been a weight on the mind, hidden in the sleet and squalling clouds. Now, he gazed at a bold and rugged coast jutting into the ocean, the rocks torn into fanciful shapes by millennia of wind and ice. Beyond, distant glaciers glittered, and once he glimpsed movement, as a huge chunk of cliff tumbled down and fell into the sea. Cape Horn looked exactly the way he had expected — except for the mild blue skies and placid sea.

There was a jubilant yell from the quarterdeck, on the roof of the afterhouse. When Wiki turned to look at the group of officers there, they were waving their hats in celebration. The ship was now to the south and west of the Cape Horn, and had officially doubled the grim landmark. All the officers were there, he saw. Walker and Perry were leaning over the rail, studying something floating on the surface. Pilson stood next to Lee, and Matthews was on the other side of the first lieutenant. Russell and the unpleasant, pockmarked Blackmer stood apart, a few yards away.

Jerkin, Sweetman, Plison, Lusser, Clamber. Jerkin was Jenkins, Plison was Pilson, Lusser was Russell. *And Clamber was Blackmer.* It was suddenly there in Wiki's head, so clear there was no question about it.

So he had identified another suspect—which profited him absolutely nothing. Just two hours ago, he'd had only five suspects for the murder of Midshipman Dove. Now, Wiki was faced with a whole shipful.

Twelve

The next day, Sunday, the wind was both light and ahead, which meant bracing yards for every breath, with the hands constantly hauling lines and sweating at halyards.

Their goal, Orange Harbor, on the eastern coast of Hoste Island, Tierra del Fuego, was just eighty-five miles away, but it seemed unattainable. At nightfall all hands were kept on deck as the *Peacock* crept cautiously through uncharted waters. It wasn't until three-thirty in the morning that Wiki, who had enjoyed the luxury of sleep, was tumbled out of his berth by the sound of gunfire. They had fetched their anchorage at last, and the lieutenants were hailing the feat with their cannon salute.

When Wiki arrived on the narrow stretch of deck in front of the afterhouse, the smoke-filled air stung his eyes, and he had to grope his way to the landward rail. Then, when his sight cleared, he saw that they were gliding slowly into an almost landlocked harbor, with an island sprawled across most of the entrance. All about, the black landscape was lit by numbers of fires, one large, the rest as small as sparks.

Other glints in the pre-dawn dark came from lanterns hung in the rigging of four anchored vessels — the slow old storeship, *Relief,* the gun-brig *Porpoise,* and the two ex-pilot schooners, *Sea Gull* and *Flying Fish.* The big beacon fire had evidently been lit by the crews to guide the ships into the harbor, while the small ones, presumably, were the campfires of the local Fuegian natives. There was an evocative smell of wood smoke, decaying seaweed, growing trees and grass.

Orders were bellowed from the quarterdeck, echoed from all over the ship as sail was gradually reduced, until only jibs, topsails, and spanker were still drawing. The deck under Wiki's feet was settling as the ship lost momentum. The dark shape of the *Vincennes* was on the starboard quarter, moving at the same crawl that they were, and beyond her were the two tall masts of the *Swallow*.

"Brace up tops'ls!"

"Aye, sir!"

The *Peacock* was slowing further, further, as the last of her canvas lost the breeze. Wiki could hear the serene trickle of water along the hull, replacing the louder hiss of their passage.

"Clew up tops'ls!"

"Tops'ls, sir!"

"Stand by the anchor, there... Let go the anchor!"

A great splash, unseen ripples, and a quivering as the ship snubbed the chain. A soft gust brought a scent of piney scrub from the land. The air was so clear that Wiki distinctly heard eight bells struck on the *Vincennes*, twenty fathoms away. A dozen instants later, a loud echo came from the bell above the portico of the *Peacock* afterhouse, marking the start of the morning watch. The sun peeked above the silhouettes of mountains and hills, sending slants of light across the beach.

"That will do, the watch." It was Lieutenant Lee's voice, from the quarterdeck. Half the weary hands headed for the amidships hatch. Ten minutes later the sails were all furled, and still more men were sent below, reducing the number on duty to an anchor watch. In the midst of the orders and shuffling, Wiki heard his name hissed. He looked around, and saw Te Aute's tattooed face peering around the corner of the afterhouse. He didn't think that the rogue was allowed abaft of the mainmast, but was glad to see his wide grin.

"Boss," said Te Aute, and jerked his chin forward. Wiki turned, and saw the seven sealers in a cluster by the gangway rail. They were all staring his way. In the brightening light he could see that the one he had head-butted still had both eyes blackened. When they saw he was watching, they all turned away, and huddled close together as they conferred. Peter Folger was doing most of the talking. Wiki could see the sealers' leader spread his hands in a gesture, and then emphatically nod as someone asked a question. They were planning something—but what? With discomfort, Wiki saw them all turn and stare in his direction again.

When he looked for Te Aute, the Maori had vanished in his usual ghostlike fashion. Glancing back at the sealers, Wiki remembered how Pilson had stood and watched as the sealers had attacked him. They weren't allowed aft, either, but he decided it was a good idea to avoid trouble, so ducked back through the companionway door. On impulse, instead of taking the stairs down to the wardroom, he headed upwards. The narrow stairway wound up through the port quarter of the ship, past the door to the officer's head in the gallery, and opened onto the roof of the afterhouse. Lieutenant Matthews was there, having replaced Lee as officer of the watch. He glanced at Wiki, but then turned away again, with complete lack of interest.

It was the first time Wiki had ventured to this privileged vantage point, which was usually reserved for the captain and the officers of the watch. The scientifics, however, were tolerated. Peale and Hale were standing at the landward rail, so Wiki joined them. They said nothing, though they shifted to give him room.

Titian Peale was staring at the lines of penguins that straggled along the edge of the beach, upright as soldiers, all facing the sea and the ships. Occasionally he lifted his head to contemplate the squalling gulls that circled the masts. Hale was frowning at the small fires, now distinguished by their plumes of smoke. Presumably, thought Wiki, he was assembling his mental capacities for writing down the language of the people who were squatting around them.

Wiki, for his part, contemplated the scenery, thinking that if it wasn't for the penguins, it could be as homelike as New Zealand. The gray cliffs that bordered the sea were abrupt, but the rolling hills behind them were dense with forest. Some of the trees in the long valleys were huge, their gnarled upper branches visible against the growth on the slopes. On distant precipices, waterfalls tumbled. There were several conical peaks jutting up above the woodlands, some high enough to be called mountains. Their precipices, in contrast to the dark green of the tangled forest that completely covered the lower hills, were bare, glinting where fans of rubble caught the sun. Far to the west, mighty snow-capped mountains were sketched against the mild blue sky, but they were so very distant that it was as if they belonged to another world. The sun shone warmly, and the scene could actually be called picturesque. It was another surprise.

Wiki heard orders as a boat was swung out and lowered. When he leaned over the rail, he expected to see Captain Hudson heading over to the *Vincennes* to breakfast with Captain Wilkes, so that they could indulge in a spell of mutual congratulation about their remarkably placid doubling of Cape Horn. Instead, however, Mr. Spieden and Mr. Stuart arrived at the gangway. The purser had a journal under his arm, and Wiki recognized Midshipman Dove's tall blue book.

Neither Mr. Spieden nor Captain Hudson's clerk looked up as the boat pulled away. Moments later, they were at the side of the *Vincennes*. Wiki watched the two men mount the side of the flagship, and disappear. Then everything was still and quiet. The beach was deserted, except for the penguins, and the only movement was smoke from the various fires. All around, the primeval forest waited, and despite the fires there was an uncanny sense of total isolation from all civilization, as if the ships floated in an empty world. On board silence reigned, as most of the crew caught up on sleep. When the two scientifics went down to the wardroom to eat breakfast, Wiki followed.

He carried his second mug of coffee back to the roof of the afterhouse, to enjoy it in the warmth of the sun, and saw that he had arrived just in time to see the boat pulling back from the *Vincennes*. Spieden and Stuart were not on board, this time. Instead, there was an officer in the stern sheets. Light glinted on buttons and braid. So, Wiki deduced, it was either Captain Wilkes, come to consult with Captain Hudson, or it was

Lawrence J. Smith, here to parade yet again in the glory of being flag lieutenant.

Somehow, he was not at all surprised to see that it was Smith. Shouts echoed about the decks of the *Peacock*, their tone bad-tempered, warning the sleeping officers that they were about to receive the second-in-command of the *Vincennes*. Bos'un's mates' calls piped, and lieutenants emerged onto the waist deck, some still pulling on their jackets. Wiki distinctly heard Matthews curse under his breath as he headed for the ladder that led down the break of the afterhouse.

To his surprise, the officer jerked his head, and said, "You too, Mr. Coffin. You're summoned to the *Vin*."

Wondering how Matthews knew that, Wiki followed. As he joined the group at the gangway, he heard the click as the boat touched the hull of the *Peacock*, and then there was a pause, while the oarsmen hooked on to dangling boat falls. It seemed to take them a long time to get the ropes fixed, but finally Wiki heard the flag lieutenant set his boot on the gunwale of the bobbing boat. It was so quiet that the mutters of two of the boat's crew as they braced themselves to heave the lieutenant onto the short ladder of battens that led up the side of the ship seemed loud.

Smith's cocked hat bobbed into sight, along with his fist on the gangway-rope that dangled alongside. Despite the bright sunshine, Wiki was suddenly struck with such a dark sense of *déjà vu* that what came next seemed inevitable. It happened in slow motion—the massed salutes from the cluster of officers, the arrival of Lawrence J. Smith over the gangway, his stiff stance as he straightened to return the salute, a shifting in the group, and then the stumble and jolt.

A cry, a splash, and Lieutenant Smith was floundering in the glossy waters of Orange Harbor. This time, Wiki didn't pause. He was wearing just shirt and dungarees. Kicking off his sea boots, he dived over the side.

Cold green water closed over his head, and his eyes stung with salt. When he surfaced and shook his hair back, it was to hear cries, curses, and more splashes as the boat's crew struggled to grab hold of Smith without capsizing their craft. Again, the flag lieutenant had completely lost his head, and was beating off the hands that were trying to help.

Wiki was not alone in the water. Other men had jumped in, but they were thrashing around in their own blind panic, crashing into each other and thrusting madly to get free again. He could hear Lieutenant Matthews cursing one of them, and realized that he had dived in, too, but was having no better luck.

Taking on momentum with a kick against the side of the ship, Wiki managed to snag Smith's coat. The lieutenant gasped, and grabbed him around the neck, and they both went under. Wiki detached himself by pushing up Smith's jaw until the stranglehold slackened. As soon as Smith let go he gripped the hem of his coat again, and hauled him up to the surface. This time, the lieutenant didn't fight him off, and Wiki thought he'd lost consciousness, but just as he arrived at the top with his sodden burden, a hand reached up, gripped his hair, and pushed down.

Wiki let go of the coat, and deliberately sank further, thinking Lieutenant Smith was using his head as a stepping stone in his panic. As he ducked past the heavy body, Wiki felt a harsh brush of something against his cheek, of ... what? An epaulette? Stiff hairs flicked across his open eyes in a flash of quick pain, forcing him to squeeze them shut. But to his relief, he was free.

Suddenly buoyant, Wiki surged to the surface — only to be shoved down again. With a stab of horror, he realized that it wasn't Lieutenant Smith at all. The brush of hair was a *beard* — it was one of the sealers, seizing the chance to drown him in the midst of the panic. All at once, he was fighting for his life.

Writhing about, Wiki deliberately went down again, but this time he grabbed the ankles of his assailant as he sank, pulling the man with him. Hand after fist, he reached up the body, gripping clothes, getting a firmer hold, all the time sinking down, deliberately down.

The sealer thrashed like a gaffed fish, but Wiki hung on grimly, with all his strength, kicking for the bottom of the bay and dragging his catch. His lungs felt on fire and his head was beginning to whirl, but still he held on, squirming as he evaded clawed fingers that reached out for his eyes, feeling the sealer's struggles gradually weaken.

At last, with a final burst of bubbles that streamed past his face, the flailing stopped, and he was able to let go. Wiki surged to the surface — to find himself between the boat and the *Peacock*. Gasping, he thought he would be crushed, and had to fight off panic. A rope dropped and hit him. He grabbed, went under with the slack, gripped higher, and was roughly hauled up the side of the ship.

He landed on the deck on his belly, vomiting water, shivering violently, chilled to the bone by the knowledge of how close he had come to death. It was long moments before he was able to lurch to his feet, and nod thanks to the burly bo'sun's mate who had thrown the rope.

Then he staggered to the rail—to see the lifeless body of Lawrence J. Smith being rolled into the boat, followed by the corpse of the sealer.

Thirteen

Wiki was following the marine corporal along the wide corridor that ran through the afterhouse of the *Vincennes* when they were both brought up short by an infuriated shout from the chartroom.

"By God, Hudson, why didn't you cut him down like a dog?"

Without doubt, the voice belonged to Captain Wilkes. Captain Hudson answered, but so quietly and mildly that it was impossible to discern the words. Then Captain Wilkes let fly again. "The scoundrel refused to call you *captain*, and vowed that in future he would only call you *mister*? And you were prepared to *countenance* it? What kind of discipline do you keep on the *Peacock*, for God's sake?"

Again, Captain Hudson answered in a murmur. The marine cast a backward glance at Wiki that was unmistakably hunted, seeking a hint of what to do. Wiki shrugged, feeling equally helpless, and so they stood there, waiting, in the otherwise empty corridor.

Wiki was in familiar territory, because he had lived in the afterhouse of the *Vincennes* for a while, earlier in the voyage. To his left, a credenza partly hid the spacious dining saloon where he had eaten many a meal. The massive table gleamed, and the revolving chairs that surrounded it had all been turned so that they faced neatly inwards. On the righthand side of the corridor doors led to the small staterooms where the flagship scientific corps berthed. A rancid smell leaked from under one of them, indicating that Joseph Couthouy, Captain Wilkes's particular *bête noir*, still ignored strict instructions not to store ripening specimens in his room.

Then all at once the double doors at the end of the passage flew open, letting through Captain Hudson, who was very flushed and even more disheveled than usual. He put on his cocked hat as he passed Wiki, without acknowledging his presence. The corporal waited until he heard the door to the portico shut. Then at last he had the courage to move, and Wiki followed.

Then they were at the doors. After visibly bracing his shoulders, the corporal knocked. A voice called out, "Come," and he went in to inform Captain Wilkes that Mr. Coffin had arrived. A moment later he came out, rolled his eyes at Wiki, and held the righthand door open. Wiki stepped inside, heard the door shut, and then the loud steps as the marine marched back to his sentry post in the portico.

The big chartroom was as light and airy as the passage. Tables were set out under a huge skylight, and sunlight slanted onto bulkheads that were lined with bookshelves. Jars, also on shelves, gleamed, many of them holding ghostly floating specimens. Wiki felt surprised that there were so many, as all the specimens that had been collected before the landfall at the Rio Negro had been stowed on his father's brig *Osprey*, and were on the way to their destination in Philadelphia. Evidently they had been scooped out of the sea during the passage to Orange Harbor, which was another indication of how remarkably moderate the weather had been.

Most of his attention, however, was on Captain Wilkes, who looked dreadful, his long face drawn, with bluish circles under his eyes. His lips were tighter than Wiki had ever seen them before, and there were blotches of red on his high cheeks. Where Wiki had expected to see him on the verge of exploding into one of his infamous fits of hysterical rage, the commander's lean frame was rigid with unnatural restraint. Somehow, Wiki found it more disturbing than an outright tirade would have been.

As he knew well, Charles Wilkes had been under intense strain for years, long before the expedition had set sail. Throughout a decade of political and scientific lobbying, hostility from the navy yard, and petty parsimony from the administration, he had remained staunchly loyal to the aims of the expedition—indeed, from what Wiki had been told, there had been times when it seemed that he was the only man in America who had believed in the grand mission. The battle with the authorities had drained his emotional energy, and finally getting to sea had only added to his problems. No sooner had they reached their offing, than it had been discovered that the *Peacock* had not been properly repaired from a near-fatal grounding on her previous voyage, and that the storeship *Relief* sailed as if she were dragging a string of anchors.

Since then, acrimony had reigned, as scientifics battled officers who were more interested in shiphandling and furthering their naval careers than in helping with experiments. Provisions had turned out to be worm-ridden, and spare gear had proved to be shoddy. At times the fleet had been scattered to the four winds, to be collected together again only after immense difficulty and nervewracking delay. Wilkes had been forced to send the *Relief* ahead, so that the sailing rate of the other ships wouldn't be reduced to a crawl, but even then the storeship had been woefully late in making her rendezvous in Rio. There had been constant squabbles about the captaincies of the *Swallow* and the two little schooners. There had been pirate scares, runaways, and near mutinies. And then there had been all those murders...

As usual, the commander of the expedition was standing behind a desk, as if he wanted to put a barrier between himself and his audience. He was wearing undress uniform, with a black scarf tied round his upper arm, the same rig he had worn at the funeral, when Lawrence J. Smith had been laid to rest in the cold ground of Tierra de Fuego, alongside the sealer who had drowned while trying to kill Wiki. The six surviving sealers had all attended the burial, too, their demeanor savage and brooding. Wiki had kept well wide of them.

Now, he stopped a cautious two yards in front of the desk. A letter lay on the top of it, alongside a journal that looked like Midshipman Dove's. Otherwise, it was bare. So Mr. Spieden had paid attention to his broad hints, he thought—he and Stuart had come looking for the letter, and it seemed that they had found it. The journal, obviously, had been used for a comparison of the script.

Looking up at Captain Wilkes, Wiki said, "A consolation on your loss, sir. I know Lieutenant Smith was your good friend."

135

"Yes." Captain Wilkes had to stop to clear his throat. "I believe he was also close to your father, Captain William Coffin."

Wiki nodded, veiling his opinion. As well as being a neighbor in Salem, Smith had had a shared seafaring history with his father, because in his youth he had served on Captain Coffin's brig for a few months, to build up sea-time. Somehow, a friendship had developed. Wiki had not been able to understand how his father could stand him, but Captain Coffin had never been less than affable to the pompous little man.

"I do wish that I had been more pressing in my recommendation that he should consult with one of the surgeons. But who expected that those fainting fits would lead to his death?"

Wiki still kept his silence, thinking, fainting fits? Had Lawrence J. Smith staggered because he was lightheaded? He remembered how the hysterical little man had demanded that he start an investigation to find out who had shoved him.

Captain Wilkes went on, "And you and Lieutenant Matthews both did your best to save him."

"There were too many people in the water," Wiki said. "Everyone got in everyone else's way."

"All brave men—and one lost his life in the attempt."

Captain Wilkes was talking about the dead sealer. Wiki looked down at the desk again. No one had noticed he had drowned the man in self defense, which was a sign of how easily the sealer could have gotten away with murder. He wondered yet again why the man had tried to kill him, as the timing seemed so odd. Where the sealers had been determined to beat the location of the *Betsey's* sealing beach out of him, now they didn't seem bothered. So what had happened in the meantime? What had made the difference?

"Did you know that Lieutenant Smith was coming to the *Peacock* to fetch you?"

Wiki looked at Captain Wilkes again, remembering that Matthews had said something to that effect. Evidently signals had been flown. He said, "Can I ask why, sir?"

"Of course. Lieutenant Smith was carrying a message requesting your presence at a meeting I was holding here with Captain Hudson's clerk, and the *Peacock's* purser." Captain Wilkes sat down, and tapped the letter with a long finger. "Mr. Spieden informed me it was you who alerted him to this."

Wiki nodded, wondering what else the purser had told him. He hoped that the IOUs had not been mentioned. Not only did he have some sympathy for Passed Midshipman Jenkins, but he could imagine Captain Wilkes's incoherent rage when he learned that gambling was rife on the expedition ships.

"Can you tell me what happened, in your own words?"

"Aye, sir. I went to see Mr. Spieden, and told him about a conversation in the wardroom. I asked for his opinion, because I was puzzled about what was said."

"Conversation? With which officers?"

"Lieutenants Lee, Pilson, Blackmer, and Russell, sir."

A curt nod, as if this confirmed something. "So tell me what happened."

"Lieutenant Blackmer asked me why I'd been going through Midshipman Dove's chest."

Captain Wilkes frowned, and said, "That is a question I would ask myself."

"Lieutenant Lee had instructed me to write a report on Midshipman Dove's death—which was a violent one, after all."

"But his *belongings*, for God's sake!"

"I was making an appraisal, and nothing more than that. Anyway, when I told Lieutenant Blackmer it was part of my official role, Lieutenant Pilson suggested that I was looking for Mr. Dove's suicide note."

Captain Wilkes said slowly, "He told you there was a suicide note?"

"He was only speculating, sir, but then he called it a letter. Well, sir, letters—unlike notes—are generally mailed, so I wondered if Mr. Dove had written a letter while the *Betsey* was waiting for our mail. But then I was informed that there was no letter written by him in the bag that was put on the sealer."

"Who told you that?"

"Two men. First, Lieutenant Russell, and then Mr. Spieden. Mr. Spieden said he hadn't noticed anything written by Mr. Dove when he put the letters in the bag, which corroborated what Lieutenant Russell had already told me."

"And what else did Mr. Russell tell you, pray?"

Wiki paused, troubled by Captain Wilkes's sarcastic tone, but merely said, "That the letters were checked by the officers, so if Midshipman Dove had written one, he would have seen it. But there wasn't one—so I wondered if it had missed the mail for the *Betsey*, and had been put in another bag."

Ignoring this last, Captain Wilkes said, "Checked?"

"Aye, sir."

The commander's voice became even more cutting. "Censored for scurrilous gossip?"

Wiki said uneasily, "Lieutenant Lee told me that it was according to your instructions, sir."

"*Lee!*" The word was a hiss. Then there was a short silence, punctuated by clicks as Captain Wilkes tapped a pencil on the top of the desk. Finally, he said, "In view of that, I'm sure you will be as astonished as I am that *this* managed to get into the mailbag ready for the next ship, *despite* Lieutenant Lee's instructions to have every letter checked." He lifted the pencil to gesture at the letter, and said grimly, "Please read it."

Wiki picked it up, and unfolded it. The scrawl was large and childish, and the letters formed with the same elaborate care as the names Dove had printed on the tops of the chits.

Hon'red father

I know the Disappointment this will bring to your heart, and how your Dearest Ambition was to see my successful Establishment in the Great Service of the United States Navy, but I swear I cannot Abide it, not a day longer. When we left the Hampton Roads, ev'ry man in the Expedition was devoted to the Person of Captain Wilkes, but now we all believe he is a Monster, and no one more than Myself. He should be Proclaimed a Cruel and Malignant Villain, a self-serving prey to Pride and Ambition, and completely Unfit to be the leader of an Expedition. I cannot and should not recount all his Atrocities, not having the Heart. Others will write to the Department in Washington and the Truth will come out. Vis consili expers mole ruit sua. But I cannot Bear it any More. Please Kiss my dear mother and tell her Goodbye.

Y'r Devoted and Unworthy Son, Mid'n Valt. Dove

139

Wiki put the page back on the table. He looked at Captain Wilkes and said flatly, "Midshipman Dove didn't write this."

"You're sure of that?"

"Absolutely. You've seen Midshipman Dove's journal? It just isn't possible that a man who was incapable of writing anything but gibberish could write this letter. It *has* to be a forgery."

Wilkes nodded, as if it confirmed what he had concluded already. Then he said, "Do you have any idea why Dove normally wrote gibberish?"

"Mr. Stuart told me that Captain Hudson received a letter from Midshipman Dove's family before we sailed from Norfolk, saying that their son had a congenital idiosyncrasy that prevented him from reading and writing. Accordingly, they begged his indulgence and understanding in the matter of his journal."

"Then how the hell did they expect him to ever pass his examinations?"

Wiki shrugged and spread his hands.

"And that quote from Horace—if he couldn't read or write English, he certainly couldn't have written that! Have you heard of Horace?"

As it happened, Wiki had certainly heard of Horace, though he had no Latin. George Rochester was fond of quoting Horace at every opportunity, saying that he would've liked to have made the acquaintance of the Roman poet, as he was a jolly fellow who loved to dance, admired beautiful women, and enjoyed his glass of wine.

Instead of revealing this, Wiki confessed, "I'm curious to know what the quotation means."

"*Vis consili expers mole ruit sua* – dictatorship without wisdom collapses of its own weight. For God's sake!" Wilkes exploded, losing his unnatural calm. "The writer is calling me an ignorant tyrant! Do you have any idea – of the damage this – this – this *forgery* would have done to me if this – this *libel* had reached the Dove family?"

Choosing his words carefully, Wiki said, "I agree with you that it does seem strange that this letter got into the mailbag without being checked and stopped."

"And it must have been an *officer* who put it in the bag."

"That does seem obvious," Wiki admitted.

"So it has to have been an *officer* who forged it."

"And that's logical, too."

"Someone who *seized* the opportunity offered by Mr. Dove's tragic suicide to discredit my name with his family – who would certainly have passed the forgery on to the Navy Department in Washington."

"Aye, sir," said Wiki, though very thoughtfully. When he had read the letter, it had seemed likely to him that it had been forged by the man who murdered Valentine Dove to convince his family that the poor fellow had committed suicide. But, when he remembered the mutinous talk he had overheard from the wardroom pantry, Captain Wilkes's theory was equally plausible. Would the Dove family have passed on the letter to influential friends in Washington, triggering Wilkes's summons back to the States? Yes, he thought. Given their state of rage, regret, and grief, it seemed very likely indeed.

"There is a mutinous *cabal* in this expedition!" Captain Wilkes exclaimed. "A cabal of officers who owe me perfect and unquestioning loyalty, but instead work against me at every opportunity — officers who congregate with their juniors to corrupt their minds in the same direction!"

Wiki said nothing, and fought down the urge to shift uneasily from foot to foot. Captain Wilkes was breathing hard, and rubbed his sweating forehead as if a pain nagged. Then, in a more normal voice, he went on, "I tackled the shameful situation in Rio, after having learned that some of the more senior officers were miserably remiss in carrying out the observations required of them — that they threw the burden on the zealous young men, and then laughed at them for being so dutiful. I called a meeting of all of the officers, and told them what I thought of that in the strongest language possible — I informed them that I was fully determined to detach sinners and laggards, and send them back to Washington, where they could explain their strange actions to the Navy Department! But has that fixed it? Evidently not! But I know their names, and I know what to do about it — and your testimony has added the names of Lieutenants Blackmer, Russell, and Pilson to the list!"

Feeling very alarmed about what was likely to happen in the wardroom when the news of this got out, Wiki said quickly, "Captain Wilkes, sir, could I please be reassigned from the *Peacock*?"

"You would prefer not to live in the same nest as those vipers?"

Wiki blinked, thinking it was true enough, but he wouldn't have phrased it quite that way. He didn't need to answer, however, because Captain Wilkes waved a hand and said, "Absolutely understandable.

As of today, you are reassigned to the *Vincennes*." Then, on an afterthought, he added, "In the meantime."

While the first part of the sentence was a relief, the last part seemed ominous. Wiki repeated warily, "In the meantime?"

Wilkes made another impatient movement. "I know I can rely on your discretion, so you may as well hear the rest. In fact, you can perform as my secretary and write to my dictation—just as you did in Rio."

"But, sir, that was because of my Portuguese," Wiki protested.

"Are you trying to pretend that you can't write in English?" Captain Wilkes demanded. Then, without even waiting for an answer, he continued, "First, I want you to make out orders for Lieutenant Lee to report to Lieutenant Commander Long of the *Relief*, for passage to the United States, he being dismissed from the expedition."

Wiki exclaimed, "*I beg your pardon?*" Hastily he added, "Sir?"

"I have abundant reason, believe me. When informed that he was not going to be promoted to the post of flag lieutenant that was made vacant by the sad loss of Lieutenant Smith, the scoundrel wrote me a most impertinent letter. And today I have learned that he has also insulted Captain Hudson—his commanding officer!—by telling him that he would call him *mister* from now on, as he was not fit to be called *captain!*—simply because Captain Hudson refused to approve a flogging that Lieutenant Lee had ordered, considering that the circumstances did not warrant it. Dismissal is a disgrace he fully deserves—good riddance to the insolent rascal!"

143

Wiki's thoughts were flying. Lee had expected to replace Lawrence J. Smith? Greatly daring, he said, "So who *is* Lieutenant Smith's replacement as flag lieutenant?"

"Lieutenant Craven."

Wiki blinked. Craven had been flag lieutenant of the fleet, right up until the night on the Rio Negro when a drinking spree had been discovered on the brig *Porpoise*. The men who had been charting the shoals in small boats had congregated there when a storm blew up, and had proceeded to celebrate their survival. Lieutenant Craven hadn't even been there, but he was in charge of the small boat flotilla, and so Wilkes had seized the chance to dismiss him.

Captain Wilkes sniffed and said, "I decided to reinstate him after I received a written apology — once he had rewritten it to correct grammar and spelling and moderate the over-obsequious tone." He set to tapping his pencil again, so obviously arranging his thoughts that Wiki took the hint, and fetched paper, pen, and ink from a drawer, and sat down at a nearby desk.

Firing Lee was the priority, it seemed, because his order of dismissal came first. Then the commander embarked on a general bulletin. "The squadron having successfully rendezvoused at Orange Harbor, all captains are directed to the *Relief* for supplies to refit for the making of the Southern cruise to the Antarctic," Wilkes dictated. "The *Swallow*, *Peacock*, and *Porpoise* will proceed south, with the *Flying Fish* and *Sea Gull* as tenders. While the season is a little advanced, due to the delays caused by the tardiness of the *Relief*, and misadventures in port, I am confident of reaching

Captain James Cook's *ne plus ultra*, 71° 10' South, the farthest south yet reached by man."

Wiki, writing this down in the flowing script that had been taught to him as a child by a drunken beachcomber who had once been a respected Martha's Vineyard captain, had trouble not shaking his head. Not only was the mission doomed to failure, in his private opinion, but it was pointless. Many Stonington men would argue that Stonington sealers had sailed farther south than Cook's *ne plus ultra*, and in smaller vessels, too—and the southern summer was almost over! Captain Cook had abandoned any thought of trying to penetrate further south in *January* 1774, and here the month of *February* was well advanced. Soon ice would make the sea impassable, while floating icebergs would be a constant hazard.

This was followed by letters to more than a dozen officers, shuffling them about the different vessels in the squadron. Pilson, Blackmer, and Russell were moved to inferior positions on the *Vincennes*, while Lieutenant Matthews was seconded to the brig *Porpoise*. The six surviving sealers were to be collected on the *Porpoise* too, advising on conditions in the Antarctic Ocean, and fulfilling their role with the expedition at last. And then there was the business of allotting commands for the southern venture. George Rochester, thank God, would stay in command of the *Swallow*, but Captain Wilkes himself would take over the quarterdeck of the brig *Porpoise*, relegating her captain, Cadwallader Ringgold, to the status of second in command, while Knox and Reid, the two passed midshipmen who had brought the schooners *Flying*

Fish and *Sea Gull* from Norfolk to Orange Harbor, were to be replaced by lieutenants.

Wiki headed up one paper after another, meditating that pride was bound to be hurt, and high ambitions dashed, and there was going to be hell to pay. Captain Wilkes, however, didn't seem to care a whit about what chaos he might be triggering, looking energized, instead. The next order was to Lieutenant Craven, who instead of enjoying high adventure in the Antarctic would be left in charge of the *Vincennes*, which would be safely moored to serve as a base for the observatory that would be set up on shore.

After that, secret instructions to the favored captains who were off to the Antarctic were dictated, informing them that while the advertised rendezvous at the end of the southern mission was Orange Harbor, if insurmountable difficulties in making Hoste Island were encountered, then the expedition fleet should be rejoined at the next rendezvous point, the Chilean port of Valparaiso. Wiki hoped fervently that orders would be ignored, and the ships would head for Valparaiso as soon as the impossibility of doing anything significant in the Antarctic Ocean was recognized. His memories of lashing sleet, blizzards, and bitterly cold gales during the battle to get around the Horn and into the Pacific were just a hint of how horrible it was going to be in the far south. Conditions on the *Peacock*, with her scant freeboard, would be particularly atrocious.

Feeling concerned about his compatriot, he said, "What about Te Aute, sir?"

"I beg your pardon?"

"Jack Sac. He's currently a supernumerary on the *Peacock*."

"Surely that doesn't disqualify him from the greatest adventure of all? But if you think otherwise, tell him he has my permission to remove to the *Vincennes*."

Wiki said, relieved, "So we'll be together, sir."

"As I said, you will be on the *Vincennes* in the *meantime*," Captain Wilkes snapped. "Once Lieutenant Forsythe's preparations are made, you will sail with him on the *Peacock*'s biggest launch to the islands sixty miles south of the southern tip of Tierra del Fuego. And then you will assist him in surveying and charting the archipelago, concentrating on the Wollaston and Hermit Islands."

Wiki exclaimed, "*What?*"

"You've done it before, and you can do it again."

Wiki was silent. He certainly had sailed in the thirty-foot launch before—for five cramped, uncomfortable days and nights that had been about the worst in his seafaring career. And that had been in the tropics! The scatter of ironbound islands that Captain Wilkes described were only just to the northwest of Cape Horn, where storms could sweep down at any moment, and temperatures would be freezing.

Captain Wilkes said, "You don't like the idea?"

"I wonder what use I would be to Lieutenant Forsythe, sir."

"You're the linguister, are you not? Lieutenant Forsythe will need you to mediate with the natives you encounter."

Wiki blinked, but supposed Captain Wilkes had a point. While the very idea of sending a relatively small boat to chart the islands about Cape Horn was insane, it should be possible to make camp on shore each night—

which would certainly mean interacting with the locals, along with grappling with their language.

He said, "So Mr. Hale will be coming with us?"

"Certainly not. Mr. Hale—like the rest of the scientific corps—will be seconded to the storeship *Relief.*"

That made sense, Wiki thought. While the *Peacock,* the *Porpoise,* the *Swallow* and the two schooners were off on this most ill-considered foray into the Antarctic, the scientifics would be able to study the plants, animals, natives and topography of Orange Harbor at their leisure. It was an excellent idea to house them all, meantime, on the storeship.

"Which," continued Captain Wilkes, "Captain Long will take to Breaknock Passage, and then through the Cockburn Channel and Magdalene Sound into the Straits of Magellan. He will then make a circuit of Tierra del Fuego, keeping to the northern shore but not neglecting to explore the many and various channels that have not yet been charted. After that, he will return to Orange Harbor."

Wiki stared, aghast. Not only would the passage up the coast of Chile to the western entrance of the straits be dangerous in the extreme, as the old, slow, unhandy ship would be constantly blown towards the reefs and rocks by the westerly gales, but once the *Relief* had negotiated the terrifyingly tortuous straits, she would have to beat against the prevailing winds to get west again—in one of the most gale-wracked times of the year. Captain Wilkes had had plenty of trouble with the rebellious and complaining scientifics, but was he really trying to kill them?

"Your pen," Captain Wilkes reminded him in a snap.

Wiki came out of a daze. So he hadn't finished, he thought numbly. "Aye, sir," he said, and was set to writing again.

Fourteen

The afternoon was well advanced by the time Wiki was finally dismissed.

The orders to Lieutenant Lee and all the other officers would have been delivered by now, he realized, and he earnestly hoped that no one recognized his writing. But when he arrived on the *Peacock* it was to find that the wardroom, thankfully, was empty. Perhaps, Wiki thought, Captain Hudson was holding an urgent meeting with his officers. He went into his stateroom, and packed his sea-chest, then sat on the edge of his berth to wait for the summons to the boat that would take him to the *Vincennes.*

As time passed, he slumped forward with his forearms on his knees, staring down at the planks in deep thought. He had two crimes now — the murder and the forgery. Was his original feeling right — that the man who had killed Midshipman Dove had forged the suicide letter to cover up the murder? Or was Captain Wilkes correct, and one of the officers who hated him so much had seized the opportunity to discredit him — a man who'd had nothing to do with the actual murder at all?

For it was murder, Wiki was convinced of that — but murder needed a motive. Poor Dove had most likely been killed to wipe out a debt, which meant that every man in the ship who had borrowed money from him was a suspect. Or was that really so? The trace of blood inside the sleeve of the oilskin coat betrayed that the killer must be one of the officers — one of the men who had initialed the chits. Which narrowed it down to Pilson, Jenkins, Blackmer, Russell, and the mysterious Sweetman.

And, if money was indeed the motive for the murder, then Sweetman was the most likely killer, because he owed the enormous sum of one thousand, three hundred dollars, while the others owed relatively trivial amounts, just... Wiki couldn't remember for sure, so he roused himself, and fetched down his Guernsey to check the figures.

The woolen smock felt different, lighter somehow, and when he felt about in the inside pocket his hand came up with nothing. The pocket was empty. The notebook was gone.

There was a coldness in his stomach. Theft was particularly despised on shipboard, as seamen had so few possessions, and this loss had ominous implications. Swiftly, Wiki checked his sea-chest, throwing everything out that he had packed so carefully. Then he hunted every corner and cranny of the little stateroom, but all he accomplished was to make a mess. Which, he thought ruefully as he surveyed his cluttered berth, meant that he couldn't be sure that an intruder had gone through his room. He didn't even know for certain if the book had been stolen — he could have left it somewhere.

The purser's office, for instance. He dashed down the ladders, and was relieved to find Mr. Spieden still at work. Unfortunately, however, while the purser seemed pleased to see him, he shook his head in reply to the urgent question.

"The last time I saw that book," he said, "you were putting it inside your Guernsey."

"Damn," said Wiki. He could think of nowhere else it might be. The inescapable conclusion was that it had been stolen.

"Was the notebook important?"

"I'm not sure," Wiki said slowly.

The notes on the early pages, all to do with his investigations on the Rio Negro, had been incorporated into a report to the sheriff in Portsmouth. That, he thought, should be on board the sealer *Betsey*, as it had been put in the *Vincennes* mailbag before they had sailed from Patagonia.

"The only important page was the list of what was on the chits," he said, and then frowned. There was something nudging at the edge of his mind, but he couldn't pin it down, so he left it, saying, "I suppose you know that I was summoned to the *Vin* this afternoon."

To his surprise, instead of answering the purser rang his little bell for the boy, and after the redheaded lad arrived at a run, he was sent off for a pot of coffee. Just as before, it seemed, Mr. Spieden wanted a quiet chat.

When the door was shut and locked, and they were settled on either side of his counter with their steaming mugs in front of them, he said, keeping his voice low, "I'm sorry I wasn't there, Mr. Coffin. Captain Wilkes flew into a shocking passion when he read the letter we found in the bag. As you probably know, he sent for you right away, but tragedy intervened. How was he with you?"

"He asked me what I thought of the letter, and I told him that I was sure it was forged. He agreed with me, but wanted to know how the letter had got into the mailbag without being checked."

"That *is* a scandal," Mr. Spieden energetically agreed. "If the officers are not doing their job, then any number of scurrilous, ill-founded accusations could make their way to the States!"

"Aye," said Wiki, and sighed. "Captain Wilkes made up his mind that it was Lieutenant Lee's fault."

"Well, he *is* the first lieutenant on this ship."

"I know. And Captain Wilkes was already angry with him. When I arrived I overheard quite a row between Captain Wilkes and Captain Hudson, apparently something to do with Lieutenant Lee and insubordination."

Spieden nodded. "Lieutenant Lee ordered a flogging, and Captain Hudson refused to approve it. So Lieutenant Lee lost his temper, and told Captain Hudson that he wasn't fit to be called *captain* any more."

Wiki paused, impressed by his inside knowledge, and then said, "Anyway, Lieutenant Lee has been banished to the *Relief*, to be sent back to the States in disgrace."

"And as a result, officers are being redistributed all about the fleet." Then the purser changed the subject, saying, "You probably gathered that I didn't bring the matter of the IOUs to Captain Wilkes's attention. He was upset enough already."

"I think you were wise." Wiki hesitated again, then made up his mind, and said, "I learned the other day that the chits were only the tip of the iceberg, so to speak. Midshipman Dove loaned money to men all over the ship."

"Good lord," said Mr. Spieden. He pushed his eyeglasses up his nose, his raised eyebrows having dislodged them. "So that's why —" He broke off, shook his head, and said, "I wondered why so few men have come to me for advances on their pay. Good lord," he said again. "And he was charging interest?"

"So I was told, but I don't know what the rate was."

"How foolish of the men to get involved in such a disadvantageous arrangement!" Then Spieden added on a philosophical note, "But sailors are traditionally foolish with their money."

"Do you think that draft for five thousand dollars that I found in his pocket might have been repayment on a loan?"

"It seems too much — though a couple of those IOUs were for significant amounts."

Sweetman's, in particular, Wiki mused. He said, "You haven't had any more thoughts about the officer Dove called *Sweetman*?"

"I did wonder if his muddled mind made a play on the meaning of the name. Sweetman could be translated into something like Pastrycook."

Wiki laughed at the comical idea, but then sobered. "Or Baker," he said.

They looked speculatively at each other. Mr. Spieden said, "Baker opens up the field too much. I can think of several men called Baker."

"So can I," said Wiki. He sipped his coffee, feeling depressed and defeated. The solution of the Sweetman name was important, as it could be the key to the mystery of Midshipman Dove's brutal murder. Yet it was so elusive, slipping further out of reach all the time.

Finally, he said, "Something else that has puzzled me is that there was no money in Dove's clothes, or in his chest. He must have had coins ready to lend out, so where is it?"

"And you wondered if the midshipmen pocketed it before they delivered his chest to me?"

Wiki smiled. "The thought did cross my mind."

"Well, you can set your mind at rest, because moneylenders — like bankers — don't work like that. As soon as a debt is repaid, the money is loaned out again. They simply find another borrower."

"Are you sure?" said Wiki, astonished.

"Before I joined this expedition, I worked as a clerk in the Navy Yard for more years than I care to remember, and I assure you that that is the way moneylending works. Money that is laying around is wasted income, because it isn't earning interest."

"Good heavens," said Wiki. His people in the Bay of Islands were sharp traders, but this was a very new view of the way business was done.

"What puzzles *me*," said Mr. Spieden, "is that there were only fourteen IOUs, and yet you say that a whole host of seamen owed money."

"He didn't actually need IOUs. Dove kept the figures in his head — without a single mistake, or so his messmates told me. He had a prodigious memory for numbers."

The purser's brows shot up so high that he had to push his eyeglasses back into place again. "And yet he couldn't write a sensible sentence?"

"It could have been part of his congenital idiosyncrasy."

There was a pause, and then Spieden said shrewdly, "And though Mr. Dove had this prodigious memory for figures, he still made the officers sign IOUs. Do you think he meant to humiliate them?"

Wiki grinned. "I don't think he liked them very much."

"Bullyragged to a bone from the first day of the voyage?"

"I'm sure you're right."

"I've seen it often," said Mr. Spieden, and shook his head sadly. "Even the keen young lads can be beaten and hazed into a state of abject misery, and Mr. Dove was never a keen mariner."

Eight bells rang from high above, a tinny echo from the open deck. Wiki drained his mug, and said, "I thank you for the coffee, but I should get going."

"To the *Vin*," said Mr. Spieden, as all-knowing as ever. To Wiki's surprise, he stood up and shook hands. "Good luck," he said. "I know you have a dangerous mission ahead of you."

Wiki's face creased in a rueful grin. "It's going to be interesting," he said. Then he remembered that he had a message to pass on, and said, "Do you have any idea where Te Aute — Jack Sac — might be?"

Mr. Spieden shook his head, and Wiki took his leave, wondering how to track down the rascal. As he arrived at the foot of the ladder to the berth deck, however, Te Aute materialized, almost as if he had been eavesdropping.

"Boss," he said, and winked.

"You're coming with me to live on the *Vin*," said Wiki. "The boat should be almost ready to carry us there, so you'd better get your duds together."

"Excellent," his compatriot said, and turned to leave.

"Just a minute," Wiki said. There was something Mr. Spieden had said that he wanted to check, and he reckoned Te Aute was as all-knowing as the purser. So he said, "Did you know that Midshipman Dove loaned money to the seamen?"

Without even having to think about it, Te Aute nodded.

"Did you borrow money from him?"

Te Aute laughed. "Not me, boss."

It was nothing less than Wiki had expected. Borrowing was an alien concept at home, just as it was throughout the Pacific. Everything that hadn't been already claimed by the chief was communal property, and so everyone just took what he or she needed. It was a customary practice that had led to the Polynesians' terrible reputation for stealing.

"But you know how he went about it?"

"He had an office. Men who wanted money arranged to see him there."

"Office?" Wiki blinked. "Where?"

"The pantry."

"The *pantry*?" Wiki was even more surprised.

"The pantry of the midshipmen's room," Te Aute said, and led him there.

As expected, it was a miserable little cubby hole. The freckled boy who acted the midshipmen's steward was stacking dishes in a rack. His eyes went

157

wide when he saw Wiki and his tattooed friend, and he backed away as far as the tiny space allowed.

Wiki said without preamble, "How much did Midshipman Dove pay you?"

"I don't know what you're talking about, Mr. Coffin."

"Yes, you do. He bribed you to keep out of sight while he carried out business transactions."

"But I wasn't here, sir, I never seen a thing, sir."

"Then you won't mind if we turn your pantry out," Wiki said, and he and Te Aute set to. There were bins below the dry sink, but they proved to hold nothing but basics like flour, molasses, and saleratus, plus a small store of luxury foodstuffs like raisins and pickles, which the midshipmen would have had to supply themselves. Otherwise, there was just the little butt of fresh water, spirit stoves for heating food, and the barge holding the hard ship's bread that was the staple for everyone at sea.

Wiki straightened, looking around. "It must be here," he said.

"What, boss?"

"A bag of coins. I don't believe Mr. Dove had no cash money. He had to have it to grease this lad's palm, for a start."

They both contemplated the boy with their fists planted on their hips, and he backed away again, his round eyes going from one face to another. Finally, he admitted, "Aye, sir, he did have a leather bag of coins."

"So where do you reckon it is?" said Wiki.

The boy wavered, seeming ghoulishly fascinated by Te Aute's facial tattoo. Then he looked back at Wiki, took in a breath and said, "I don't know for certain, sir, and I swear to God I never stole nothing, sir, but it might be a good notion to have a real good look at the bread barge."

When the lid was taken off, the wooden keg appeared to be full of nothing but big round crackers. Close investigation proved, however, that it was made up of two kegs, one fitting tightly inside the other. Prying out the inside keg revealed that it was shorter than the outer keg, so there a space at the bottom, in which there was indeed a leather bag. It was only half full, but sagged heavily when Wiki hauled it out.

The boy licked his lips nervously, and said, "What are you going to do with that?"

"I'm taking it to the purser, who will send it to Mr. Dove's family, along with the rest of his stuff. And if you keep as quiet as a little mouse, I'll forget to report that Mr. Dove bribed you to let him use your pantry as an office."

"Aye, sir," said the boy, very rapidly indeed, and Wiki shouldered the bag, nodded his thanks to Te Aute, and headed back to Mr. Spieden's office. The purser, he meditated, was going to be quite chagrined that his theory about Dove not keeping cash in hand had been proved so wrong.

When Wiki arrived back in the wardroom, it was to find Titian Peale sitting at the table with his sketchpad in front of him, and a decanter of Madeira at his elbow. He was still there when Wiki came out of his stateroom after repacking his sea-chest, and was apparently still absorbed in his drawing, but as Wiki passed, he said, "Do you think you might have forgotten something?"

Wiki stopped, but before Peale could say anything more Lieutenant Lee came down the stairs, followed by three other officers in a tight, confrontational group. Wiki had only a glimpse of Lee's rigid, white face and glittering eyes before he found his arm gripped. It was Peale. The naturalist pulled him through his stateroom door, and closed it with a decisive snap, shutting out the clamor of angry conversation on the other side. Then he let go of Wiki's arm.

Wiki set his chest down and looked around. The naturalist's stateroom was a mess, with sketches and diagrams pinned up all over the walls, and the desk piled up with more papers. Chests and trunks filled all the corners, chocked up with blocks of wood. There was a distinct smell of sea shells with rotting contents.

Peale had his back to him, and was prying out a botanist's frame that had been stowed between two chests. Then, after unstrapping it, he detached a document from the papers that had protected it, and handed it to Wiki, saying, "We did a good job. It's as good as new."

It was the certificate from the sheriff's department of the Town of Portsmouth, Virginia. *He had forgotten his letter of authority.* Feeling extremely chagrined, and very relieved to have it returned, Wiki took it from the naturalist. It was not quite as good as new, as the ribbon and the seals were still travelworn, but the certificate was now a lot less likely to fall to pieces at the folds. After thanking Peale profusely, he put it in the inside pocket of his Guernsey.

Then he said, "Did you know you're being reassigned to the *Relief?*"

"I do," said Mr. Peale. "And I'm not." His face was set in an even more determined expression than usual.

Wiki said blankly, "You're not what?"

"I have sent a note over to Captain Wilkes, demanding an interview. I am not, categorically *not*, moving to the *Relief*. I am determined to sail south with the *Peacock*."

Good lord, thought Wiki. He admired Mr. Peale's obstinacy, and thought that Captain Wilkes might have met his match. "I wish you luck," he said.

"I *know* it will be damnably uncomfortable—what else could it be on this excuse for a ship?—but I refuse to miss out on the great opportunity."

Wiki said dryly, "It could also be a lot safer on the *Peacock* than on the *Relief*."

He wondered if Peale had any idea of how dangerous the leaky old *Relief*'s assignment was going to be, and then thought that the naturalist was probably bloodyminded enough to change his mind and decide to join the expedition to the Straits of Magellan and beyond, if he did. So, instead of elaborating, he said, "You wouldn't happen to know where my notebook got to, as well?"

"What notebook?"

Wiki sighed, though he hadn't felt any real hope that Peale might have it. He said, "The one where I make notes of my investigations. It has disappeared, which is a nuisance—and not just because I'll have to start a new one."

"But there's nothing to investigate here."

"Midshipman Dove's death *was* a violent one."

"And so was Lieutenant Smith's, by God." Peale opened the door in response to a knock, and nodded to the steward, who had come to tell Wiki that the boat was ready. Then he went on, "I've never seen anything so desperate as that struggle to save the poor drowning man."

As Wiki shouldered his chest he studied Peale cautiously, hoping that his battle with the sealer had been too deep in the water to be seen from the deck. While he felt no guilt whatsoever about the death of the sealer, having killed in self-defense, the prospect of an inquiry was very unwelcome. But Peale said nothing more, so Wiki bid him goodbye, thanked him again, and left.

The wardroom table was surrounded by lieutenants with glasses in their hands, who stared at him inimically as he headed for the companionway. Wiki paid little attention, though, because he was still thinking about the attack, feeling puzzled yet again that it had happened at all...

Then all at once he knew the answer.

The stray thought that prodded the edge of his mind while he had been trying to remember exactly what was written in the notebook was suddenly clear. *There had been a note of a position in the Antarctic Ocean — a position Captain Noyes had given him.*

The position had been that of the corpse-carrying iceberg, not the rookery, but the sealers, obviously, had jumped to the wrong conclusion. Believing that they had the location of the *Betsey*'s great haul, they had thought it was safe to wreak their overdue revenge.

But that led to another puzzle. The book had been stolen from his stateroom, where the sealers had no access, not being allowed in the after part of the ship. So it must have been one of those officers now sitting at the table who stole the book and handed it on to the sealers.

But which one?

Fifteen

Six days later, Wiki stood at the larboard rail of the *Vincennes* and watched the *Relief* weigh anchor.

Early the previous day, the *Porpoise* had taken her departure, followed by the schooner *Sea Gull*. With Captain Wilkes in charge, they had headed rapidly to the southwest. The triangles of the schooner's sails had disappeared first, and then, scant minutes later, Wiki had seen the last of the gunbrig's topgallant as the *Porpoise* rounded the headland. Just an hour later, the *Peacock*, *Flying Fish*, and *Swallow* had followed in their wake, but to take up a different course in the attack on the Antarctic.

At the time, the northerly breezes had been gentle, the pewter water rippled by cats' paws of wind, but at four in the afternoon a gale had got up, and the *Vincennes* had bucked at her anchors. And now, the *Relief* was to venture out into this region of vicious storms, complete with her cargo of scientifics. Wiki heard the rhythmic cries as the men manned the windlass to heave the anchor. Another loud order, echoed all about the decks, and topmen sprang aloft to loose the three topsails. At the same time two of the jibs were set, to pay her head off as the topsails were sheeted home. Then, as she slowly gathered way, plucking up her anchor as she went, the mainsail, foresail, and spanker were set. Round came her stern, and within minutes she was gone, hidden from sight by the island at the head of the harbor.

Wiki turned and went into the afterhouse, his footsteps echoing. Yet again, he was struck with how different the ship felt since Captain Wilkes had gone. Partly, it was because the ship echoed emptily. Ten men, with an officer and three civilians—the expedition pastor, one of the draftsmen, and Wilkes's physician— were on shore in the observatory, and the *Vincennes,* stoutly moored and with her topmasts struck, was manned by a much reduced crew, including all the invalids of the fleet. But the main difference was that no one cringed in anticipation of another tirade from their overwrought commander. Wiki often fancied he could hear the general sighs of relief as overstrained nerves relaxed.

On the larboard side of the corridor all the stateroom doors were shut, and just one man sat at the big table in the dining saloon on the other side of the credenza—the conchologist, Joseph Couthouy, who was now Wiki's only companion at meals. By rights, he should have sailed with the other scientifics, but, like Titian Peale, he had stoutly refused to move onto the *Relief.* His reason, however, had been much saner. A seasoned shipmaster out of Boston, Couthouy was acutely aware of the awful dangers that faced the storeship.

"They're gone," Wiki said now.

"To a watery grave."

"Dear God, I hope not."

"Their chances are bloody slim. Have you seen the only charts they have, the ones made by Captain Philip Parker King a whole damn ten years ago, when he was with Fitzroy of the *Beagle*? There are notes on them saying that no shipmaster in his right mind would entangle himself in those labyrinths—that venturing into that tortuous maze is begging for shipwreck!"

Wiki said glumly, "Captain Long doesn't even have King's charts."

"*What?*"

"All they were given is King's directions."

"Oh, my God," said Captain Couthouy, and gulped wine.

"Exactly," said Wiki, and listened to the wind whistling through the rigging. The *Vincennes*, though stoutly moored, was bucking every now and then. A gale was on the rise, yet within days the cutter was supposed to be sailing perilously close to Cape Horn, on a crazy mission to chart islands sixty miles south of Tierra del Fuego. He reached gratefully for the coffee pot when the steward carried it in.

Then, as he sipped, he contemplated Captain Couthouy. The conchologist's immense russet-colored beard fairly bristled with all the confidence of a shipmaster who expected his orders to be obeyed, by God, and so it was not hard to guess that Captain Wilkes had given in without too much of a struggle when Couthouy had flatly refused to leave the *Vin*. Couthouy was also an eccentric. Shell-collecting being his passion, he had made up his mind to sign up with the expedition long before the fleet actually got underway, informing no less a person than President Jackson that he would ship before the mast, if necessary. It was a boast that Jackson had found so entertaining that Couthouy had been shipped on the spot as a scientific, but Captain Wilkes had not been at

166

all amused. He and Couthouy had disliked each other on sight, and since then their relationship had become bitterly acrimonious.

"And you know why Wilkes has bundled the scientific corps on that floating coffin and sent it on its way into the rocks?" Couthouy expostulated now. "He never wanted to ship civilians in the first place, reckoning he could do all the astronomical work necessary to make it a *scientific* expedition. And he would've certainly sailed without 'em, if the Navy Department could have found any *scientifically* competent navy officers. But what do you expect of navy officers? Absolutely nothing outside their sphere, because they're just saltwater tars with ambitions for command and nothing more than that. One and all, they lack the required interest and attention. In fact, they are bloody uncooperative. I had six jars of precious specimens dangling down the side to keep 'em alive in the water, and those jars were smashed by the boats as they came up alongside. Deliberately, I vow, because they know that Wilkes is set against me."

"Tut," said Wiki, who was already very familiar with Captain Couthouy's battles with Captain Wilkes. Most of them, he had noticed, had been quarrels about Couthouy's habit of collecting dozens of specimens instead of the one of each species that Wilkes repeatedly specified.

"As it is," said the shipmaster, "he's thought up this way of getting rid of his pestilential civilian scientifics, because he reckons they will grab all the credit when the ships get home, just as Joseph Banks and Daniel Solander did, when Captain Cook's *Endeavour* got back to England. Setting them on that mad course in that sailing disaster is his way of forestalling that. Even if they make it back to Orange Harbor—which I strongly doubt—the scientific corps will be so terrified by the experience that they'll all take passage home at the very next port."

"Surely not," said Wiki.

"They will be lucky to weather Noir Island and find the roads, let alone fetch the entrance of Cockburn Channel. If Andrew Long has any sense, he'll disobey orders, steer for Juan Fernandez to get a good offing from the lee coast of Chile, then head for Valparaiso," said Couthouy, and drank deeply from his glass, as if making a toast.

Wiki said nothing, though he was tempted to strongly agree.

"It's because Long is one of Jones's boys, of course," said the shipmaster.

Wiki came abruptly to attention, as this was an interesting statement with equally interesting implications. Commodore Thomas ap Catesby Jones, a famously hot-tempered but thoroughgoing seaman who was unstintingly revered by those he commanded, had been the Navy Department's first choice to take charge of the expedition. Getting the fleet assembled, provisioned, manned, and under way had proved to be a much more tortuous and difficult task than expected, though, and finally, fed-up beyond bearing with the politics and palaver, Jones had flown into a passion and resigned, reducing the department to giving Charles Wilkes the job.

In the meantime, many of the officers had been appointed by Jones—lieutenants who felt a great deal of loyalty to him, and who emphatically resented his replacement by a man who was not only a mere lieutenant himself, but had the reputation of an ill-tempered martinet. Wiki already knew that Samuel Lee had been appointed by Catesby Jones, and wondered now if that had played a part in the decision to dismiss him. Had Blackmer, Pilson, and Russell been recruited by Commodore Jones, too? And what about the pantherlike Matthews? If they were all Jones loyalists, it could account for their hatred of Captain Wilkes.

The door of the afterhouse slammed open, and the sound of the wind increased to a howl. Then the noise became muffled again as the door crashed shut. Lieutenant Forsythe strode around the end of the credenza, bulky in oilskins, with traces of snow flurries on his shoulders. He shed the wet gear, dumped it on the floor, and thumped his broad backside into one of the revolving chairs without so much as a by-your-leave, let alone a greeting. He had no right to be in the afterhouse saloon, as his proper place was down in the officers' wardroom, but Captain Couthouy made no comment. Not, Wiki supposed, that it would have made any difference. For obstinacy and aggressiveness, Couthouy and Forsythe were well matched.

Wiki lifted his coffee mug in a silent salute, and said, "Are we sailing in the morning?"

Forsythe shook his head. "Nope. We have provisions for thirty days to load, and the job ain't half-finished, yet."

"So when?"

"When the dunnage is in—and the barometer drops."

"*Drops?*"

169

"Aye. That's the only way of foretelling fair weather in these goddamned infernal regions. Didn't you know that?"

"No, I didn't." On his previous voyages in these regions Wiki hadn't been high enough in the ship's social scale to have access to the barometer. He said, "But I always thought that a rising barometer meant improving weather."

"That's in the *proper* bloody part of the world. Down here, the barometer tells opposite."

Couthouy's face was a picture of mingled disbelief and pity. He said, "Did they teach you that in the Gosport Navy Yard?"

"No, they did not." Forsythe reached over, snared Couthouy's wine bottle, and splashed a generous measure into Wiki's empty mug, which he then drained in one thirsty gulp. "But it's logical," he said, coming up for air. "Stands to bloody reason."

Well, thought Wiki, it was obvious by Forsythe's reckoning that right now the barometer was on the rise. The *Vincennes* was bucking at her moorings, while the hardest gusts hit her broadside as if in elemental determination to send her up on the beach. He could hear shouts from the quarterdeck for a heave on the spring that had been put on the anchor cable, evidently in response to orders from Lieutenant Craven to bring her bow round to the eye of the wind. Night had fallen, and he knew it would be as black as a witch's pocket out on deck. Then he wondered how the *Swallow* was faring in the icebergs—and the *Peacock*, too, with Titian Peale on board.

"I don't blame you for wanting to procrastinate," Captain Couthouy said to Forsythe. His knowing smirk was only half-hidden by his beard and his lifted wineglass. "In your position I'd grab every excuse going, simply to save my own hide, not to mention the lives of my men. If that launch is caught out in a gale in the Mantello sea way..."

The glance Forsythe cast at him was savage, but he said nothing, because what the Boston shipmaster had said was nothing less than brutal reality. As Wiki was also acutely aware, the cutter was too small and top-heavy for the highly dangerous assignment. Caught out in a southwest gale, it would be driven off the land, never to be seen again, and if the tempest blew the other way, the coast that should have been their refuge would become the sailor's dread, a lee shore. Survival would mean a battle against a wind that threatened to send them crashing onto the rocks.

The steward came in again with a tray of cutlery and plates, fiddleboards under his arm to keep them steady on the table top, the ship's movement becoming even more lively. Evidently supper was nigh. Forsythe looked broodingly at Couthouy's wine bottle for what seemed a long while, but instead of reaching out for it he sighed heavily, and went.

Before he headed for his berth, Wiki took a lantern and tried the double doors of the big chartroom. The righthand one opened, and he went inside the big, shadowy room, holding the lamp high. The light bounced back from glass cupboard doors, and glimmered on ghostly shapes that floated inside jars. The gilt lettering on the spines of racked books glinted discreetly. Eventually he found the barometer, and bent down to peer at the reading. Memorizing the figures, he went to bed. After a surprisingly good night's sleep, he checked the instrument again. Then he went out on deck, where he found Forsythe harrying the six men of the cutter's crew into loading more gear, and a calm, mild morning.

He said, "We're still not leaving today?"

"Don't you ever bloody listen? No, we're not."

"The barometer's on the rise."

"Which means a gale is on the way." And, to Wiki's amazement, at seven bells in the forenoon watch the first squall ripped down from the hills, sending the beech trees tossing like the sea, followed by a succession of gusts that were accompanied first by hail, and then by snow. And so it was over the twelve days after that—mild dawns with a rising barometer, followed by vicious weather in the afternoon.

"It's really quite remarkable," said Dr. John Fox.

The physician was stationed on shore with Chaplain Elliott and Drayton, one of the expedition draftsmen, but the three supernumeraries had come to the afterhouse of the *Vincennes* for the usual Saturday feast. Now they were gathered in the chartroom with bottles of wine and decanters of Madeira while the table was being laid. The officer in charge of the observatory, Lieutenant Carr, was down in the wardroom, toasting the day with the resident lieutenants.

Wiki studied the speaker. Dr. Fox hailed from Salem, Massachusetts, the same town where Wiki had spent his first four years in America, and as John Fox was only three years older than Wiki himself, Wiki had often seen him walking in and out of the prestigious Salem Latin School, where he was a noted scholar.

However, he had never deigned to admit that he recognized Wiki Coffin, though he must have known about his colorful past, Wiki having been the subject of so much scandalous talk, back home.

"Remarkable?" said Couthouy.

"Yes. Gales here are always heralded by a rising of the barometer, quite contrary to atmospheric behavior in the northern hemisphere."

"Good lord," said Wiki. He couldn't wait to tell Forsythe.

"Remarkable indeed," said Couthouy. His expression, Wiki thought, was interesting.

"Not as remarkable as the Fuegians," said the Reverend Gillespie, who obviously didn't find the vagaries of barometers noteworthy at all. "Have you conversed with the natives?"

Wiki had done his best, both on board and on shore. However, he was saved from answering by Couthouy, who said, "Three canoes came to the ship over the course of the week. Primitive craft, bits of tree bark sewn together with scraps of whatever they can find—shreds of whalebone, sealskin, twigs. It's one of God's wonders that they keep afloat. And it's the women who paddle 'em! Though the men pull them along by grabbing at the kelp," he added. "Whole damn families on board, entirely naked to the weather, warmed only by a little fire—an open fire in a canoe! Only the men consented to come onto the deck. Entirely naked, as nude as God made 'em—and yet, when they were given cloth, they merely tied strips of it about their heads! Have you ever heard of anything so damn primitive?"

"They are people, Mr. Couthouy, people—God's creatures, just like us," said the cleric, his tone chiding. "And I'm sure they have an idea of a deity. When I folded my hands in prayer, I looked about to find the men who were standing about their wickerwork wigwams folding their hands in prayer too. It is a testament to the fact that we can find the virtues of humility and a craving for betterment even in the most uncivilized societies of men."

"They're the most complete mimics," Couthouy said dampeningly. "So I wouldn't pay much attention to that."

"It's true," said Drayton, the draftsman. "They even whistle in exact imitation when I play my violin. When I endeavored to find out their word for head, I pointed at my own head, and said, *head*, but when I then pointed at the native's head and looked enquiring, he simply said, in perfect imitation, *head*. And so it was with eye, ear, and hand, until I simply gave up. Before he left on the *Relief*, Mr. Hale was tearing his hair with frustration, and I guess it is the same for you, Mr. Coffin."

Wiki smiled wryly, in agreement. Even listening to the Fuegians' language was problematical. As each canoe came alongside, the fellow who appeared to be the captain stood up and harangued the ship in a twittering kind of speech, but when Wiki tried to engage the Fuegian men in conversation they either imitated what they heard, or whispered to each other, so he'd made scarcely any headway at all.

"What I would like to know," said Dr. Fox, "is what that word means. The word that is constantly on their lips."

They were all looking at Wiki. He said, "*Yamask-una?*"

"Good lord," said Drayton. "You've got it exactly. They say it over and over again—I often think it is the only word in their vocabulary."

"It means, *be good to me.*" They looked at him blankly, and Wiki shrugged and said, "They're asking you to be generous."

"They're *begging?*" said the reverend in horror.

"I'm afraid so," said Wiki, and escaped to the midshipmen's mess, where he was their invited guest for the Saturday feast.

The invitation had come from Midshipman Keith, Wiki's erstwhile stateroom companion on the *Swallow*, who had been moved from the brig to the *Vincennes* in the throes of Captain Wilkes's reshuffling. Welcomed with enthusiasm, Wiki sat down and looked around. This was the room where he had first been a guest at a midshipmen's Saturday feast, the same mess that had been decorated like the parlor of a bordello. Now, the damask on the couches was frayed and sadly stained, and the tablecloth had been the target of many splashes of wine. The weapons displayed on the forward bulkhead were as shiny and well-greased as ever, however, and the hash pie was as good.

Evidently the Madeira was as good as ever, too, because the boys very quickly became merry. Wiki was entertained with several songs, and Constant Keith told embroidered tales about the adventures they had shared on the *Swallow,* and after that Midshipman Dicken boasted extravagantly that he and friend Keith would climb the tallest hill within reach, as soon as the weather cleared for more than two hours.

"Think of it," he said. "We will be able to take a view of the Pacific and of the Atlantic at exactly the same time!"

"Good lord," said Wiki cooperatively, though he wasn't at all sure that such a view was possible. Then he observed, "I was invited to a feast at the midshipmen's mess on the *Peacock*, too."

Highly interested, they pressed him for a description of the food, the wine, and the quarters. "Much less luxurious," he said. "And not nearly as merry, though they did their best to be polite and entertaining. Mind you," he added, "they had only just lost a messmate."

They looked vague.

"Midshipman Valentine Dove," he prompted.

Silence reigned as they all recollected the tragedy, apparently with some difficulty, judging by their frowns. Then one said with an air of embarrassment, "Didn't Dove finish himself off, sir?"

"Cut his throat?" said another.

Another silence, as they waited for Wiki to go on, but he merely waited, too. Finally, Dicken said tentatively, "I heard that Dove was an oddity, sir."

"An oddity?"

"Aye. A sort of genius in the mathematical way, but hopeless with everything else."

"He hated the expedition, the *Peacock*, and the officers, everyone knew that," said another boy, who was named Gibson. "Scuttlebutt had it that he would've discharged himself at Rio, if he'd been allowed off the ship."

176

"Deserted?" said Wiki, astonished.

"Well, being from the family that he was from, he probably would have managed it more respectable like, by contacting an agent, or someone locally important. But he couldn't do it anyways at all, as nobody was allowed on shore, except for a few."

"Like us," said Dicken with pride, poking a thumb in Constant Keith's direction. Both boys had managed to have an adventure by climbing Sugar Peak—not once, but twice. It was a feat that they had commemorated with a sketch, now hanging on a bulkhead, of the two of them reclining at the top of the mountain next to the white handkerchief they had flown on a staff as a signal, the lords of all they surveyed.

Then Dicken told everyone all over again about how they planned to repeat the great accomplishment by climbing the highest hill in Orange Bay, which was just to the south of a deep eastward inlet. When the weather settled. They would have to penetrate primeval forest to get to the foot of the mountain, but that would not deter them.

"But even we wasn't allowed in the city proper," said Keith, reverting to the topic of Rio.

"True," said Dicken meditatively. "Very true. All on account of those bloody Brits, if you remember."

Wiki remembered it very well indeed. The battleship HMS *Thunderer* had also been in port at Rio, and as regular as clockwork, at eight bells every evening watch, the British marines had struck up "The *Chesapeake* and the *Shannon*," just to taunt the patriotic Americans, who couldn't wait to get on shore and teach the saucy bastards a lesson. Accordingly, Captain

Wilkes had stopped all liberty, forestalling a lot of broken heads and black eyes. It had been one of his wiser decisions.

One with interesting implications, Wiki realized now. He said, "If Midshipman Dove had managed to get on shore at Rio, do you think he planned to join another ship — one that was steering back to the States, perhaps?"

"He was going to set up in business, or that's what I was told," the knowledgeable Gibson said. "He had plenty of money to invest, and all the right contacts, and he was going in for some kind of banking. An agency, he called it."

"Moneylending?"

Gibson looked doubtful. "Don't know, sir, not without moneylending is part of all the other business that is done at banking agencies. All stuff I don't understand, like bills of exchange, drafts on merchants, things like that. He was a genius with figures, as Dicken said."

All the boys were smiling at him, in a tipsy sort of fashion, but Wiki didn't smile back. Instead, he said sharply, "Did any of you borrow money from Midshipman Dove?"

They all shook their heads at once, their amiable grins unshaken. But, he then realized, it was obvious that none of them were short of the ready. This lavishly furnished room and the well supplied table were testament to that. They were much more likely to be lenders than borrowers, and he had been foolish to think otherwise.

"Do you think he cut his throat on account of he was so disappointed and dispirited at not being able to escape the expedition at Rio, sir?" one of them asked.

Wiki did not, but avoided the question, saying, "What happened to the money he was going to invest, do you think?"

He expected it to be a rhetorical question, and for the boys to shrug and shake their heads. Instead, Gibson smiled brightly, and said, "The best cove to ask about that would be Lieutenant Forsythe, sir."

"*Forsythe*?"

"Yes, sir, Mr. Coffin, on account of what I heard he got up to after he was allowed to go into the city of Rio."

Sixteen

To Wiki's surprise, after a lot of searching he found Forsythe in the chartroom. The men attached to the observatory had gone back on shore, so the room was otherwise empty. Then Wiki saw that one of the decanters of Madeira had been left behind, which was evidently the attraction.

Forsythe, with a glass in his hand, was moodily regarding the barometer, and cast only a backward glance when he heard the door open.

Wiki said, "You were right."

"Which time was I right?"

"About the barometer. It reads the opposite way, down here. Your theory has just been confirmed by the folks at the observatory."

Forsythe swung around, and snarled, "It ain't a theory, it's a goddamned fact."

"So it seems."

"And there's been a bloody gale every day we have been here."

Wiki nodded, because that was certainly true. Then he wondered about Forsythe's foul mood. He couldn't work out whether the Virginian was chafing at the bit because he wanted to get away, or was bad-tempered because he was anxious about putting his men into danger.

He said, "Is the cutter ready yet?"

"As ready as it can be," the southerner grunted. During the calm mornings, Wiki had seen Forsythe supervising the cutter's men as they braced the two masts with preventer stays, and lashed all the moveable gear. The provisions had been stowed under the floor of the little decked-over cuddy, and were packed snug, too.

"But I ain't makin' a move until the barometer drops and stays that way."

"So we wait," said Wiki, with a sigh. He didn't know if he would rather sail away in the cutter and get it all over and done with, or have the mission delayed by the weather until after the *Porpoise* got back to Orange Harbor. The prospect of Wilkes's thunder and fury when he found that they hadn't obeyed orders was almost as daunting as the dangerous charting of the islands.

Then he wondered why Forsythe was spending so much time in the afterhouse. Oddly, the southerner passed the gale-wracked evenings at the table in the saloon, listening with highly uncharacteristic patience to Couthouy's interminable complaints. The only times he went down to the wardroom, where he properly belonged, was for meals and sleep, and Wiki had found this intriguing, as he couldn't think of a reason.

Deciding to find out, he said casually, "I'm surprised you spend so much time with Captain Couthouy and me. Do you really prefer the company here?"

Unexpectedly, Forsythe snorted with one of his flashes of humor. "Are all Boston shipmasters whining windbags?"

"I'm sure Captain Couthouy would be better company on board his own ship. The expedition's been a disappointment to him."

"Ain't that the truth," said Forsythe, and looked around, refilled his glass, and sat at one of the desks. "But those bastards what came over from the *Peacock* could give even Couthouy a lesson in complaining."

Pilson, Blackmer, Russell. Wiki sat down at a neighboring table, and said, "They complain about the expedition?"

"Mostly about Wilkes. I have my gripes with him myself, but the way they go on and on about him is just plain bloody mutinous."

"Even though Lieutenant Craven is there?"

Unexpectedly, Lieutenant Craven had chosen to stay in his room off the wardroom instead of taking over Captain Wilkes's berth in the afterhouse, as he was entitled to now he was in command of the moored *Vincennes*. Perhaps, thought Wiki, he didn't like the thought of living with the spirit of the irascible commander, even though the body was not actually present.

"Not when he's in hearin' distance, no. Even they wouldn't dare. But when Craven's on deck..." Forsythe's voice drifted away, and then he burst out, "It's as if they have some sort of plot going—the coy bastards smirk at each other, and whisper, like they've got a secret what they're cuddlin' to themselves."

Wiki exclaimed, "They're still at it?"

"*Still*? What the hell do you mean?"

"They carried on like that on the *Peacock,* too, but I thought that once Lieutenant Lee had gone with the

Relief, whatever they are plotting would have died a natural death."

Forsythe's eyes narrowed. "You reckon he was their leader in this mystery stuff?"

"Well, I thought so."

Silence, as the Virginian stared at him, and Wiki became aware once again of the shrewdness that lurked beneath Forsythe's bull-like exterior.

Then Forsythe said abruptly, "Tell me more."

Wiki hesitated, thinking about the officers' wardroom in the *Vincennes*, which was directly below the afterhouse. He had only been in there once, but remembered the shafts of light that had slanted down from the galleries. Wondering if sound penetrated there, too, he lowered his voice as he said, "Captain Wilkes thinks there is a mutinous cabal of officers in the expedition."

"Wa-al, that ain't news. Everyone knows he doesn't trust the men that was recruited by Commodore Jones."

"He reckoned that this cabal was led by Lieutenant Lee, but from what you say it seems he was wrong."

"That ain't necessarily so," Forsythe said, and tossed back the contents of his glass. After refilling it, he said, "Sam is a natural born rebel. He don't like Washington, and he don't like the way the country is going. It's a political matter, a lot of it to do with cotton and slaves, and nothin' what a half-breed like you would understand. It'll come to something, just you see—but it'll be back home in Virginia, not on the expedition."

Feeling both intrigued and curious, Wiki said, "So you think Captain Wilkes was right to fire him?"

Forsythe shrugged heavy shoulders. "Where there was one, there's always a bloody 'nother."

"Leader, you mean? But who could it be?" *Pilson, Russell, Blackmer. Sweetman.*

Another shrug. "They whisper among themselves. Drive a man crazy with their smirks and whispers."

Wiki laughed. "And to think I thought the reason you spent so much time in the afterhouse was that Lieutenant Craven wouldn't allow card play in the wardroom."

The look Forsythe cast him should have scorched, but Wiki was too used to this to pay any attention. He said, "Talking about gambling, did you owe Midshipman Dove any money?"

Forsythe shouted, "Not a bloody cent!"

Wiki's eyes widened. "So you did know that he was a moneylender?"

The lieutenant grimaced, realizing he had given himself away. "All the officers knew it."

"All the officers of the expedition?"

"Not everyone, but most."

"And they all borrowed from him?"

"Only those what needed it," Forsythe said sourly. As Wiki knew, his lack of funds, combined with his passion for gambling, constantly irked, particularly as many of the officers were privately wealthy. It was a major reason for his vile temper.

Which meant, Wiki deduced, that it was highly unlikely that Forsythe had not availed himself of Midshipman Dove's monetary services. He said, feeling sure of it, "But you did borrow money from him."

"Before Rio," Forsythe admitted. He concentrated on refilling his glass from the last of the Madeira in the decanter—to avoid meeting his eyes, Wiki thought, but then the Virginian lifted his head to stare at him challengingly. "But by the time the squadron set sail from Rio I didn't owe him nothing."

Wiki thought a moment, and then reflected, "You went on shore in Rio."

Forsythe said combatively, "No one was allowed liberty time in Rio, as you might remember."

"But you were there—as a witness in a murder trial." Wiki recollected it well, because he had been a witness, as well—and interpreter, too. "And you left the court the moment you had given your evidence."

"Nobody stopped me."

"But you didn't head back to the ship." Wiki had caught up with Forsythe in a taberna, where the southerner had been drinking as if he'd had something to celebrate.

He said, "Did you pay your debt to Midshipman Dove in coin, or did you do it by doing him a favor?"

There was a long silence as Forsythe stared at him, his blue eyes unfocused. Then he shook his head and said, "By God, there are times I forget that you really are a sleuth. Next thing, you'll tell me what that favor was."

Wiki slumped forward in his chair, forearms laid on his knees as he stared at the floor in deep thought. On first reflection, it seemed like an impossible challenge, but then he remembered the boys telling him that Dove would have jumped ship in Rio, given the chance—that he had contacts there, and the investment to set up an agency. Then he remembered what he had found in the dead man's inside pocket, drenched in blood but legible once unfolded.

He straightened, stared at Forsythe, and said with confidence, "Your job was to deposit a bag of five thousand dollars in coin into a bank in Rio, and collect a draft in exchange, which you then gave to Midshipman Dove. And in return he canceled your debt."

Forsythe blinked in astonishment. Then he grunted with wry amusement. "You believe I'm that honest?"

"Yes, of course I do."

"You reckon that Kit Forsythe—who's known to be a real bastard—is honorable enough not to run off with five thousand dollars, when he could've gotten away with it so easy?"

"Run where?" asked Wiki. "But yes, I do believe you are honorable."

"Bloody hell and good lord above," said Forsythe, and laughed again. Then he lifted his glass in an ironic toast. "I'm honored. And you're right." He gulped down the last of his wine, then said, "I brung Dove the draft, and he ripped up the IOU and gave the pieces to me."

Wiki said curiously, "How did he spell your name?"

"What?"

"It would've been written on the top of the chit. How did he spell it?"

"I didn't check."

"Then how do you know he ripped up the right one?"

"I trusted him—and he bloody well trusted me." Forsythe reached down to the floor, and came up with an unopened bottle of wine. Tucking it into the crook of his elbow, he said, "I reckon this will do me nicely on the cutter, when we're camping with those heathen Fuegians in some godforsaken cove on Wollaston."

On that note, Wiki expected him to get up and leave, but instead Forsythe stayed in his seat, apparently pinned by curiosity, because he said, "How did you know about the draft?"

"I found it when I searched Midshipman Dove's clothes. It was tucked into a little inside pocket of his jacket."

"So where is it now?"

"I gave it to the purser, who locked it in the strongbox of the *Peacock*. It'll be sent to Dove's family from Valparaiso, perhaps, or maybe Mr. Spieden will wait to hand it over when the expedition gets back to the States."

"If it ever gets there," Forsythe said sourly, and they both listened to the wind in the rigging. As usual in the late afternoon, the weather was deteriorating. Wiki thought that the quartet from the observatory had been wise to be expedient about getting back on shore.

He said, "There was a slip of paper attached to the draft, but it was so soaked in blood I couldn't read it. Any idea of what it might have been?"

"The fellow in the commercial agency wrote out a couple of names and addresses in Valparaiso, and stuck them to the bill, sayin' they'd be of use to Dove when he got there."

So it was an open secret that the expedition would drop anchor at Valparaiso, Wiki mused, despite Captain Wilkes's obsessive secrecy. It was also interesting that Dove's contact in Rio de Janeiro didn't know that the young man couldn't read. Then his meditations were interrupted, as Forsythe said, "You asked me how I knew Dove ripped up the right chit—so what other chits were there?"

"I found fourteen, hidden away in his chest."

Forsythe's brows shot up. "Just fourteen?"

"You're surprised?"

"Wa'al, I thought a lot more folks availed theirselves of his services."

"I'm sure you're right." Then Wiki changed the subject, not wishing to risk insulting Forsythe by telling him that only officers were made to sign. "Have you heard of a man named Sweetman?"

Forsythe thought, then shook his head. "Was one of the chits his?"

"Four of them. He owes a total of one thousand, three hundred dollars."

Forsythe's lips pursed in a whistle. "And you've no idea who he is?"

"Not a notion."

Silence, as the southerner stared at him.

Then Forsythe said flatly, "You don't think Dove killed himself, and knowin' all this, I don't think so, neither. He was too rich and had too many plans to want to put himself away."

"You're right," said Wiki. "Someone gripped his hand around the razor, and forced him to drag it across his own throat."

Forsythe grimaced. "How d'you know that?"

"There were no hesitation cuts, which are usual when men are steeling themselves to cut their own throats—or so Dr. Holmes told me. And there were bruises on his hand where someone had gripped it hard. I can't prove it was murder, but I'm certain he didn't take his own life."

"And you reckon that cove Sweetman did it? To save paying back all that cash?"

Instead of answering, Wiki slumped forward in his chair again. His forearms rested on his thighs, and his hands were lightly clasped between his knees as he contemplated the floor, deep in thought. He could hear Forsythe's heavy breathing, but the southerner was otherwise quiet as he waited for an answer.

To save paying back all that cash? Was that really the motive for the murder? Wiki remembered what Midshipman Dove had said — *But I hear you never fail to identify the killer, sir — that you have a kind of sixth sense about men's motives for committing crimes, which successfully leads you to the identity of the murderer.* He remembered finding Dove's body, hunched on its side, curved around itself in a pathetically helpless posture; he remembered the deep, decisive gash in the throat. And he remembered the traces of blood on the inside of the sleeve of the wet oilskin coat he had plucked off the rack at the entrance of the officers' wardroom on the *Peacock*.

Finally he straightened, and looked at Forsythe.

"All I can tell you," he said, "is that the murderer was definitely one of the *Peacock*'s lieutenants. And that I am not at all sure of the motive."

Seventeen

$\mathscr{S}$unday dawned as serenely as on the day Wiki had arrived in Orange Harbor, and continued calm past dinnertime, so it was no surprise to see Forsythe and his men busy in the cutter, to all appearances getting set for a departure.

Wiki jumped down to join them in the boat where it floated in the lee of the *Vincennes*, and said, "Tomorrow?"

"Perhaps," said Forsythe, who was stowing charts. He was frowning, though, and kept on straightening to eye the oyster-colored clouds that scudded across the sky.

Wiki hesitated, and then said, "Te Aute wants to come with us."

"*What!*"

"Jack Sac." Wiki had seen Te Aute several times since coming on board the *Vincennes*, the Maori materializing every now and then in his unusual unsettling fashion. He had made his request several days before. At first Wiki had tried to laugh it off, and then he had argued, but finally he had agreed to pass it on to Forsythe.

"You're joking."

"I'm afraid I'm not. He's adamant."

"But why the hell would you want a sworn enemy in the same cutter?"

"He's not a sworn enemy."

190

"You wait until he's cold and surly, and remembers old grievances. He'll drop you like an unwanted pup."

"I'll take that risk."

"But why, for God's sake, does he want to come?"

Wiki shrugged. Te Aute hadn't told him. He had wondered if the Maori felt a sneaking admiration for the big, rough, competent southerner, but it was just as likely that Te Aute was exercising the Polynesian love of charging out into uncharted seas, just for the hell of the adventure.

"And you expect me and my men to tolerate a cannibal savage as well as a half-breed on board our cramped little craft?"

Wiki smiled, knowing that he was being tested, rather than insulted.

Silence, as the southerner stared at him. Then, with total unexpectedness, Forsythe let out one of his dour grunts of laughter. "Fine," he said. "Tell him to come—and not to bloody complain when he finds out how nasty it's goin' to be."

"I will," said Wiki.

Doing his best to hide his amazement, he set off to find Te Aute.

Late in the afternoon the breeze strengthened, blowing onshore with occasional drifts of snow. When dark fell, Wiki passed Forsythe in the corridor of the afterhouse. The southerner was heading for the outside door from the direction of the chartroom, evidently to check the weather. "The barometer's dropping," he said, but didn't look happy. "Your tattooed friend is a complete blind idiot, wishing to come with us, but it looks as if we're off at dawn." Then he was gone.

Wiki joined Captain Couthouy at the table. Eating supper and only half-listening to the conchologist's monotonous conversation, he didn't feel happy, either. So they were off in the morning, he thought, and wondered greatly about their chances of returning. Then all at once the outer door slammed open, and Forsythe beckoned from the other side of the credenza.

Puzzled, thinking that surely they were not taking their departure now, Wiki followed him to the open deck, and over to the rail. The wind had dropped completely away, and it was uncannily calm. Then he heard the massed sighs floating in from the sea, followed by the hiss of fountains of fine spray. The sounds were so loud, rhythmic, and constant that it was like listening to the surf on a beach.

Wiki whispered reverently. "Dear lord, I can *smell* them." He couldn't believe it—the moored *Vincennes* was completely surrounded by whales. In the light of the moon he could see the double dandelion puffs, backs like half-sunk logs in the troughs of the swells, the occasional upward flick of short flukes, and the pale roll of a pleated under jaw as a whale sounded. There were many hundreds of the great fish—*hundreds*. Perhaps thousands.

He could also see Forsythe's evil grin in the light of the nearest cresset. "Ain't it a sight to break your spouterman's heart?"

"It would certainly break a whaling skipper's heart," Wiki agreed. "They're finbacks, mostly too big a proposition for our lances and harpoons. And they would sink like stones if we did manage to kill them. But if your barrels were very low and the voyage had been very long, it would certainly be heartbreaking to see so many whales, and yet know that it was useless to haul aback and lower boats."

"Someone will invent a whale-killing gun one day."

"But still they would sink," said Wiki. He'd heard of attempts to invent guns that fired explosive lances, but didn't like the thought. Whaling was bloody and brutal, but the fight between a great whale and six men with wooden-handled harpoons in a twenty-foot cedar boat was an honest one. It just didn't seem sporting to venture into the whale's realm with a bomb-firing gun.

But of course he didn't share that opinion with Forsythe. As a mercenary in the employ of a New Zealand chief, the southerner had sniped with a rifle at Maori warriors armed with just traditional wood and stone weapons, and he would have laughed with derision at such a fanciful thought.

Then all at once the whales vanished. As one animal, they arched, lifted flukes, and sounded.

A primeval sense had warned them, it seemed, because the wind abruptly squalled up. The fringes of Wiki's poncho flew out on the gust. Forsythe said, "Those bloody stupid young fools are out in this."

Oh God, no, thought Wiki. "Dicken and Keith?"

"Aye. Went out this morning, and haven't come back."

Wiki had forgotten the boys' boast about climbing the hill, but now he remembered it with a clutch of foreboding. When Captain Cook's *Endeavour* was moored in a bay that was not too far from here, Joseph Banks had taken a party ashore on exactly the same mission as the boys, and come back with the bodies of two of his servants, both frozen to death.

He said, "Search party in the morning?"

"That's what Craven has ordered—as soon the weather allows. So, while we'll take the cutter to the beach, we won't leave until the stupid young sods are found."

Eighteen

*B*y dawn, as usual, the gale had abated.

Wiki was in the maintop, scanning the coastal forest and the stony slopes that lifted against the sky beyond, when Forsythe's infuriated yell warned him that the cutter was about to get underway. In the distance, he could see thin lines of men straggling into the trees, but no hint of the signal that the two junior midshipmen should have had the sense to raise. Before Forsythe could let out another bellow, he moved fast, sliding down a backstay to deck, and jumping down the side into the launch. Te Aute was there, his tattooed face stretched in a grin of delight. No one else, Wiki noticed, looked nearly as happy.

The moderate breeze was blowing onshore, so it was an easy matter to sail northeast along the coast. Forsythe was at the tiller. "Where d'you think they were headed?" he demanded.

Wiki pointed beyond the next deep inlet, to the hill that had looked the most mighty from the *Vincennes*. It was merely a fifteen hundred-foot mound when compared to Sugarloaf Peak in Rio de Janeiro, but was harder to reach, because of the blanket of thick forest that clothed its foot.

He said, "That one, there."

"You're sure?"

Wiki shook his head, and Forsythe cast him an impatient look before navigating the cutter across the

195

outward flow of the inlet, and then coasting her safely through the scatterings of rocks that were heavily bearded with kelp, and up to the shore. She hit bottom, but the bilge rails on either side of the hull kept her upright.

When Wiki stared up beyond the tops of the trees, the mountain looked a larger proposition to climb than it had seemed from the water, a great pyramid composed of a series of steep shingle slopes that were interrupted by gullies and ridges. Immediately beyond the beach a dense, tangled jungle of birch, willow, and winterbark sprouted, some of the beech trees being fifty feet high or more. All the trees were bent to the northeast, driven by the prevailing winds.

On the beach, he contemplated the challenge. Once that gnarled forest was negotiated, they would reach a level terrace, and after that they would have to climb steep inclines of slippery gravel screes, which were patched by parched looking grass and furrowed by ravines.

Despite the arid look of the hill, when Wiki entered the perimeter of the forest his boots sank into bog. What looked like grass proved to be scum-covered mud. A stench of rotting leaves and general decay wafted up with every step, along with a cloud of tiny insects, which he irritably waved away.

When he looked over his shoulder, Forsythe was wading through the undergrowth to join him, and brushing at insects too. So Wiki waited in the dense shadow of an immense tree.

"Wa-al, then, this ain't going to be bloody fun," Forsythe said, catching up. "But my plan is that you and I tackle this side of the hill. I've told the boys to take the cutter back to the inlet, and get up far enough for two of them to climb the western side. The other four will sail the cutter further still, to where there is a eastward curve. Once they're there, two more of them can search the northern slope, leaving the two others to look after the launch, along with Maori Jack. If they find those silly young bastards, they'll bring the cutter back after collecting up all the men, and fire a signal."

"Sounds good," said Wiki. He headed for where the trees seemed to be thinnest and the misty light slanted down, and almost immediately got bogged down in marsh that was studded with great clumps of rank grasses. Trying to skirt around these meant stumbling into hidden mud wallows, so he was forced to jump from one clump to another. He could hear Forsythe swearing as he followed. Then he found a trail cut through the tangled undergrowth, and the going was easier, though uphill.

Then suddenly a thicket of bushes barred his way. When he pushed through these, he blundered onto a Fuegian camp that was set into the sheltered end of a terrace, where it was guarded by bushes on three sides and a steep gravel slope on the other.

Short, squat, spindly-legged men stood in a bunch in front of this encampment, and stared at him from under their matted hair. Some were holding fish spears, but as usual the reception wasn't at all hostile. They were an unhealthy looking set, Wiki meditated, covered with grease and grime, and so thin that their skin hung in folds. In fact, he thought, the wonder was that they were alive at all. The air smelled of snow as well as of smoke and decay, but their nakedness was merely emphasized by a small, ragged hide of some animal that was thrown over one shoulder.

Wiki heard a crashing in the shrubbery. Forsythe arrived, and stopped short at the sight of the Fuegians.

"Wa-al, Mister Linguister," he said. "This is your chance to show off your talents."

Wiki grimaced. How could he possibly ask if two midshipmen had passed by here the day before, and expect to get an intelligible answer? Sign language was his only hope. He pointed at Forsythe and then himself, then pointed at the sun, waved his hand in a circle to indicate the passage of time, and pointed up the mountain. The Fuegian men stared at him stolidly, and then one who had a strip of red cloth bound about his head said, "*Yamask-una.*"

"What the hell does that mean?" said Forsythe.

"He wants us to give him a present."

"You're bloody jesting."

"I'm afraid I am not."

Wiki went through the same signing again, but this time all the men put out their hands, wiggled their fingers, and then chorused, "*Yamask-una.*"

"Get away from me, you avaricious little buggers," snarled Forsythe, and headed across the terrace and then up the scree slope beyond, shingle spraying back from his boots.

Wiki looked at the Fuegians. When he spread his hands apologetically, he saw them spread their hands in exactly the same gesture, before he started climbing, too. He looked back after a while, but none of the natives had attempted to follow.

Twenty hard, arduous minutes later, he and Forsythe had mounted the first ridge. When Wiki looked back again, there was not a sign of the Fuegian camp. "Someone gave that fellow the red material he had round his head," he said.

"You reckon it was Keith and Dicken?"

Wiki shrugged, but it was a possibility. From the corner of his eye, he glimpsed movement, and when he turned to stare, he saw a single figure climbing the ridge to the east of them. It couldn't be one of the cutter's men, because they were searching the slopes to the north and west, he thought, and felt reassured that someone else from the *Vincennes* had chosen this hill as the most likely one.

He pressed on, descending into a small, bare gully, and then climbing again through sliding gravel, his arms spread for balance, listening to the racket that Forsythe made as he followed. The southerner was nimble enough, considering his bulk, but he had given up cursing in favor of catching his breath.

The top of the next ridge dropped abruptly into a gully that held a small thicket far down at the bottom, bushes clustered about the thin glimmer of a stream. There was an equally precipitous slope on the other side. Wiki stopped to contemplate this new hurdle, glumly thinking that it was going to be a frustratingly up and down effort to get to the top of this damnable mountain. When he looked up to estimate how far they still had to go, he saw the figure again. Whoever it was, he had found an easier route, because he was a lot higher than they were.

As Wiki watched, the man was joined by two others, who appeared from the other side of a ridge. Then they were standing in a row on the crest. One of them moved, slinging something forward from over his shoulder. Wiki glimpsed the glint of a rifle barrel as it was raised and aimed.

At him. Diving headlong, he grabbed Forsythe around the legs, and rolled with him down the slope.

They both knocked bruisingly on rock and gravel, and Forsythe struggled and swore. When they arrived at the bottom, Wiki had to thump him once, to keep him down.

Then Forsythe stilled abruptly, as a second shot passed narrowly over their heads.

"What the hell?" he said, and started to stand up.

"*Get down!* They're shooting at us," said Wiki. His voice was shaking.

Another shot. This time the bullet whacked against a nearby rock. Obviously, they were still a clear target.

"Jesus," said Forsythe, and flung himself at the bushes, rolling to a stop against a spindly trunk with his nose practically in the trickling water.

A fourth shot whined by as Wiki landed on his belly alongside the southerner. His face was buried in rough grass, and he could smell dirt as well as dust. He was trembling with fright—and anger, too.

"Why didn't you bring your rifle?" he demanded. "I've never seen you ashore without your bloody rifle before."

Forsythe glared at him. "Left it at the cutter so they could make a signal, didn't I—and you never bloody warned me, did you, that something like this could happen."

"But how could I possibly guess it would happen now?" said Wiki. He still couldn't stop his voice from shaking.

"What the hell do you mean, *now?*"

"Well, it isn't first attempt to kill me—or even the second. But it can't be the bloody sealers, this time—they're with *Sea Gull* and *Porpoise*."

"How the hell do you know that?"

"Because I was the one who wrote down Captain Wilkes's orders to the fleet."

Forsythe's hard eyes went narrow. "You have some explaining to do, my boy," he snapped. Another shot pinged into the bushes. They both flinched, but it was three yards to one side.

"Shockin' poor shooting," muttered Forsythe. "Which at least is somethin' in our favor—but how the hell we get out of here…"

Wiki shook his head as a horrid presentiment stirred inside him. "They're not shooting to kill," he said.

"What?"

"They would've got us by now, if they were. Think about it—they've had at least two chances. They're shooting to pin us down—keep us trapped in this gully."

"Who, for God's sake?"

Wiki shook his head again, though he was certain now that he and Forsythe had been overheard as they talked in the charthouse. "They don't want our bodies to be found with bullet holes in them. One will keep sniping to trap us here, and the others will come and club us down."

Silence. Then Forsythe said, "You're certain?"

Wiki said more calmly, "I think so. If we're battered to death it would look as if we fell by accident."

"You'd better bloody well be sure, because I'm making a break for it. If it comes to a fight, I'd rather be in the open. There's two of us, and only two of them."

"And the one with the rifle," muttered Wiki, but followed when Forsythe jumped to his feet and plunged through the bushes.

They zigzagged up the next slope at a headlong pace, and flinched as another shot droned past, though it was a yard to one side. As they reached the crest, and leaped the narrow ravine on the other side, Wiki could see another steep slope ahead. This time the stony ground was bare, except for stunted grass sprouting between flat, primeval rocks.

Above, and to their right, the two figures were running diagonally down the slope to confront them, followed more slowly by the third. All three had guns, but the leading two had theirs slung on their shoulders. Except for the intent, fast way they moved, they could have been any party from the ship hunting for game or specimens.

"They mean business," said Forsythe grimly. He stood with his legs braced and his fists clenched, while Wiki wavered, keen to keep moving, but reluctant to leave Forsythe behind. Then the distant rifle fired. The bullet hit a stone and ricocheted so close to Forsythe's head that it clipped his ear. He cursed, flicked away blood, and moved fast up the next slope, dodging every now and then to avoid projecting rocks, with Wiki close behind.

Another shot, nearer, close to Wiki's heels. He ran faster, his chest laboring, feeling like a hunted rabbit. He could hear Forsythe panting, again too short of breath to swear. The two men running to intercept were now gripping their guns by the barrels, as if ready to use them as clubs. Wiki recognized Blackmer and Russell. The man in the distance, the one with the rifle, had to be Pilson.

Forsythe lurched to a halt, again on the crest of a little ridge. "Come on, you foul bastards," he said, though not loud enough for them to hear. He stooped, and came up with a fist-sized rock in his hand.

Then, with complete unexpectedness, two more figures abruptly materialized at the top of the next shingle scree. Incredulously, Wiki recognized Keith and Dicken. So they really had climbed the mountain, he thought. The boys jumped up and down and yelled, and waved the white flag they had on a stick, and then started sliding pell-mell towards them.

All other movement stopped short. Russell and Blackmer were just twenty feet away. For another moment they stood frozen, and then, slowly, they swung their guns round, and slung them over their shoulders again. They came forward, still moving slowly, watching Forsythe all the time. Pilson, his rifle slung likewise, was coming down the hill at an angle to the two midshipmen, who were still fifty yards away.

When the three lieutenants arrived their faces were expressionless. "What the devil were you bastards thinking?" Forsythe growled.

"Us?" said Pilson. His eyes flickered to Wiki and then back again. "We were firing signals to let you know we'd raised the two lost men."

"Like bloody hell you were. You were shooting at us."

"If we were shooting at you, you'd be dead," said Blackmer, and spat to one side.

"We heard the shots," Dicken panted, arriving in a crash of scattered pebbles.

"Thank God you came," Keith said, his chest heaving as he lurched to his own halt. "I swear it was the only thing that kept us going when the snow came down, knowing that we'd told you where we were headed, Mr. Coffin."

The two boys had endured an appalling night. Dicken's cheeks were brightred, as usual, but otherwise both boys were white-faced, their lips chapped, and their eyes surrounded by dark circles, and they shivered convulsively. The words tumbling out of them, they described making a cairn of rocks, and covering the leeward side of it with twigs and reeds, then lighting a little fire, which was all that had kept them alive. By the time morning came they were so cold, exhausted, and confused that they had lost all sense of direction. And then, they had heard the rifle shots.

Turning to Pilson, they thanked him profusely. He smirked, and told them they were welcome.

"You will notice," said Wiki to Keith, "that Lieutenant Forsythe didn't have his."

Midshipman Keith blinked, then frowned. "His?" he echoed.

"Rifle," said Wiki. He smiled grimly. "It can make matters quite complicated when you're not armed, and the other men are."

Keith shook his head, still very puzzled.

"When you see Captain Rochester, and relate the story of your misadventure, be sure to tell him that you arrived in the nick of time to save us."

Keith said nothing, but his frown had become thoughtful.

Forsythe, who had ignored all this, was staring at Pilson with eyes that were as hard as stone. "How did you get here?" he said curtly, and Pilson gestured down the mountain to the inlet. Their boat was moored just downstream of the cutter, which was how they had known that Wiki and Forsythe were climbing the southern side of the hill.

"Wa'al," Forsythe said after digesting this, "we can leave these lads in your tender care, and get on with our proper business. And when we get back, I'll be tackling you about this little matter of pinning us down for the slaughter. Nice trick, I suppose, but I didn't enjoy the experience."

The pockmarked Blackmer merely twitched his lips in a thin smile. "*If* you get back," he said. "We're laying bets on the outcome, and the odds surely don't look good for you and your uppity half-breed friend. We don't think you're going to make it back at all."

Silence, as they grimly contemplated each other.

Then Forsythe said, "I wouldn't mind making a bet, myself. A hundred says we'll see you back at Orange Harbor."

"You're on," said Blackmer. "Not that I expect to be paid," he added, and laughed.

"Bastard," said Forsythe, and turned and led the way down the mountain.

Gravel spurted from his heels while Wiki followed. Both of them had their arms spread wide to keep their balance, and neither of them looked back.

There were dark clouds scudding across the sky, and below them the sea was broken. Wiki fervently hoped that the barometer was falling, because they had a nail-biting voyage ahead — with a long passage across open sea, before they could find refuge at an island.

Nineteen

Thirteen hours later, just as the cutter had almost reached Wollaston Island, the wind abruptly squalled up.

That was bad enough, but then it veered around the compass. Within just a horrifying handful of minutes the gale was blowing due west, coming from behind and driving them directly onto the rocks. They were within a half-mile of potential disaster—Wollaston Island, their target, was now a dangerous lee shore.

When Wiki looked at Forsythe, his face was drawn and grim. The southerner had no choice but to drive southeast, stretching for the Hermit Islands, which were now invisible. The long string of rocky islets should have been silhouetted in the long southern twilight, but were unseen in the gathering murk. All that the cutter's men could hope for was that Lieutenant Forsythe's reckoning was right, and they lay somewhere ahead.

No sooner was the launch settled to their new course than the wind grew to hurricane force, accompanied first by rain, and then with sleet. Even though the canvas was hurriedly reduced, the cutter was bounding from wave to wave, the masts whipping with the terrific strain. It was bitterly cold, the lines encased in ice, and the decking forward swathed in frozen snow. Yet every man kept staunchly at his station, hanging on while the cutter leaned far, far over, slicing through the white-capped sea. Wiki could see Te Aute by the foremast, clinging desperately to the gunwale as the launch shipped one green wave after another.

It was impossible to see where they were going, as the snow was flying in huge, wet, blinding curtains of flakes. When something bumped hard against the bow several men cursed with fright, and everyone flinched as the bumping progressed aft. It was only a harmless lump of ice, sweeping past them, but that there might be larger pieces — or even a sheet of ice — was a new terror. Every minute, Wiki expected the fatal crash.

Then the sky cleared a fraction, exposing the moon just enough to see the outline of a nearby island. It was veiled in mist, its shape blurred by wind and water, but Forsythe let out an exultant yell. Orders were bawled, and the cutter settled on a new heading, steering for a rocky headland.

Then they were almost there. With Forsythe's usual nervewracking audacity they came within two boat-lengths of the rocky point before they tacked, but then they were safely about it. The noise and tumult of wind and surf faded into almost total silence. For a dazed moment, Wiki thought he'd gone deaf. Then sense prevailed, and he realized they were safe from the storm. They had left the mist and murk out at sea, beyond the tall headland, and ahead was a sheltered cove.

Forsythe let out a gusty breath as the cutter coasted into shallows and settled, and said in a voice that sounded far too loud, "I name this bay Bloody Well-Timed Reprieve."

Everyone laughed. The sound was shaky, but the sense of relief was palpable.

Quickly, the cutter was secured to a mooring line, and provisions were passed on shore, along with a tarpaulin. Within ten minutes the cutter's crew and Te Aute were busy making a camp on the beach. But, when Wiki moved to follow them, Forsythe jerked his head in the direction of the little cuddy.

"Leave 'em to it," he said. "I want to have a word."

Wiki complied very reluctantly indeed. It was almost midnight, after a real hell of a day. All he wanted was to help the others collect wood and start a fire, then dry out in front of the flames while a pot of coffee boiled. And then, after eating a cracker with a slice of cold salt beef, find a bed.

Instead, he was forced to follow the Virginian into the cramped, dank space, where they both sat cross-legged on the deck between the two narrow berths, facing each other with their elbows on their knees and their heads between their shoulders because of the low deckhead.

Forsythe reached up and lit a lantern, and then rummaged around in the starboard berth, coming up with one of the bottles of wine he had purloined from the *Vincennes*.

Eyeing Wiki as he did it, he pulled the stopper with his teeth. Then, after taking a long swig, he said, "Wa'al, that's the first time my fellow officers have done their damnedest to murder me, not without it was a shoreside brawl. Any idea of the reason?"

Wiki paused to get his tired mind in order. He could smell the wet wool of his poncho, and Forsythe's sour sweat. "My best guess is that sound travels from the chartroom of the *Vin* to the wardroom of the *Vin*, the one being right above the other."

"What sound?"

"Us, in the chartroom, talking about Midshipman Dove's murder."

Forsythe's lips pursed as he worked this out. "The time you told me you reckoned it was one of the *Peacock* lieutenants what dragged that razor across Dove's throat?"

"Aye."

"And those who were stalking us were all officers from the *Peacock*."

"Aye."

"So the man that put Dove away must've been one of them."

Blackmer, Russell, Pilson. Wiki nodded, though the man Dove had called *Sweetman* hadn't been one of the stalking party — whoever he was.

"Which means it can't have been Sam Lee what did the murder," said Forsythe, and drank more wine. His tone held a certain satisfaction, and Wiki remembered that Forsythe and Lieutenant Samuel Lee were neighbors back in Virginia, undoubtedly with a lot of shared history.

Then, still with that shrewd glint in his eye, Forsythe observed, "But it wasn't them that planned to kill you the other two times, because you acted so surprised."

"That's true," Wiki admitted. He could hear the cutter's crew moving about on the beach, and rattles and scrapes as a fire was lit.

"The first time, it was the sealers," Forsythe said.

"Aye," said Wiki. Forsythe was thinking of the nighttime attack on the deck of the *Peacock,* obviously, so he added diplomatically, "And I thank you for the rescue."

"If Pilson had clapped you and Te Aute in the brig with the sealers, you would've come out of it as dead as last week's mutton," Forsythe said with a complacent grin. Then he frowned, and said, "You reckon that was the plan?"

Wiki hesitated, thinking that if he was right, it implicated Lieutenant Lee, but then said, "Yes."

Forsythe tilted the bottle and swallowed. When he lowered it Wiki saw that he was studying him quizzically again, one hard little eye half-shut. Then he said, "Tell me about the second try to kill you."

Wiki bit back a sigh, listening to the distant chat on the beach and wishing that Forsythe had not chosen this moment to play the sleuth. It had been a very taxing day, and yet his cross-examiner seemed as fresh as when they had started.

"One of the sealers did his damnedest to drown me while I was trying to save Lawrence J. Smith," he admitted. "He shoved me under the water so hard it felt like he was standing on my head."

"You're sure it was one of the sealers?"

"When I ducked down and away, I felt his beard brush across my face." Wiki paused, remembering the flash of sharp pain across his open eyes, and then said, "I somehow made it to the surface, but managed just one gasp of air once before he shoved me down again. So I grabbed his legs and took him down with me — and held him down until he stopped struggling."

"That was how the bastard got drowned?"

"It was a case of which man could hold his breath the longer."

Forsythe's evil grin became a snigger. "You were bloody lucky no one noticed, or you could've been up for courtmartial—with Wilkes in charge of the court."

"There was such chaos—there were too many men threshing about in too small a space, getting in each others' way. It was impossible for anyone to tell what was happening."

Then Wiki was struck by a thought that was so startling that for the moment he forgot his impatience at being closeted with Forsythe in this cramped, cold space.

He said slowly, "Do you think that the water being so crowded could have been deliberate?"

"It do seem strange that so many were so keen to save the pompous little bugger."

"It does indeed," said Wiki. They stared at each other in speculation for a second, and then were interrupted by a holler from the beach. The tin of tea had boiled, and grub was being shared out.

But still Forsythe didn't move.

Wiki said promptingly, "What?"

"It seems odd to me that the silly little bastard was in the water at all."

"He'd made a habit of falling in," Wiki said.

"You're bloody joking!"

"No, I'm not," Wiki assured him. "The same thing happened after poor Dove's funeral—in fact, it almost happened twice. The officers and Captain Hudson were all lined up at the gangway, when Smith stumbled and grabbed Captain Hudson's arm. He stumbled next, and hit an officer, and they all hung onto each other and the whole lot nearly went over. Everyone considered it a joke, but then when Smith had another go at climbing down the side he stumbled again, and into the water he went. Lieutenant Matthews jumped in and saved him, so everything ended happily—but then Smith pointed the finger at me and reckoned I should start an investigation to find out who had pushed him."

"*Pushed* him?"

"That's exactly what he reckoned—and hotly, too. But then Lieutenant Matthews spoke up. He insisted that Smith had stumbled."

"The same man who jumped in and saved him?

"Aye." Wiki paused, then added, "But I don't think Smith believed him, despite the act of bravery."

Forsythe snorted with laughter. "The mistrustful little bugger. So who did push him in? You?"

"Now you're being ridiculous. In fact," Wiki said slowly, "there's a lot about the business that is odd."

"Why? Does it bother you that Smith was so clumsy?"

"Yes, it does. But there's something that bothers me even more than that."

"What?"

"Lieutenant Lee."

Forsythe's tone took on a note of aggression. "What about Sam Lee?"

"Captain Wilkes said that Lieutenant Lee made a fuss—because he hadn't been promoted to flag lieutenant after Lieutenant Smith was drowned."

Forsythe's tone became impatient. "And you reckon that's important?"

"I don't know. It seems strange that he expected to get the job, when there were so many well-qualified men, but apparently he wrote Captain Wilkes a very insulting letter."

"A lot of officers made a fuss about a lot of things, particularly when the commands for the southern expedition were handed out. And Sam was a lot better qualified than you appear to think," said Forsythe dismissively, and to Wiki's relief he moved at last.

One at a time, they backed out, and straightened with a creaking of stiff sinews. Then Wiki stood and looked around.

The cuddy had felt chilly and dank, but outside it was bitingly cold. The cove was now shrouded in gloom, the fire leaping brilliantly against the black backdrop of trees. The air here was as calm as before, but Wiki could hear the thunder of the surf on the other side of the little headland, and glimpse the stirring of the highest leaves against the gray sky.

He started to move with alacrity towards the camp, looking forward to toasting himself in front of the flames. But Forsythe held him still.

He was looking about, his head cocked to one side as he listened. "Let's hope the bloody wind backs," he said, his voice troubled. "For if it holds a steady northwest gale and no one bothers to come to the rescue, we could be windbound here all winter."

"Surely not," said Wiki with a wince.

Three weeks later, everyone had glumly decided that Forsythe's dire prediction was nothing less than the nasty truth. Sometimes hope had flickered, for it had looked as if they might manage to escape from the dubious refuge of Bloody Well-timed Reprieve, but whenever they managed to sail out and get a good offing, it was to be beset by yet another onshore gale, which forced them to flee for the nearest haven. Once, it had been a rock-strewn bay on one of the other islands, but every other time it had been their old camp. As a refuge, it had become too damn familiar.

After three weeks of this, they looked like rogues, their clothes stained and frayed from living in so much weather. Even Wiki, who normally had trouble growing much facial hair, had a lot of stubble, while Te Aute's ferocious *moko* was heavily blurred by black whiskers. Not only did it alter his appearance drastically, but it had helped Wiki make up his mind about something that he had been cogitating for years — which was whether or not to get a facial tattoo. Now, he had definitely decided against it, because he thought Te Aute looked rather comical — like his grandfather, Koro, when Koro had forgotten to shave, but without the venerable dignity.

The cutter's crew, with their tough weathered faces, their thick beards and their hair straggling over their collars, simply looked piratical. As resourceful as buccaneers, too, they had made themselves remarkably comfortable, considering the sleet and snow and the hostile terrain.

There was the decked launch for a base, and a tarpaulin with thatched branch walls for shelter, and always a roaring fire. Even more importantly, there was plenty of fresh water, and an abundance of fine fresh fish to go with their hard bread and salt beef. They had even managed to enjoy themselves, when it wasn't hailing or snowing hard. Part of the time had been used up in snowball fights, part in teasing the Fuegians who came to visit — which always ended up in giving them any bits of clothing that someone could spare—and the rest in yarning about the fire, occasionally interrupted by a song.

But all the time there was the nagging worry about being trapped here for months.

Wiki, like everyone else, had watched Lieutenant Forsythe brooding darkly over the one little chart he'd been given, along with Captain King's sketchy sailing directions. It was little wonder that his temper was even fouler than usual, or that he went off on increasingly longer excursions.

The solitary expeditions were triggered by his determination to shoot something edible. Forsythe prided himself on his marksmanship and his record of providing his men with tasty fresh game, and he refused to believe that it wasn't possible here. And so, every day that they were trapped in this place, he set off into the convoluted coastal forest, slogging through the marshes and wallows with his gun. Once, he had shot at an otter—which with unbelievable agility had slid into the water apparently unscathed—and another time he had come back with a large, stringy bird, which had been dutifully stewed up, but had proved inedible.

As far as the men were concerned, the only benefit of Forsythe's dogged determination was that they were spared his bad moods while he was away, and that it left them free to grumble about the impossible mission and their probable fate. Their usual target was Dick Gates, Forsythe's coxswain, who was forced to withstand questions like, "I mean, Dick, I ask you, are we goin' to die for *nothing*?" and, "What the hell is the *point* of charting these godforsaken islands?" As there was nothing he could do about it, he usually didn't bother to answer, but that didn't stop the griping.

"It ain't just the charting of the different islands that the expedition is all about, you know," said one by the name of Jake. "That scientific, Mr. Dana, he reckons that he's a-goin' to make hisself uncommon famous by distinguishing how they were formed. He give us a talk on it, one day on the foredeck, all to do with volcanoes and coral reefs and somesuch. Quite interestin' really, not that us understood it."

"But Mr. Coffin here already knows how the islands were made," said a New Bedforder by the name of Michael, and winked.

Wiki grinned, and said, "You're thinking of Maui."

"Aye, that was the name."

"It was Maui who made the islands of the Pacific—Maui the demigod. He picked up South America by its skirts, and shook it until pieces flew all over the ocean. And wherever they landed, isles and atolls grew."

"You should tell that to Mr. Dana," said Jake.

A crashing in the undergrowth signaled the lieutenant's return. Judging by the smell that preceded him, Forsythe had trekked about the coast, forcing a way through mud that was thick with seal dung. As usual, his game bag was empty, and his expression was grim. Forsythe, Wiki deduced, was badly in need of a drink, but was going to be frustrated in that as well, as the bottles he had brought along had been emptied days ago.

The men hurriedly made a place for him by the fire, and after planting his seat on the ground with a grunt, he reached out for the tin plate that had been kept warm by the coals. They watched as he picked up a fish in his grimy fingers and ate it ravenously, spitting out bones with every mouthful. Another fish disappeared the same way, and then he poked a fork at the mound of boiled greens that remained on his plate, observing, "I s'pose our two brown bastards are responsible for this."

Everyone looked at Wiki and Te Aute. As usual the Ngati Porou man had been keeping a low profile, crouched quietly at the edge of the group, listening to the conversation but without contributing to it. The boat's crew had accepted Wiki long ago, respecting him as a thoroughgoing seaman who had been trained in a hard and efficient school. His compatriot, however, was still an unknown quantity, so while the Fuegians were endlessly fascinated with Te Aute, gathering about him in crowds, the cutter's men kept their distance.

Te Aute, however, gave no hint of being offended by this. Now, he smiled amiably at Forsythe, and said, "Just me, boss."

The first time they had been stranded here, he and Wiki had fossicked for cresses together, conferring in *te reo Maori* as they groped through childhood memories to a time when they had been taught what was edible and what was not. They had both tried the herbs out, too, when Forsythe and the cutter's men had flatly refused to eat them until the harvesters had proved they weren't poisonous. Both had survived the trial, and so the cutter's crew had consented to try the dish, which they had pronounced both tasty and healthful. Since then, herbs had been part of the daily menu, the plants being so abundant that a half-hour of foraging by just one man got enough to feed them all.

"It's good for you, boss," Te Aute said.

As everyone had noticed long before, he was not afraid of Lieutenant Forsythe. Indeed, Wiki had definitely come to the conclusion that he admired him. "Stops the scurvy, eh," he went on. "I ate lots, back home. Makes you grow, boss."

"So why is Wiki a lot bigger than you, huh?"

"Born a big bastard, boss."

Wiki grinned, because that wasn't true at all. The credit for his impressive physique was owed to his stepmother's household management. Mrs. Coffin might have been humiliated by the sudden appearance of her husband's illegitimate son, but once she had rallied she had set out to make something of the skinny little Maori boy who had arrived at her kitchen door. Accordingly, he had been fed very well indeed—even in the middle of winter, which had certainly not been the case back in the Bay of Islands.

Forsythe ate one forkful of the boiled greens, threw the rest into the fire, and announced, "The barometer's falling."

And everyone looked at the sky. It was gray and blotched with dark clouds, as usual. They all believed him, though—and knew what it augured, too.

"Aye," said Forsythe with sour satisfaction. "We'll have a gale tonight, and an offshore breeze at dawn. It'll be our chance to get away for once and for bloody all from this godforsaken spot. And we're goin' to forget Cap'n Wilkes and his *hazardous* mission. We're headin' back to Orange Harbor."

219

Twenty

Forsythe, as usual, was right.

The next day dawned with a fine offshore breeze and the mildest weather they had experienced since leaving the *Vin*. Yet, despite the favorable conditions, he was as obstinate as ever, too. Still determined to ignore instructions, he set a brisk course for Orange Harbor.

Within an hour the tall headland that sheltered Bloody Well-Timed Reprieve was lost in the mists astern, and the launch was dashing smartly from wave to wave, kicking up foam as she headed northwest. Then Wollaston Island — the focus of the suicidally impossible charting mission — was a mere smudge on the sternward horizon.

Two hours later, they were sailing across the Mantello Pass, the launch a mere speck in a vast immensity of open water. An increasingly choppy expanse of sea surrounded them on all sides, the distant silhouette of the southeastern coast of Tierra del Fuego the only sign of land. Though very few words were said, Wiki could feel the mounting tension. This was the precarious part of the passage. Black clouds were piling up to the west, and if the weather blew up...

The wind freshened with a rush, bringing a hard rain mixed with sleet. Within seconds Wiki's poncho was streaming, and like everyone else he was hunched against the nearly horizontal onslaught. The sea rose too, becoming lumpy and then breaking, and the rain on his face tasted of salt, because of the whipping spray. Their passage became a series of wild surges and sickening plunges, but Forsythe grimly hung on to his straining, sodden, rain-blackened canvas. Taking on water with every dive down the slope of a wave, leaning over precipitously as she surged to each crest, the cutter tore on through the murk. Her masts were lashing like coach whips, but Forsythe clung with nail-biting nerve to a course that would take them to Orange Harbor. If the storm didn't destroy them first.

Then, above the tall crest of an oncoming comber, Wiki glimpsed the white tips of two high topmasts. The great wave surged upon them, slid under the long bowsprit, the cutter rose and rose—and he saw the whole of the oncoming vessel.

He recognized her at once. "*Sea Gull!*" he cried.

For a moment he thought his words had been blown away by a gust, but then he saw Forsythe's exultant grin. "Luff," the lieutenant said, and brought the cutter up into the wind.

Moments later, they were lying under a deep-reefed mainsail, forestaysail and jib, as they waited for the schooner to run down. Ironically, the wind dropped, in one of the dramatic changes of weather so familiar in this region, turning into a fair breeze that would have carried them to Orange Harbor. Even the sea was abruptly less violent. Wiki looked at Forsythe inquiringly, but he made no move to get under sail again.

The *Sea Gull* was arriving fast. Then she was so close that Wiki could hear the shouted orders as sail was taken in. She seemed magnificent as she loomed over them, her two masts stretching into the sky—and yet she was the second-smallest vessel of the squadron, just 110 tons, and less than 75 feet long. Even the step up to the gangway seemed high.

Forsythe went first. Then, after taking one stride onto deck, he stopped so abruptly that Wiki bumped into him. Forsythe didn't seem to notice, because he was staring so intently at the officer who was waiting at the forward end of the deckhouse that bulked between the mainmast and the stern. Then Wiki, edging around the southerner to stand beside him, saw that it was Lieutenant Pilson.

Pilson. He was wearing the same smirk he had worn when Dicken and Keith had thanked him for saving them from their ordeal on the mountain. Forsythe's grip visibly tightened on his shouldered rifle, ready to swing it around.

He snapped, "Who's in command here?"

Pilson didn't answer. Instead, another officer arrived at his shoulder—Matthews. The clouds broke at that precise moment, and the light slanted on the waxlike texture of the long scar on his cheek.

"Passed Midshipman Reid," Matthews said, in reply to Forsythe's question. His tone held the disdain that the lieutenants always betrayed when reminded that the commands of the small vessels of the expedition had been handed on to more lowly officers.

"Reid? But I thought Lieutenant Johnson took the *Sea Gull* into the Antarctic?"

Wiki remembered that, too. Not only had he written the order, but a great fuss had followed. Lieutenant Walker, who had been given command of the slightly smaller *Flying Fish*, had complained to Wilkes that the difference in size made him feel slighted.

Matthews said, "You're right. Johnson did take her south. But when the schooner got back to Orange Harbor, Reid was returned to the command, and I was seconded as his first lieutenant. And given the job of finding you," he added.

"So we weren't all lost and forgotten," Forsythe remarked. His tone was ironic.

Wiki interrupted, saying quickly, "How did the *Swallow* fare?"

Matthews gave him one contemptuous glance, before turning back to Forsythe. Wiki tensely waited, but instead of repeating the question, Forsythe demanded, "So where the hell is Captain Reid?"

"Passed Midshipman Reid? Sick." Matthews jerked his head at the door to the deckhouse, where—as Wiki knew from his stint on the *Sea Gull* while on the Rio Negro—there were three small staterooms and a pantry surrounding a surprisingly spacious cuddy.

Forsythe's brows lowered. "So why was Jim sent out, if he wasn't fit enough?"

"Only just got sick. Started complaining a couple of hours ago. I'm in charge right now," Matthews went on smoothly, "being second in command."

So why was Pilson here? Two lieutenants were one more than necessary, especially when they technically outranked the captain, who was only a passed midshipman. Everything about the schooner felt wrong. Wiki turned to look at the foredeck, where the *Sea Gull*'s sailors were watching the cutter's crew mount the side of the brig and file forward after securing the launch to the stern.

Then his pulse jumped, as he recognized six heavily bearded faces. *The sealers.*

Forsythe had seen them too. He shifted his grip on his rifle again, and muttered in Wiki's ear, "I don't like the look of this."

Neither did Wiki. There was a cold knot in his stomach, and he very much wished that Forsythe had taken advantage of the improved weather to keep on to Orange Harbor. But it was too late for them to change their minds. Matthews had spoken to Pilson, and the junior lieutenant was headed to the foredeck, shouting orders. Men moved to halyards, some of them surprisingly half-heartedly, and slowly the sails were hoisted again.

That sense of wrongness returned. A few of the hands chanted as they hauled, but otherwise the work was silent and unnaturally awkward. It was the sealers who were holding up the process, Wiki realized. Not only were they clumsy, but they were lazy, too, leaving most of the work to the sweating seamen.

It seemed a long time before the great sails cracked full with wind, the spars were swung, and the schooner was underway again. Pilson's steps rang irritably on the planks as he returned to the amidships deck.

Forsythe growled, "Those sealers are about as much use as a bishop in a brothel."

"Tut, Kit," said Matthews. "Don't be so unkind. They weren't shipped as able seamen."

"That's exactly what I mean. Those men are seal-killers, not proper mariners. Everyone knows that they might be fine in small boats, but that they're bloody hopeless on board ship. To them, a schooner is just a conveyance that ferries them to the sealing beaches and then puts them on shore, and hopefully comes back for 'em when they've got their load of pelts. They don't steer the ship or work the sails, and they don't go aloft neither, because real seamen do all that work. But this ain't a sealing mission. So why the hell are they takin' up space on this schooner?"

"They were here already."

Wiki frowned, remembering the clerking session with Captain Wilkes. Surely the sealers had been divided between the *Porpoise* and the *Sea Gull*? It had been logical enough, because it meant that Captain Wilkes, in command of the gun brig, would have access to their expert knowledge of the Antarctic, as well as Lieutenant Johnson in the schooner.

Lieutenant Matthews had also been on the *Porpoise*, he remembered. So why was he lying?

Matthews went on, "And we were short of men, because so many are sick."

Forsythe said, "What do you mean, sick?"

"The able seamen who sailed on the *Sea Gull* south are all on the *Vin*, confined to their berths by orders of the surgeon."

"Reid is sick, and they're sick, too? Is there a bloody epidemic?"

Matthews smiled.. "A little scurvy aboard the *Porpoise*, yes, but the *Sea Gull*s got sick for a different reason. After Wilkes gave up chasing Cook's *ne plus ultra*, he sent the *Sea Gull* to Desolation Island, in order to retrieve a maximum-minimum thermometer that was left there ten years ago by a British scientific expedition. It was a hell of a job getting there, as they had to beat upwind, and even worse getting out, because a gale blew up from the other direction, and kept them windbound for days. So the men killed penguins for fresh grub, and the penguin stew made them sick. By the time they limped back to Orange Harbor, only the sealers—who knew enough not to try to eat penguin—were fit to haul on a rope."

"Then it's a wonder the schooner got there," Forsythe derided.

Still smiling, Matthew said, "Come into the cabin, and we'll see about finding you a berth. Coffin and the rest of your men will have to find a soft plank on deck or in the foc'sle, I'm afraid. Maybe we can rouse out a couple of spare hammocks, but because of the rush to come out and get you we're not all that well equipped."

Forsythe snapped, "The linguister berths aft."

"I beg your pardon?"

"Mebbe Sam Lee forgot to pass on the message that Deputy Coffin is a scientific, not a seaman."

"I know places—such as on board the *Swallow*—where there would be much debate about that, Kit."

"Wa'al, Nat, there ain't any debate here. Deputy Coffin bunks aft, and that's it."

Wiki shifted uneasily. When he had been stuck for a bed on this schooner on the Rio Negro, he had found a cozy spot between the folds of a spare sail, and his definite preference was to do the same now. Bunking in the afterquarters with Pilson and Matthews was almost as unpleasant a prospect as swinging a hammock in the foc'sle with the sealers, and he also didn't want to abandon Te Aute. The sealers had already proved that they had long, vindictive memories, which made Te Aute a target, and though the Maori might be as quick and sly as a lizard, there were uncommonly few hiding places on a vessel this small.

And he had noticed something else — something that was even more worrying.

He said, "Lieutenant Forsythe..."

Forsythe ignored him. Instead, he said to Matthews, his voice heavy and deliberate, "You heard me?"

"You're making a big mistake, Kit."

"Allow me to be the judge of that."

"He's a *half*-breed, for God's sake. It's gossip that will go down very strangely in Virginia."

Wiki interrupted, saying urgently, "Why is the schooner steering south, instead of making for Tierra del Fuego?"

Forsythe blinked, and then cast a quick look at the sky. Frowning, he turned back to Matthews, and said, "When do you expect to fetch Orange Harbor?"

"Who knows? Our next job is to finish the mission that I don't believe you even started."

"*What?*"

"Charting the Hermit Islands and Wollaston."

"What the hell? I mean," said Forsythe, echoing what his men had muttered over the campfire, "what the hell is the point?"

"Orders," said Matthews, and shut his mouth with a snap.

Silence, as the two men stared at each other. Finally Forsythe shrugged, and said, "Right, then. You know your orders, and I know that the linguister bunks aft. So I guess we understand each other, now."

"And I fail in my duties as a host."

"What?"

Matthews's smile became knowing. "I'm sure you could do with a drink."

Forsythe pursed his lips. However, he said nothing, following Matthews instead. He jerked his head at Wiki as the two officers turned for the deckhouse door, but Wiki said hastily, "I'll join you later, Lieutenant."

"What?" Forsythe stopped short. His expression became a suspicious scowl.

"I'll just be a few moments." Then, before Forsythe could demand a reason, Wiki scooted up the mainmast.

As he arrived at the crosstrees he looked down, to see both officers looking up at him.

Forsythe was looking both angry and surprised at his insubordination, and Matthews's scarred face was amused. He said something in Forsythe's ear, then urged him onward with a prompting hand on his shoulder. The deckhouse door creaked as it opened, and both officers ducked their heads to step down the short companionway. Then the door clapped shut.

When Wiki looked aft, beyond the sternward end of the deckhouse, Pilson was standing by the helmsman, his head tipped back, his mouth hanging open. Wiki gave him a sardonic wave. Then he straightened to gaze all about the horizon again, searching for any sign of land.

The shadows of Wollaston and its companion islands were entirely lost to sight, while the mountains of Tierra del Fuego were disappearing fast. Again, he felt a strong conviction that there was something very wrong on board this schooner, emphasized by the certain knowledge that Lieutenant Matthews had been lying, and not just about the sealers. The schooner was certainly sailing southeast, but not to complete the cutter's mission of charting the islands of Cape Horn. So why? And what did it have to do with all six sealers being on board?

Despite the gentleness of the breeze, the mast was swaying. If the wind strengthened, it would swoop in sickening circles, as Wiki knew well from having been aloft on this schooner on the Rio Negro. Right now, he was very secure, though, standing on the crosstrees and holding onto a lanyard with his back set firmly against the topmast shrouds. Seventy feet below, he could see the streams of froth running along the schooner's sides to join with the bubbling wake, where the cutter bounced along at the end of her rope, her two masts dipping from one side to the other and her long bowsprit flicking up water every now and then.

Though late afternoon, the weather was still pleasant. Clouds clustered, but there was enough sunlight to send sparks off the tops of the slowly heaving waves. It was impossible to think of a greater contrast to the sleet and murk when he had first sighted the *Sea Gull.*

Then his attention was seized as a glint caught his eye, far astern. A little white flicker had showed up against the shadowy outline of Tierra del Fuego. Then it vanished. Wiki shaded his eyes and stared until his eyes stung and teared, but it didn't reappear.

When his sight cleared, he looked down — to see the six sealers clustered on the amidships deck, directly below. Their beards jutted out as they stared up at him, waiting for him to come down the mast.

The cutter's men, with Te Aute, were in a tight group on the foredeck, watching. Their silhouettes were tensely braced. Apart from Lieutenant Pilson and the man at the tiller, there was no one else in sight.

Wiki reached up to the spring stay — the great tarred rope that led from the mainmast to the foremast, and spanned the amidships deck. After hooking his ankles over it, he slid rapidly forward, hand over hand. Sliding down a foremast backstay, he arrived with a jump in the middle of the group of cutter's men, who scattered to give him room, and then gathered close again.

Dick Gates, Forsythe's coxswain, was looking from the slowly advancing sealers to Wiki and then back again. However, he merely said, "Come to join us in the foc'sle?"

"Unfortunately, no. I would prefer it, believe me, but the lieutenant is adamant that I berth with him aft."

Gates nodded. Like them all, he was well aware of Forsythe's moods and whims, and the hazards of trying to argue when he'd made up his mind. "At least you'll have a hammock," he said. "They don't seem very hospitable, here."

"You're right about that," Wiki said. "According to Lieutenant Matthews, you're welcome to a soft plank, if you can find one."

"Is that so?" Dick Gates's mouth pulled down.

"When I was on board of the *Sea Gull* while on the Rio Negro, they stowed a couple of spare sails under the foretopgallant deck, alongside the galley stove, and I found them quite comfortable." Wiki paused, glanced again at the sealers, and then said in a lower voice, "I'd feel happier if you didn't berth in the foc'sle."

"On account of what?"

"On account of the sealers. I'd appreciate it if you'd keep an eye on Te Aute."

"Jack Sac?" said Gates, puzzled.

"Yes," said Wiki, and looked at Michael, the New Bedforder, who was the only man in the cutter's crew who also belonged to the *Swallow*'s boat's crew.

Michael said to Gates, "That time Mr. Coffin was attacked by the sealers on the deck of the *Peacock*, Jack Sac stood alongside of him. They would've murdered both of 'em, for sure—that is if the lieutenant hadn't arrived and sorted things out, with us boat's crew to back him up."

"Ah." Dick's eyebrows went up, and then he nodded. "So that's it, then," he said, and shifted from foot to foot, watching the sealers. "We can handle whatever's coming," he said. "Though there's something..."

"Yes?"

"Oh, it's probably nothing. Idle threats, that's all. But they keep on saying there ain't room for all these extra souls on this here schooner—that it's too damn crowded by far. And they reckon they're goin' to do something about it."

"What could they possibly do?"

Dick paused. But though Wiki waited, he said nothing.

Finally, Wiki shook his head, and said, "Idle threats, you're right."

The sealers were very close, their shoulders hunched, their demeanor belligerent as they all stared at him. So, thought Wiki, he was the first focus of their aggression, though it could quickly turn into a general fight. Lieutenant Pilson, still at his station in the stern, could easily see what was happening, as the roof of the deckhouse was just three feet proud of the deck, and his view was almost unimpeded, with only the cabin smokestack and a couple of skylights being in the way. The officer, however, was as unmoving as ever, so Wiki removed himself from the scene by heading back up the foremast.

When he arrived at the crosstrees, he paused, looking down, but nothing had happened. The six sealers were disappearing down the hatch to the foc'sle, leaving the foredeck to the cutter's men and Te Aute, and as far as Wiki could tell nothing had been said. As he swung out on the spring stay, however, he thought about those idle threats with a deep sense of foreboding.

Because of that, when Wiki was back on the maintopmast crosstrees he turned to look down at the deck. Pilson, to his surprise, was gone, leaving the quartermaster alone at the helm. A man wearing an apron—the steward, perhaps—was walking forward from the deckhouse. He disappeared into the shadow of the foretopgallant deck, and after a couple of moments came out again with a kid of cooked food and a steaming bucket that held either coffee or tea. The cutter's crew gathered around him, and a meal was handed out. Instead of returning to the deckhouse, the man in the apron went back to the galley, and after he had gone the cutter's crew and Te Aute sat in a line in the lee of the larboard bulwarks to share out the meal.

Pleased that they were being looked after, Wiki wondered if he just might have misjudged the situation on board the schooner. While he thought about it, balancing Matthews's lies with this unexpectedly hospitable behavior, he returned his gaze to the empty, slowly heaving sea. Because of the long evenings in high latitudes at this time of the year the sun was still above the horizon, though half-hidden by growing masses of dark purple clouds. Then all at once the clouds thickened, and the sun was gone. A wind whisked up, flicking at the fringes of his poncho, and fat drops of rain smacked icily onto his cheek.

Forsythe, if there, would have announced that the barometer was rising and a gale with snow was on the way. Wiki turned, ready to clamber down the mast. He was about to step off the crosstrees when a sudden change in the light caught his eye. The clouds had parted, and a shaft of light slanted down far astern, misty with rain, silhouetting...

It was the little shape again, still a very long way off, but perceptibly closer. By squinting, Wiki could see that it was double, like two tiny square clouds. Then, as he strained to see better, the two little clouds narrowed, and became triangles — a two-masted vessel, tacking to counter the bad weather that was blowing down fast.

Then the clouds closed, and dark murk descended. A vicious gust of rain with sleet slashed across Wiki's face, but he descended the shrouds with a heart that was very much lighter.

Twenty-one

When Wiki opened the door of the deckhouse, he was met by a hot draft, from a cabin stove that was going full blast.

He ducked under the low mantel and went down the four steps of the short companionway, to arrive in a room like a gentlemen's den, complete with a dense fug of tobacco smoke. The cuddy was as spacious as remembered, with such a generous deckhead that he could stand easily upright. Four doors, all closed, led to three tiny staterooms and the pantry, and there was a square table with four chairs.

Matthews, Pilson, and Forsythe were seated about that table, with bottles, glasses, little piles of wooden chips, and a pack of cards. Wiki wondered who was in charge of the deck. The boatswain? Forsythe was on the starboard side of the table, his brawny shoulders hunched over his hand of cards. Even though he was in shirtsleeves, his face was flushed and he was sweating.

He said, "The cutter's crew get their grub?"

Wiki nodded. So Forsythe had organized it, he thought. It was typical of him that even though he cast his foul abuse around freely, he made sure to look after his men. He also noticed that the words had been slurred. Forsythe, he realized with dismay, was drunk, and wondered how it had happened so fast. Because it had been so long since Forsythe had had a drink? Or perhaps the heat of the stove?

Pilson said with a sly grin, "Like to join us?"

What Wiki really wanted was a private word with Forsythe, but that was obviously impossible. He shook his head, and said, "How is Captain Reid?"

"Sleeping. Keep your voice down." And Pilson returned to his cards.

Wiki pushed the spare seat nearer the fire, then pulled off his poncho and hung it over the back of the chair, where it immediately began to steam. Then he had another look at the table. There was no sign of food, but he could smell coffee, so he went into the pantry, to find a coffee pot keeping warm over a spirit stove. When he sipped after pouring a mugful, it was to find that someone had sweetened it, while he preferred his coffee bitter. However, it was hot, and went well with the ship's bread he found in a bin, along with some pickles from a jar.

Eating and drinking as he stood at the bench, he listened to Matthews telling the others about his experiences in the Antarctic. Forsythe seemed to be too drunk to be interested, because he contributed very little to the conversation, but Wiki, in the seclusion of the pantry, listened intently, and learned a great deal — just as he had from the pantry of the wardroom of the *Peacock*.

Matthews was telling his unresponsive audience that Captain Wilkes had steered first for the South Shetlands, a Mecca for sealers just twenty years ago. Wiki knew that the rocky outposts had been abandoned after just a couple of seasons, the rookeries devastated, but now he learned that the seal populations were recovering fast, because Matthews described finding a beach with reasonably abundant seal life. From there, the *Porpoise* and the *Sea Gull* had crept south, steering for the tip of the nearest Antarctic peninsula, taking in sail and heaving to at night, for fear of running into icebergs—a cowardly move, in Matthews's opinion, but one that Wiki thought was eminently sensible. Wilkes had given up and turned for Orange Harbor after just one week! And he wasn't even a competent navigator, Not long after the *Porpoise* had started fleeing north, Wilkes had damn-near run her onto the rocks of Elephant Island, just because he couldn't do his dead reckoning.

Then there was a stray mention of encountering a homeward bound whaleship, along with derisive comments about dirt and grease. The yokel of a New Englander captain had reported three thousand, eight hundred barrels of oil, and had seemed pleased about it, Matthews said. Wiki was amused, thinking that many whaling skippers would have been envious of that report, but then he was distracted by the next tidbit of news—Wilkes had put letters on the ship, the captain having agreed to forward the mailbag to Washington. Dear lord, Wiki thought, feeling shaken. If Spieden and Stuart hadn't found that forged suicide letter, it would be on its way to Midshipman Dove's family.

Throughout Lieutenant Matthews's monologue, his words were punctuated with the slap of cards. When Wiki, having finished his meal, went back into the mess cabin, it was to see that the disposition of the gambling chips had changed. Now, most of them were piled beside Matthews's elbow, while Forsythe had only a half-dozen left. Forsythe looked drunker than ever. He had a bottle to himself, which he was helping himself to freely, while the other two officers were sharing another.

Wiki said nothing, going to the stove and checking his poncho. It was dry, and when he picked it up it was hot to the touch. The fire was roaring, the outer iron glowing. The steward was still conspicuously absent, so obviously it was the officers who were keeping it well stoked. Why? Because Matthews was chilled by his memories of the Antarctic? Or to keep Forsythe drowsy and slow-thinking? If the latter, it was certainly working. What with the heat and the drink, it was amazing that he was still awake.

Wiki took off his Guernsey and spread it on the chair back. He had not a notion which stateroom had been assigned to Forsythe, so looked at the card players with his eyebrows raised. Forsythe merely stared back owlishly. It was Matthews who waved a hand, indicating a door. As Wiki opened it and went inside, he saw Forsythe take another swig from his glass, all the time blinking at his hand of cards, as if he had trouble focusing.

The hanging lantern revealed a room that was even smaller than the stateroom where Wiki had lived on the *Peacock*. There was a sidelight high in the bulkhead that opened out into the narrow alley between the wall of the deckhouse and the larboard bulwarks of the schooner, but otherwise the cabin looked very similar, having a bank of lockers with a thin mattress on top, and a tiny desk by the head of the bed. Despite the cramped space, a hammock had been slung diagonally from the wall above the desk to the wall by the bottom corner of the bed, ready for the linguister. Wiki was touched. Forsythe, to all appearances, was intent on getting drunk and losing whatever money he had left, and yet he had made sure that his men were fed, and his linguister had a place to sleep — and not on the floor of the stateroom, either. Not only had he insisted that Wiki should share his room, but he'd organized a hammock.

On impulse, instead of turning in, Wiki went back through the cabin to the pantry, and poured a mug of strong coffee. Then, very firmly and pointedly, he placed it by Forsythe's elbow. He knew Pilson would snigger — which the officer did — but he didn't care. Ignoring the derisive snort, he headed back to the stateroom.

Before he got to the door, however, he was halted by an explosive curse from Forsythe. Wiki turned, to see him push the last of his tokens across the table to Matthews, then shakily pick up a pencil and write out a chit. At that moment, he seemed almost sober.

He said to Matthews in a bitter tone, "You bloody gammoned me."

Matthews's thin smile widened. "*Si possis recte, si non, quocumque modo rem.*"

"What?" Forsythe's broad, red face went perfectly blank.

"*If possible, make money honestly — if not, somehow.*"

Wiki stood frozen. *Horace*, he thought fleetingly — the aphorism was from Horace, the Roman poet George Rochester liked to quote. But the overpowering realization was that he now knew who had forged Midshipman Dove's suicide letter. *Vis consili expers mole ruit sua*, the forger had written. Back then, just like now, Lieutenant Matthews couldn't resist a display of his superior scholarship.

Then he saw that Matthews was studying him alertly. The one steady eye in the scarred face was focused on him, and Wiki felt very aware of the cold, intelligent mind behind it.

Matthews said sharply, "Mr. Coffin?"

Wiki said, "Sorry," and backed blindly away. When his shoulder hit the wall, he reached around for the door handle without looking, and pulled it open. He took one step inside before he realized it was dark — that he was in the wrong room.

This time it was Pilson's voice that ripped through the afterquarters. "What the hell do you think you are doing?" he snapped. "I thought I told you not to disturb him."

Wiki's face felt numb, and he had to school himself to move slowly. He came out of the stateroom, and closed the door very carefully, keeping his back to the men while he concentrated on picking up his warmed Guernsey. He heard his own voice mutter, "Sorry, I wasn't looking" — but all the time his mind was screaming, *Captain Reid is dead!*

Still keeping his back to the table, Wiki opened the correct door, stepped inside, and closed that door as carefully as the other. Then he sank onto the edge of Forsythe's berth, clutching the Guernsey in both his trembling hands. The instant he had stepped into Captain Reid's room, he had known that he was in the same space as a dead man. It had been dark, so that he had only seen the shape of the still form on the berth, but he had known without a single doubt that there was an awful absence where there should have been life.

He was shaking uncontrollably, cold sweat pouring off him, and the sugary coffee and acid pickles kept on rising into his throat. When there was a loud rap at the door, his heart jerked so hard that it hurt. Bracing himself, he stood and opened it.

Lieutenant Pilson was on the other side. He said, "You oughter do somethin' about your friend."

Friend? Then Wiki saw that Forsythe was slumped with his head on the table, the bottle he'd been drinking from lying by his outstretched hand, leaking a black puddle that dripped onto the floor. Wiki went over, gripped his shoulder, and shook him hard. Pilson and Matthews were watching him with amusement, and made no attempt to assist, even when Wiki was forced to heave him up.

The increasingly sharp movements of the ship helped, along with the fact that Forsythe stirred a little. Slowly, Wiki negotiated the way to Forsythe's berth, staggering with every pitch, and once almost losing his burden. Dropped onto the mattress, Forsythe began to snore. His open mouth dribbled, and he was visibly sweating, and yet the touch of his skin had been clammily cold.

Looking down at the sad sight, Wiki thought a moment, then went back through the messroom to fetch a bucket from the pantry. The cabin was empty, but he didn't bother to wonder where Pilson and Matthews had gone. Instead, he placed the wooden pail on the floor by Forsythe's snoring head, and covered him with a blanket. Then he clambered into the hammock, after shucking his boots and tugging on his woolen jersey. Clutching the fringe of his poncho with cramped fingers, he tugged it around himself as he settled.

Then he lay and thought about the dead man who was just inches away, on the other side of the partition between this stateroom and the next. Because of the overworked stove, it was almost as hot in the stateroom as it was in the cabin, but Wiki couldn't stop shivering. His head felt as if it was stuffed with cotton, and his mind didn't seem to work properly. He had kept on his socks—good thick stockings, knitted out of greasy, water-resistant wool—and he thought about the girl who had knitted them for him, wishing she was there, because he very much needed the comfort of a warm body to hold. Then, after a timeless interval, he was jerked back to the present by a commotion out on deck.

Angry shouts were followed by the sounds of a scuffle, and then the thump of a boat against the hull. Dazedly, Wiki dropped out of his hammock, and ran out into the mess cabin, silent in his stockinged feet. It was still empty. The ship pitched, and Forsythe's empty bottle fell off the table and crashed into the puddle on the floor.

Wiki took two strides up the companionway and flung open the outer door, to be met by a rush of icy air. It took seconds for his sight to adjust, but then he saw the struggling huddle by the gangway—the cutter's men being shoved over the side, one by one. When Wiki ran to the rail, the cutter was bobbing just below, kept in place with ropes held by two of the schooner's seamen. As he watched, the last of Forsythe's handpicked crew was tumbled down, to be caught by his fellows. The light from the single cresset gleamed down—on dark whorls in a dusky face. Te Aute.

241

Wiki roared, "What the hell is happening?"

An unknown voice said, "This here schooner's too crowded, so we figured to do something about it."

"But for God's sake, there's a gale on the way!"

"Best seamen in the fleet, ain't they?"

I have to do something, Wiki thought dazedly. The movements of the *Sea Gull* were growing increasingly agitated, and he could hear the hull creak as wind whistled briefly in the rigging. Even if the launch didn't founder in the storm, the nearest land was many miles away. Nevertheless, he braced himself to jump down.

The voice said, "No, you don't, you're staying right here, you crafty bastard." Several rough hands gripped him. *The sealers.* Wiki struggled desperately. He didn't want to leave Forsythe to cope with the murderous sealers on his own, yet he was frantic to get into the cutter, because he was the only one who knew…

His numb mind focused, and he started shouting — in *te reo Maori.*

One of the sealers rasped, "What the hell?" Wiki ignored him, evading fists that cuffed his face, still shouting out his urgent message in his native tongue. The rushing clouds in the sky were abruptly broken, revealing patches of stars, and he added more precise directions, but before he had finished the cutter was forcibly shoved off.

He cried to Te Aute, "*E pai ana nga mea katoa?*"

"*Hei aha,*" came the reassuring reply, muffled by the crash of a wave that blew apart on the breast of a gust, then a very faint, "Yes, boss!"

"*Kia tere!*" Wiki briefly saw the wave of a hand, and then a sail was set, followed by another. A deluge of spray came over the rail, and Wiki ducked. When he straightened, the cutter was half-hidden by a cresting wave. Another wash of spray was followed by a last glimpse of the launch heading north under a press of sail. Then she was gone. Wiki couldn't even see the tips of her masts.

Wiki turned, faced the sealers, and said bitterly, "So, having sent them to their deaths, is it time to kill me?"

"Here's a taste, you interfering bastard." It was the big leader, Peter Folger. Two men held Wiki still despite his struggles, while Folger's vicious fist slammed into his stomach—once, twice—again. Wiki doubled over with an agonized gasp, fighting for breath, holding his chest with his tightly folded arms. By the time he managed to straighten the sealers were gone, leaving the echoes of their laughter behind them.

His gorge rose, and he swerved back to the rail to empty the contents of his tortured belly into the sea. The spasms seemed to go on a long time, but by the time he was finished, and had drenched his face with handfuls of salt water from a bucket, he felt a great deal better. Despite the distraction of the pain in his abdomen, his mind felt much clearer—and despite the remains of bile in his mouth, he could still taste the sugary coffee he had vomited. With abrupt, horrified realization, he grabbed up the pail of salt water, and ran through the cuddy to Forsythe's berth.

Forsythe was as he had left him, snoring loudly, clammy with sweat. Where his face had been florid, however, it was now leaden. Bracing himself against the pitch of the ship, Wiki slapped one cheek, then the other, lifted his shoulders and shook him violently. Still Forsythe was out to the world, unmoving, and when

Wiki bent to listen to his chest his heartbeat was so slow that for a horrid moment he thought he was dead.

Not dead—*dying*. Another frantic shake, and then a rattle of slaps. To Wiki's intense relief, Forsythe stirred, moaning and tossing his head. Opening bloodshot eyes, he uttered a stream of slurred curses, and then demanded water.

Wiki filled a tumbler with salt water and poured it into his mouth, and Forsythe drank thirstily. Then he reared up. "You *bastard*," he hissed, leaned over the side of the berth, and was violently sick. To Wiki's relief, most of it went into the pail he'd put there earlier.

"More," said Wiki, when the long bout of heaving was finally over, and held out another glass of seawater.

"*What the hell are you doing?*"

"You've been poisoned."

"*What?*"

"Drugged. And you need to get rid of it all."

"For God's sake!" But with huge distaste Forsythe emptied another glass, and then vomited again. Finally, when nothing was left to come up, Wiki went to the pantry and fetched a tumbler of fresh water, which Forsythe emptied in two gulps before demanding in a cracked whisper for more.

He was sitting more or less upright when Wiki returned from the pantry with the refilled glass. Though he still looked dreadful, his color was returning. He tried to speak, wiped his face with the wet cloth Wiki handed him, and said huskily, "What the devil happened?"

"There was some sort of drug in my coffee—in the sugar, I think. Did you drink any coffee?"

Forsythe shook his head, and then winced, because the movement hurt.

"So it must have been in your liquor. You had a bottle of your own, while Pilson and Matthews shared the other."

"So that's why you gammoned me into drinking salt water? To force me to discharge my locker?"

"I think I saved your life."

Silence. Forsythe stared at him. After a long moment he rasped, "So I bloody owe you," and didn't look happy about it. Then, to Wiki's alarm, he flopped full length on the berth with his eyes half-open and showing just the whites, the irises rolled back into his head. Reassuringly, however, he started snoring.

Wiki stared at the sprawled form for a long moment, wondering if Forsythe would be alive in the morning. He had done all he could, he wearily decided, and after covering the lieutenant up, he clambered back into the hammock.

Twenty-two

When Wiki woke it was dawn.

He scrambled out of the hammock to check Forsythe, and to his relief, though the lieutenant was still deeply asleep, he was definitely alive. It was cold, so Wiki adjusted the blanket over Forsythe to cover him completely, and then picked up his poncho from the hammock and pulled it over his head. The officers must have let the cabin stove die down, he thought.

While the weather had calmed, the schooner was rolling uneasily on a heavy swell, with every now and then a muted crash as she hit floating ice. Above the creaks and bumps, Wiki heard noises outside—steps and voices as men assembled on the amidships deck. Then Lieutenant Matthews's voice echoed from directly above. Evidently the officer was standing on the roof of the deckhouse, using it as a quarterdeck.

When Wiki opened the little sidelight, the words became clear. He heard Matthews announce that Captain Reid had passed away in the night, and that he, Lieutenant Matthews, was to be called *Captain Matthews* from now on, having taken over the command. Then, without a pause for any reaction from the men, the burial of Reid's body commenced. The traditional liturgy was recited in a matter-of-fact tone, and then Wiki heard the splash as the corpse was slid into the sea. *Haere e te hoa, ko te tatou kainga nui kena,* he thought with a shiver, hoping the confused ghost

246

would understand the command to tread the sacred path of *Tane*, and join his ancestors in the heavenly abode. Then he heard Matthews dismiss the men, and their steps and their ordinary conversational voices diminishing with distance as they went forward.

When Wiki turned away from the sidelight, he found that Forsythe had pushed the blanket aside, and was sitting on the edge of his berth. He was cradling his head, which obviously hurt like hell, but looked up when Wiki moved. His eyes were more bloodshot than ever, his beard was spotted with dried vomit, and he clearly felt awful, but he looked a great deal more alive than he had in the night.

Forsythe started to speak, coughed, cleared his throat, and said huskily, "What's happening out there?"

"They've just buried Captain Reid."

Lines of pain creased the weathered face. "Jim Reid?"

"I'm afraid so."

"When did he die? And how, for God's sake?"

"I blundered into his room last night, and he was already dead. I expect that he was dead before we even boarded the brig."

Forsythe said bitterly, "And I s'pose you're goin' to say he was murdered."

"Yes. But I don't know how—though he might have been drugged, like we were. And I don't know who did it."

"So, aren't you goin' to do something about it? You're a sheriff's deputy! How about doing your job?"

"I would love to do that, but it just isn't possible."

"Why?"

"Lieutenant Matthews has taken over the schooner. He's seized it."

"*What!*"

Wiki paused. He was thinking, *Plison, Jerkin, Lusser, Clamber, Sweetman.*

Then he said, "Matthews is Sweetman."

Forsythe's eyes went blank, then focused again. "The same cove who owed Dove the most money?"

"Exactly." One thousand, three hundred dollars, spread over four chits.

"What makes you think that Matthews is Sweetman?"

Any discussion of aphorisms from Roman poets was bound to be doomed, so Wiki said, "Try spelling the name backwards."

He watched Forsythe's lips move as he went through the letters—S... W... E... Then he clutched his head again, having been unwise enough to nod emphatically. "Oh God, that hurts," he said. "You reckon there's any laudanum on this here brig?"

"You've had enough drugs," Wiki said. "Would it help if I loaned you my bandanna to tie around your head?"

"I'll try anything, damn it."

Wiki fished the bandanna out of the inside pocket of his poncho, spread it out on the bunk, and then rolled it into a tube, which he flattened and tied about Forsythe's forehead. Then he stood back and surveyed the result. It made the beefy southerner look more disreputable than ever, but Forsythe seemed to think it helped, because he left it on.

"So Matthews murdered Midshipman Dove?" he said.

"Or Pilson did. Or both of them. One could have held him still while the other closed his hand about the razor." It was a horrible thought—Wiki shivered again. "It was dark, it was raining, and it was in the maintop. No one would've noticed."

"But it had to be Matthews. Since he's Sweetman, he was the one who owed the most money, so he had the most to gain."

Wiki paused, thinking that it was indeed the obvious motive for the murder—*ko nga take whawhai, he whenua .. for the source of trouble, look at property.* And one thousand, three hundred dollars was a lot of money. But then he remembered the day of Midshipman Dove's funeral, and the impression that there was a strong family connection between Lieutenant Lee and Lieutenant Matthews.

He said tentatively, "I've noticed that the first families of Virginia seem to be pretty tight-knit."

"Mebbe so," grunted Forsythe, who was deep in his own thoughts. "What of it?"

"I just wondered if you were related to Lieutenant Lee."

"Sam? Sort of, I guess. On my mother's side. But why the hell are you asking?"

"And what about Lieutenant Matthews? Is he related to you?"

"*No!* Wa'al, I don't think so. God, I hope not."

"So he's not related to Lieutenant Lee, either?"

Forsythe stared challengingly. "Are you trying to involve Sam Lee jest because their parents are connected?"

Wiki said, startled, "Both parents?"

Forsythe shrugged. "Sam and Nat Matthews are sort of double cousins, I guess. But what the devil does it matter?"

"They're close?"

"They've been friends all their lives, but why the hell are you barkin' on about that—when this schooner has been pirated? United States property—it's a capital crime, for God's sake! How the hell can Matthews get away with it? And why? Where do you think they're steering?"

"That's a very good point," said Wiki. He could hear Pilson and Matthews talking on the roof above his head, the words indistinct. Silent in his stockinged feet, he slipped into the cuddy, looked around the empty room, and then quietly opened the next door, the one that led to the stateroom that had been Captain Reid's. He had to brace himself to go inside, but was rewarded by what he had hoped to see—the *Sea Gull*'s log, lying on the little desk by the head of the berth.

The last entry was a day out of date, but was a good indication of the direction the schooner was heading. Wiki could still hear voices from above, along with an indistinct yell from aloft, and then shouts as orders were conveyed to the helmsman, so he went to the third stateroom. It was a mess, with clothes and other gear scattered over the floor as well as the berth—but there on the desk was something unexpected.

His own notebook. And he now knew, beyond the slightest doubt, exactly where the *Sea Gull* was headed.

To the position that he had noted, the position of the corpse-carrying iceberg—and they should be there very shortly.

Wiki scooped the book up, returned it to the pocket inside his Guernsey, and hurried back to Forsythe's room. Forsythe met him in the doorway. He was carrying his rifle, and had a determined expression.

"What are you doing?" Wiki exclaimed.

"Goin' to take back this schooner, ain't I," Forsythe snapped. Then he shoved roughly past him to the stairs and the deck.

"But you can't!"

Grabbing up his boots, and stumbling into them, Wiki set off in pursuit—too late. When he arrived Forsythe was on the amidships deck. Matthews jumped down from the roof of the deckhouse, his expression startled. He let out a shout, but Forsythe ignored him, heading forward and yelling for his coxswain, Dick Gates. Getting no reply, he plunged into the forecastle.

Without seconds he was out again, his expression furious and frustrated. The sealers, on the foredeck, were grinning. He looked around wildly, then came aft again, stopping short in front of Wiki.

"Where the hell are my men?" he demanded.

Wiki paused, feeling very conscious of Matthews close behind him, and that Pilson, who had gone into the cabin, could also hear every word.

Before he could answer, Pilson spoke. Then Wiki turned, it was to see him standing at the door of the afterhouse. He was holding a rifle, which was aimed at Forsythe. With his usual unpleasant smirk, he said, "They decided to abandon us."

"What? What the devil? When?" Forsythe's eyes flickered from Wiki to Pilson, and then to the gun Pilson leveled. Though his own rifle was slung from his shoulder, it was obvious that he wouldn't have time to swing it around before Pilson fired.

"Last night," said Pilson, his smirk widening. "They decided they preferred the cutter to our company."

Forsythe turned on Wiki again. "What the hell is he talking about?"

Wiki spread his hands in a helpless gesture. "They were overpowered and forced to get into the cutter, and then it was shoved off. The last I saw of them, they were under sail, steering northeast."

Slowly, as he absorbed this, Forsythe's eyes became glazed with pain. Then his face turned red with fury, and he shouted at Wiki, "And you stood by and let it happen? What kind of cowardly bastard are you? Why the bloody hell didn't you sail with them?"

It was no use trying to explain, not with Matthews and Pilson listening—and there was something else that Wiki badly needed to know. So he escaped the thunder and fury by springing onto the mainmast and scrambling hand over fist for the crosstrees.

As he secured his back against a topgallant stay, he could hear the echoes of Pilson's derisive laughter, along with more shouting from Forsythe. Then the voices faded. When he looked down, Forsythe was standing impotently on the amidships deck, this time without his rifle. Matthews had taken it off him. Pilson leaned indolently against the side of the deckhouse with his rifle at the ready, and Forsythe's gun propped against the bulkhead by his knee.

So he and Forsythe were both trapped and without weapons. With Forsythe on deck, and himself aloft, there wouldn't even be a chance to consult and make a plan. Wiki abruptly realized that it might have been a bad mistake to climb the mast.

He scanned the horizon rather desperately — and stared, riveted, at what lay close to hand, just five miles ahead.

An island — *an island*. The *Sea Gull* had arrived at the position that Captain Noyes had given for the iceberg, but where Wiki had fully expected to see a patch of empty, heaving ocean, the berg having drifted on, he saw a tall mass of rock towering up from the sea. Its sheer sides were colored dun and pale green by some sort of encrustation, so that it almost blended in with the oyster-gray sky, but it was indubitably an island, one of the demi-god Maui's most far-flung specks of land.

Astonished, he wondered how Noyes had mistaken it for an iceberg. There were good reasons, he supposed — the *Betsey* had blundered upon it during a thick snowstorm, and because of the spray flung high by the gale, the abrupt, terraced cliffs would have been sheathed in ice. Noyes and his crew had also been panicked, because the huge obstacle had appeared so suddenly out of the murk. They had come perilously close to collision, and at that fraught moment, it would have been easy to jump to the wrong conclusion. And then there had been the distraction of that frozen corpse...

In this clear morning light, in calm weather, it was obvious that it was land, not ice. The island was shaped like a comma, the tall granite stack trailing off into a curving tail, which formed a treacherous embayment made up of rocks that stuck out of the sea like a warped row of teeth.

Otherwise, as far as Wiki could see, breakers dashed against sheer cliffs. It was the most inhospitable place imaginable. The only reason anyone would try to get ashore on this gale-lashed pile of granite was that it was exactly the kind of place that seals chose to give birth to their young.

That it was — or had been — a seal rookery meant that at last he could make sense of Captain Noyes's strange story of a corpse. Obviously, a gang had been landed here, and at some time during the devastation of the seal breeding ground one man had been clubbed to death, presumably during a fight with another. The only question was whether it had ever been reported. Wiki strongly doubted it. Sealing being such a dangerous trade, the loss of one man would have been easily explained. He had been killed in a fall — or so they would have said — and it would have been readily believed. The dead man would have been crossed off the crewlist, and his killer would have been discharged when the sealing vessel got home, without any questions asked.

But why was the corpse stuck to a cliff, and not buried or dumped in the sea? That it was frozen into place didn't seem so likely now, as the island was far enough north to be affected by summer temperatures.

Then Wiki was distracted by a flurry of orders from the quarterdeck, as the *Sea Gull* was brought round to the south. Gradually, more of the cliff face was revealed, but still Wiki couldn't see anything that looked like a body. More orders, and seamen heaved on halyards. With a great creaking of gaffs, sail was taken in until the schooner was lying quietly a mile from the shore. The weather was remarkably calm, thought Wiki—almost menacingly so, as if a tempest was lurking just over the horizon. Then he was distracted again, this time by a vibration in the rigging.

He looked down. Matthews was climbing up the mast.

Wiki shifted defensively, ready to swing out onto the spring stay, but the scar-faced lieutenant stopped at the top of the shrouds, steadying himself with a fist that gripped the crosstrees at the level of Wiki's stockinged feet.

Wary of a sudden grab about his ankles, Wiki crouched to lower and center his weight, and reached out to secure a good hold on a backstay. Then he waited.

Matthews said nothing, instead studying him impersonally while the suspense dragged on. Deciding it was a good idea to try to shake that cold confidence, Wiki lifted his brows, and asked, "Is this what happened on the night that you killed Midshipman Dove? Were you alone when you came over the futtock shrouds with the razor in your hand, or was your lackey Pilson with you?"

Matthews's mouth tightened. He hissed, "*Mister* Pilson to you."

"Or perhaps you were alone," Wiki meditated aloud. "It's logical enough. *Mister* Pilson didn't owe nearly as much money as you did."

"Money? I don't know what the hell you mean."

"Yes, you do. And a one hundred and ten-dollar debt is pretty insignificant when compared to a sum of one thousand, three hundred. But," Wiki went on, "while getting such a big debt wiped out was certainly an advantage for you, I don't believe that's the one and only reason you killed Valentine Dove."

Matthews's laugh was scornful. "You reckon there are a number of these so-called reasons?"

"Yes indeed, and they add up to quite a story, one that goes back to something that happened after Midshipman Dove's funeral. As he was leaving the ship, Lieutenant Smith stumbled rather comically — which meant that everyone was watching when he stumbled again. The second time, he fell overboard, and after he was rescued he swore he'd been shoved. He demanded that I should start an inquiry, but no one took it seriously, because you stepped up and testified that it was all his own fault, which made Lieutenant Smith look like an hysterical idiot. But, in fact, he was right. He was indeed pushed — and it was you who pushed him."

The good eye widened, and then Matthews snapped, "You've forgotten that I was the one who jumped in to save him — which you did not."

"Ah, but that was part of your carefully laid plan. Another fall, another attempt to save him from his own clumsiness, and no questions would be asked when the rescue went wrong. And remember," said Wiki carefully, "I *did* jump in when Lieutenant Smith fell the next time, when he'd come to summon me to the *Vincennes*. And not only did he drown — because you made sure of it — but I was almost drowned, too."

"And why only almost, I wonder?" said Matthews. The tone was sardonic, but Wiki sensed a note of bafflement, too, as if Matthews couldn't understand why that part of the plan hadn't worked.

"As you know perfectly well, one of the sealers jumped into the water with the intention of killing me in the chaos. Unfortunately," said Wiki, "he came off second-best."

Silence, and then Matthews said, "You could never prove it was anything to do with me, because there's no reason why I would want Smith dead."

"Oh yes, there is. You killed him so that your cousin Lee would be promoted to flag lieutenant in his place."

He had hit a nerve, Wiki saw, because the drooping lid on Matthews's damaged eye flickered. He went on, "He was the obvious candidate to fill the dead man's shoes—in your opinion, anyway. And his," Wiki added on an afterthought. "As far as you knew, Lieutenant Craven was still out of favor with Captain Wilkes. And then, once Captain Wilkes was summoned back to Washington, his name having been discredited, Lee, being the flag lieutenant, would have a powerful role in the expedition."

"And the expedition would have been all the better for it!" Matthews flashed.

"That's a matter of opinion."

"The opinion of many! And while Lee might have been fired by that madman, the situation hasn't changed. The truth about Wilkes, his insane decisions, his hysterical temper, and his tyrannical blundering will come out—and sooner rather than later, take my word for it!"

"Ah," said Wiki, "but that is not going to happen."

The drooping eyelid twitched again. "What?"

"The so-called suicide letter that was written to discredit Captain Wilkes has been retrieved from the mailbag. It's *not* on the way to America."

Silence, while Matthews stared at Wiki. Then, as the full import of this sank in, the scarred, once handsome face seemed to collapse in on itself.

A long silence, while Wiki watched him. Matthews was staring unseeingly at the island, while the sagging eyelid twitched almost continuously. Then Matthews said, almost as if to himself, "How the hell did you find out about the letter?"

"Pilson has a loose mouth."

The scarred face contorted in a flash of open fury. "Watch your own mouth, you uppity half-breed bastard!"

"*Mister* Pilson couldn't resist dropping broad hints that a suicide letter existed, which gave me a trail to follow. And when I was asking about a possible letter, I was assured that it hadn't been put on the *Betsey*. So, if there was one, it had to be in the mailbag that was waiting for the next ship—which is exactly where your forgery was found."

Matthews shut his eyes as if they hurt, and when he opened them again he was white with rage. Pilson, Wiki reflected, was going to suffer for this.

Deliberately, he went on, "But you made it easy for me, too."

"What the hell are you talking about *this* time?"

"Because you can't help bragging. Once we had the letter, it was obvious that that it was you who had forged it, because you can't resist showing off your fancy Latin."

The distorted face went blank. "What Latin?"

"Aphorisms from Horace, to be precise."

Matthews's good eye narrowed, and then widened again as he remembered the quotation in the letter. Then Wiki was distracted by a glimpse of movement on the deck below. Forsythe was coming out of the deckhouse with Pilson close behind him.

Wiki frowned, feeling very puzzled, and then saw that the schooner's whaleboat was being lowered. The sealers were gathered by the gangway in an expectant group. Pilson, his rifle poked between the southerner's shoulder blades, was prodding Forsythe in their direction.

He looked back at Matthews, and said, "Is this when we learn your plans?"

The scar-faced officer laughed, an ominously confident sound. "You mean you haven't guessed what happens next? When you're so pleased with your own brilliance? Take a look ahead, and tell me what you see."

Wiki turned on his perch, carefully avoiding a betraying glance at the sternward horizon. He looked at the towering heap of granite, and said, "An island, in the position I copied into the notebook that *Mister* Pilson stole out of my stateroom."

"Where the sealer *Betsey* took a record haul — and where we expect to do the same."

Wiki shook his head. "You're wrong."

Matthew blinked. "What do you mean?"

"It's an island that Captain Noyes mistook for an iceberg. I copied down the position only because it was considered a navigational hazard. When he sighted this island, he was a long way north of the *Betsey*'s sealing ground."

Silence, and another twitch of the eyelid. "So this isn't the sealing beach?"

"No."

"But you know where it really is."

"I certainly do."

"So, we made a mistake—but I strongly doubt that your secret position will be a secret for long. And prying it out of you is a job I can safely leave to others. Once you get on shore at this island, and the sealers find out that there isn't any rookery—"

Wiki smiled. "I'm sure the sealers would enjoy beating the location out of me, but there's actually no need."

Then he told Matthews the position of the *Betsey's* beach, and watched as the good eye widened.

"That's in the South Shetlands!"

"Exactly."

"But they've been sealed out!"

"You said yourself that the seals are returning. But it seems most likely that Captain Noyes found an island in the South Shetlands that the original sealing gangs overlooked."

"Why are you telling me this?"

"I would have thought you would've worked that out yourself, Lieutenant Matthews. It's because you can't get there—because the South Shetlands will be iced in for months."

Wiki watched the lieutenant's face go utterly blank, as if he was turning over options while he took in the full implications of this. Then Wiki looked again at the island, contemplating fat, black clouds that were gathering beyond the mountain. A northwesterly gale was on the way, he thought, and then returned his attention to Matthews.

"The sealers who talked you into seizing the *Sea Gull* and sailing off to collect a valuable haul of skins are going to be very disappointed, because the *Betsey*'s sealing ground will be out of reach until November," he said. "Knowing them as I do, I expect them to get nasty. What I suggest is that you sail to Valparaiso, rejoin the fleet, and turn in the sealers for attempted piracy. If you're convincing enough, you might even get a commendation from Captain Wilkes."

Silence. Wiki, watching Matthews closely, could sense the cold, shrewd mind at work. Matthews looked down at the sealers, who were staring up at him, obviously anxious to get on shore. Then he nodded to himself as a decision was reached.

He looked at Wiki again, and snapped, "Get down to deck. *Move!* No, not that way," he ordered.

Wiki, who had turned to step down from the crosstrees, stopped short. Matthews said, "I don't trust you an inch, you half-breed bastard. You are *not* following me down the mainmast. Instead, you can monkey along the spring stay, where I'm a long way out of your reach. And, once you're down, you can join Forsythe at the gangway."

The lieutenant lifted his left hand, and for the first time Wiki saw that he was holding a pistol. Silently, he reached up for the spring stay and swung out on it.

Twenty-three

The sealers gathered close as Wiki arrived at the gangway.

They didn't seize him, somewhat to his surprise. Instead, they all turned to watch Matthews, who had come down the mainmast shrouds. It was obvious that they were impatient to hear his orders and get away. But, instead of joining them, Matthews took Pilson's arm, and drew him aside.

Then he talked at length in the junior officer's ear, while Pilson kept his rifle steadily aimed at Forsythe. Wiki watched expressions chase over Pilson's face as he listened—disappointment, followed by utter disbelief. He started to shake his head, then stilled as Matthews talked more rapidly, occasionally gesturing with the pistol he held loosely in his hand.

Finally Pilson shrugged, nodded, and laughed. The sound was an unexpected, ominous bark of amusement. Then both officers walked up to the sealers.

Two seamen brought the whaleboat around to the gangway with ropes, while the sealers shifted, ready to scramble into it. However, Matthews held them back, and supervised the loading. Peter Folger went down first, and was given the pistol to hold while Wiki and Forsythe were shoved down.

Then, to Forsythe's open astonishment, Pilson handed down his rifle, butt first. He grabbed it, and looked around suspiciously, while Wiki stared up at Matthews's blandly expressionless face, feeling quite confounded.

Both Pilson's rifle and Folger's pistol were leveled menacingly, so Forsythe looped the gun strap over his shoulder. Then he sat still, his meaty hand caressing the stock, a frown creasing his red face underneath the snugly tied bandanna.

A dozen cudgels were tossed into the bottom of the boat, followed by the other five sealers, who took up the oars. Once settled, the sealers all looked up at Matthews.

"Good luck with your seal hunt," he said, and smiled thinly. "This *should* be the *Betsey*'s sealing ground, being the place that Deputy Coffin noted in his book, but I'm sure you'll find another use for your cudgels, if it's not. And, we won't be surprised to hear a shot, Mr. Forsythe having made it so obvious to us all that he is so angry with his half-breed friend."

Silence. The sealers looked at Forsythe, their expressions blank, then glanced at Wiki, and then looked up at Matthews again.

With an eyebrow lifted, Matthews said, "Just let's say that we don't expect everyone to return."

The sealers nodded and shifted, understanding at last. The order to commit murder was plain.

Without any more ado they shoved the boat off from the schooner's side. As the oars dipped and swung, Forsythe's eyes flickered from the sealers to Wiki's face and then back again, while all the time his hand caressed the stock of his rifle. Peter Folger was holding the pistol steady, despite the swoop and swing of the boat. Wiki concentrated on easing his feet inside his boots, making sure his socks hadn't worked into lumps. He had a good idea that he would be running hard very soon after reaching the shore.

Petrels screamed and squalled in the sky above, swooping about the masts of the schooner, and then the sound diminished as the whaleboat left the *Sea Gull* behind. The swell from the northeast was heavy, but the sealers pulled their oars with the strength and economy of experience, so that the tall cliffs approached surprisingly fast. Then Wiki could hear the caves at the bottom booming with the thunder of the surf. Thick beds of kelp lashed back and forth in the foam.

The boat slowed, jinked about some protruding rocks, slid sideways as three oars were thrust backwards, and then surged into a narrow channel. Two powerful heaves, and the boat rushed on the breast of a breaker to a scrap of a beach.

The bottom grated on shingle, and two sealers jumped out into the knee-deep surf, and held the boat still. Peter Folger stood up, his small red-rimmed eyes intent and unblinking.

"Out," he said to Wiki, and gestured with the pistol.

Bracing a foot on the gunwale, Wiki made a long leap into the ebb of a wave, and ran up the stony slope, taking short steps to get his balance. When he stopped and looked back, Forsythe was making his jump. Peter Folger was just behind him, a cudgel in his fist, the pistol now thrust into his belt.

Forsythe wasn't as lucky with his judgment of the surf. Caught by a late-breaking wave, he stumbled, almost fell, and stumbled again as he struggled to the beach. Then, to Wiki's horror, he sprawled full length, felled by a vicious blow from Folger's club. His rife went flying further up the shingle, rattling as it landed on stone.

Forsythe lay still, water foaming about his lower legs, blood leaking from one ear. He was so obviously dead that Wiki's heart jerked painfully in his chest. Then Peter Folger rushed upon him with his cudgel raised. Surely he wasn't meant to kill him now? But apparently that was so. Confident that they were on the right island, the man had gone mad, he thought.

Looking around wildly, Wiki saw a narrow path that led up to a terrace that wound back and forth across the sheer face of the cliff. It was only a crack in the rock, but he put his head down and barged up it as fast as he could, bumping his right hand against the stone to keep his balance. He could hear urgent shouting from the beach below, but overriding every other sound was the thump of boots on rock as Peter Folger pursued him.

Up, up Wiki labored, zigzagging as he followed the course of the narrow terrace, always upwards, his mouth dry and his breathing harsh. His pulse was pounding in his ears.

A bird came bursting out of a crevice, claws flicking across his cheek, and he stumbled. The great drop yawned at his feet to his left, but his outflung right hand caught a stray clump of grass. Wiki regained his balance with a frantic lurch, and ran on, reaching for the crest of the mountain.

Then he was almost at the top, with only about fifty feet to go. The track had widened marginally, but was a lot steeper from now on. Wiki pushed himself at the slope, stumbling as his burning thigh muscles protested, unnervingly aware of the seething rocks that beckoned an immense distance below—and stopped short beneath a high overhang, because a dead man dangled before him.

The corpse was just as Captain Noyes described—the savage countenance, the dull, wide-open eyes, the great beard, the black gouts of blood. The difference was that the man wasn't standing, he was *hanging.* A gray, frayed rope was tied about the chest and under the arms, and the other end was caught about the outcropping of rock, high above. The corpse hung from it. It had never been murder—it had been an *accident.*

Then Wiki heard the pump of Folger's boots. He had been outpacing the sealer, but now Folger was coming fast, up the last steep stretch, his panting mouth wide open, his cudgel raised. Wiki turned to face him, braced for battle, trapped.

And with a cracking sound a bullet flashed past Wiki's ear. It hit the dead man. The corpse swung with the impact, and crashed against the rock face—and the rope broke.

The dead man flopped down at Wiki's feet. He grabbed the corpse up, and staggered because it was so light, just clothes with a mummified body inside them. Because of the backward stagger, Folger's cudgel missed him. Wiki felt the whisk of its passage in front of his face, then saw the club raised above the sealer's head. With all his might, Wiki flung the corpse at Folger. The sealer recoiled with a hoarse scream, stumbled, took a fatal step backwards, and fell.

There were two bumps, and then silence. When Wiki, trembling violently, looked over the edge, Peter Folger was sprawled on the rocks far below. Surf covered him every now and then, and kelp lashed about his legs. Near him, the ancient corpse floated like straw.

Further out, the whaleboat was pulling madly for the schooner, with five sealers at the oars. Wiki shook his head, unable to comprehend what was happening. When he looked around again, Forsythe was trudging up the terrace.

Wiki said, "Thank God you're not dead."

Forsythe ignored this. Instead, he inspected his rifle with a worried expression. "I was aiming at Folger," he said. "But I bloody well missed."

"Well, your miss saved my life."

"Then I don't owe you any more."

"Actually," said Wiki, having just noticed something, "I think you do."

The bruise where Folger's cudgel had hit Forsythe's head spanned the tightly rolled bandanna. Because Forsythe had stumbled as he had come ashore, the blow had been a glancing one, and the cloth had deadened it further.

But Forsythe wasn't listening. Instead, he peered over the edge of the cliff, just in time to see Peter Folger's body slide into the ocean.

"You really should stop killing people," he remarked as he straightened up. "It's gettin' to be a bad habit."

When Wiki looked at the sea again the whaleboat was thrusting along the water at a frenzied rate, as if taking part in a race. "Would you mind telling me what the hell is happening?" he said. "Why did they abandon Folger, and let you escape?"

"It ain't like you to be so imperceptive. Take a look at the *Sea Gull*."

Wiki looked, just in time to see the mainsail jerk up to the top of the mast, followed rapidly by the canvas on the foremast. The schooner was making sail, while the sealers worked frantically to catch up before she got out of their reach.

"Dear God!" he exclaimed.

"Aye," said Forsythe, as laconic as ever. "Matthews was goin' to maroon the lot of us on this rock—Folger, his sealers, you and me, and all. Ain't that a thought?" Then, with a grunt of dour amusement, he said, "I wonder who would've been the last man standing."

Wiki was sure it would have been Forsythe himself, particularly since Pilson had thoughtfully armed him with his rifle. Instead of saying so, though, he thought about the expression on Matthews's icy face after the lieutenant had realized that the *Betsey*'s rookery was far to the inaccessible south. The strong impression had been that the cold, calculating mind was coming to a decision, and now Wiki knew what the decision had been.

Forsythe said, "The sealers started yelling and screaming just as I was scrambling to my feet. They didn't pay attention to me, bein' so frantic, and when Folger didn't bother to answer they give him up, and piled into the boat. And you know what," he remarked, "I think they're going to make it."

He was right. As Wiki watched, the sealers arrived at the schooner and swarmed over the side, abandoning the boat, which bobbed away on the waves.

He glimpsed struggles on the deck, followed by the very distant sound of a shot. A moment's pause, and then the schooner set the rest of her canvas. Slowly the *Sea Gull* gathered way, steering northwest to get past the rocky tail that curved off the island.

Wiki looked beyond the schooner, to the eastward horizon. Then a gust picked up the fringe of his poncho. The wind was freshening. He gripped Forsythe's arm and urged him upwards, saying, "Let's get to the top."

"What the hell for?"

"You'll see."

"What the *hell*?"

Wiki, leading the way at a breakneck pace, didn't have the breath to answer. He hurried upwards, hearing Forsythe's labored panting as he followed, accompanied by a stream of curses. Then the lieutenant ran out of enough breath to speak, and they climbed in silence. Ten minutes more, and they broke out onto the top of the island.

They were standing on a very narrow platform. Straggling grass clung to cracks in the rock, apparently holding the vantage point together. There was not enough room to stand side by side, so Forsythe stood just behind Wiki, breathing heavily into his ear. Wind whistled harshly, trying to dislodge them, but Wiki braced his legs, transfixed, knowing that Forsythe was equally riveted.

The *Sea Gull* was having a hard struggle to get to the northwest. If she could only weather the curve of jagged rocks that formed the tail of the island, she would be safely on the way to the Pacific, but the heavy swell was driving her towards the embayment.

Wiki saw her prepare to tack further off, but then, to his horror, she missed stays. "Those bloody sealers ain't no seamen," Forsythe muttered. Wiki could hear him shifting uneasily from boot to boot. "Nothin' but a hindrance."

Wiki was silent. He could imagine the bawled orders, the panic, and the clumsiness. Again, the schooner endeavored to tack, and this time managed successfully. However, once the *Sea Gull* was on this new course, she couldn't reduce canvas. The wind and sea were kicking up hard, but the only way she could weather the tail of the island's comma shape was by sailing as fast as she could.

On the *Sea Gull* thrashed, on, until the ultimate moment when she was forced to tack again, to avoid running onto the rocks. Wiki abruptly thought with horror, *This is what will happen to the Relief*, and grief stabbed for the fine minds on board the storeship. Then he realized that the premonition was not for the distant *Relief*, but for the schooner in the foaming sea below. His sailor's mind had measured distance and leeway, and worked out that the *Sea Gull* was doomed.

Just as he had foreseen, the *Sea Gull* missed stays again. She wallowed helplessly, while the wind and swell drove her backwards onto the rocks. Wiki watched her hit the reef, and heard Forsythe swear. He saw the mainmast collapse, breaking the spring stay, and saw the rigging go by the board. And the schooner turned turtle. He saw tiny, frantic figures scramble onto her upturned bottom.

Then another wave crested. When it broke, every vestige of the *Sea Gull* was gone.

"Oh Christ," said Forsythe. "*Oh Christ.*" It was a sound of primeval pain. He sighed, and then Wiki sensed him shift as he looked at the approaching brig.

"Is that what you dragged me up here for?"

"Aye. She's been shadowing us all along."

The *Swallow* was less than ten miles away. Wiki wondered how much the lookouts had seen.

"How long have you known she was trailing us?"

"Since just after we boarded the *Sea Gull*."

Forsythe was silent. Then he said, "You calculated all along that that young pup Keith would pass on the message, after Pilson and those other two bastards pinned us down on that Orange Harbor mountain?"

"Constant Keith enjoys telling a rousing yarn, and George is a very good listener. I just hoped he would repeat exactly what I said. And if he also repeated what you said to Blackmer and Pilson, that would've helped a great deal too."

"Good lord," said Forsythe, remembering.

Then, with one of his flashes of shrewdness, he deduced, "And when the cutter's men were shoved down into the launch and set adrift, you let 'em know that the *Swallow* was in the offing?"

"I gave them the best directions I could," said Wiki, without mentioning the language employed.

"Then I hope like *hell* that they made it."

So did Wiki. He didn't have a chance to say it, because Forsythe became officious, and ordered him to take off his poncho and fly it as a signal.

Wiki protested. The wind was gusting up from the Antarctic, and Forsythe's jacket would fly just as well, he reckoned. Forsythe, or so he had noticed, seemed impervious to weather.

"Don't try to gammon me you're soft because you was born under a coconut tree, because I know you wasn't," Forsythe snapped, so Wiki scrambled down the terrace until he found a stick, and handed it up, along with his poncho. Then he waited in the lee of the slope out of the bite of the wind, leaving Forsythe to rig the signal and fly it.

Ten minutes, and Wiki heard a grunt of satisfaction. The *Swallow* had seen the signal and changed course in response.

Wiki waited, waited, and then he heard Forsythe's roar of delight. The *Swallow* was towing the launch. The cutter's men were safe.

Author's Note about Background

*O*n Sunday, August 18, 1838, the six ships of the first, great United States South Seas Exploring Expedition, commanded by Lieutenant Charles Wilkes, set sail from Norfolk, Virginia, headed for the far side of the world. The goal was the Pacific, but over the next four months the fleet surveyed the Atlantic Ocean, various calls being paid at Madeira, Cape Verde Islands, the northeast coast of Brazil, and Rio de Janeiro. The final Atlantic landfall was at Patagonia, for a survey of the shifting shoals of the Rio Negro. On February 3, 1839, the squadron got underway, bound south for Orange Harbor on Hoste Island, 85 miles northwest of Cape Horn, where a double-pronged mission into the Antarctic Ocean would begin. This is the setting of the fifth Wiki Coffin mystery.

As in the previous Wiki Coffin mysteries, the story is fictional, and many of the characters are imaginary. The seventh ship of the fleet—the brig *Swallow* – did not really exist. This, like the other Wiki Coffin books, is a novel.

However, the actual events surrounding the US Exploring Expedition have been followed as much as possible. Charles Wilkes's paranoia about mutinous cabals in the expedition, particularly among the officers who had been appointed by Thomas ap Catesby Jones, is well documented. Indeed, he wrote about it at length himself, his tirade in chapter 13 being largely taken from his autobiography, as is the firing of Samuel Lee. The insanely dangerous assignments given to the *Relief* and the launch were also exactly as described.

The difference is in the climax of *The Beckoning Ice.* While the story of Forsythe's mission to the Wollaston and Hermit islands is based on real history, and the *Sea Gull* was really sent out to rescue the crew of the cutter, Lieutenant Johnson, who had commanded the *Sea Gull* in the Antarctic, was still in charge of the schooner. After Johnson picked up the launch, along with her crew, the charting job was completed, and then the schooner returned to Orange Harbor, where Passed Midshipman James Reid was given back the command. Then the *Vincennes* and *Porpoise* set sail for Valparaiso, leaving the *Sea Gull* and *Flying Fish* with instructions to wait for the storeship *Relief.* On 28 April the storeship had still not arrived, so the two schooners sailed out of Orange Harbor—straight into a vicious storm. The *Flying Fish* ran back for shelter, but the *Sea Gull* was never seen again.

The following books are recommended to readers who are interested in learning more about the background to *The Beckoning Ice*:

Darwin, Charles. Beagle *Diary.* Edited by Richard Darwin Keynes. Cambridge, UK: Cambridge University Press, 1988.

Erskine, Charles. *Twenty Years Before the Mast.* Washington, D.C.: Smithsonian Institution Press, 1985 (reprint of 1890 edition).

Gurney, Alan. *The Race to the White Continent, Voyages to the Antarctic.* New York: W. W. Norton, 2000.

Hale, Horatio. *Ethnography and Philology.* 1846. Reprint, Upper Saddle River, N.J.: Gregg Press, 1968.

Harland, John. *Seamanship in the Age of Sail.* London: Conway Maritime Press, 1984.

Philbrick, Nathaniel. *Sea of Glory, America's Voyage of Discovery, The U.S. Exploring Expedition, 1838-1842.* New York: Penguin, 2003.

Poesch, Jessie J. *Titian Ramsey Peale, 1799-1885, and his Journals of the Wilkes Expedition.* Philadelphia, Pa.: American Philosophical Society, 1961.

Reynolds, William. *The Private Journal of William Reynolds: United States Exploring Expedition, 1838-1842.* Edited by Nathaniel Philbrick and Thomas Philbrick. New York: Penguin, 2004.

Reynolds, William. *Voyage to the Southern Ocean: The Letters of Lieutenant William Reynolds from the U.S. Exploring Expedition, 1838-1842.* Edited by Anne Hoffman Cleaver and E. Jeffrey Stann. Annapolis, Md.: Naval Institute Press, 1988.

Stanton, William. *The Great United States Exploring Expedition of 1838-1842.* Berkeley, California: University of California Press, 1975.

Viola, Herman J., and Carolyn Margolis, eds. *Magnificent Voyagers: The U.S. Exploring Expedition, 1838-1842.* Washington, D.C.: Smithsonian Institution, 1985.

Wilkes, Charles. *Autobiography of Rear Admiral Charles Wilkes, U.S. Navy 1798-1877.* Edited by William James Morgan, David B. Tyler, Joye L. Leonhart, Mary F. Loughlin. Washington, D.C.: Naval History Division, 1978.

Wilkes, Charles. *Narrative of the United States Exploring Expedition.* 5 vols. 1844. Reprint, Upper Saddle River, N.J.: Gregg Press, 1970.

Glossary

Aback — a sail is aback when it blows towards the stern. To bring a ship aback is to slow it by turning the yards so some of the sails are aback, canceling out those that are still driving the ship forward, bringing the vessel to a standstill.

Afterhouse – or **afterquarters**, where the captain (and his wife and family, if there) and the officers berthed and ate.

Afterquarters – the privileged area where the captain and officers berthed and ate. Often divided into cabins and staterooms. On many merchant ships, the roof of these afterquarters formed the **poop**, or quarterdeck. On whaleships, where the decks were flush (to make **cutting in** easy) the afterquarters were below decks.

Amidships – the middle section of the ship.

Articles – short for Articles of Agreement, a contract between the captain of a ship and a crew member regarding stipulations of a voyage, signed prior to and upon termination of a voyage. A man who was illiterate would sign with a cross, or touch the pen as someone else signed it for him

Athwartships – perpendicular to the centerline of the ship, across the width of the ship.

Barometer – a device to measure the barometric pressure. A rising barometer suggests good weather whereas a falling barometer indicates increasing storms.

Beam – the breadth of a ship.

Beat — to sail into a wind that is blowing from ahead, by making successive tacks.

Before the mast – traditionally sailors lived forward of the main mast while officers berthed aft. Sailing before the mast was sailing as an able or ordinary seaman.

Belay — to make a running rope fast, or secure, by coiling it around a **belaying pin**. Also, in seamen's slang, to disregard the last order, or to stop what they were doing.

Belaying pin — the wooden pin where running rigging is coiled, generally made of ash. Occasionally used as a weapon.

Bells — the system by which ship's time is known. The ship's bell (usually by the ship's helm) is struck eight times at the change of watch — twelve midnight, 4 a.m., 8 a.m., 12 noon, 4 p.m., 8 p.m., and every half-hour between, the number of strokes indicating which half-hour, e.g., one bell at 12:30, two bells at one, three bells at 1:30, four bells at two, five bells at 2:30, six bells at three, and seven bells at 3:30.

Bend — to attach a sail to its proper **yard** or **stay**.

Berth deck — on navy ships, the deck where the seamen swing their hammocks, and have their mess tables. If the officers live on the berth deck, it is in the most privileged part, nearest to the stern.

Binnacle – a stand or enclosure of wood or nonmagnetic metal for supporting and housing a compass.

Boatswain, or bo'sun — petty officer in charge of ship's gear, such as ropes or sails, and also directly in charge of activities such as making sail or weighing anchor, according to the directions of the captain or the officer of the watch.

Bolt-rope – a line sewn into the edges of a sail.

Bowsprit – a large spar projecting forward from the stem of a ship.

Box haul — bringing a ship on the other tack by backing her headsails. Also used in making a **sternboard**, where the ship was deliberately sailed backwards.

Brace, Braces – on a square-rigged ship, lines used to rotate the yards around the mast, to allow the ship to sail at different angles to the wind.

Brail, as in "brail up" – to gather a loose-footed sail against a mast, by means of small ropes called "brails."

Breach — the breaking of a wave, and also the surfacing of a whale.

Brig – a two-masted sailing vessel square-rigged on both masts, with a spanker (a broad quadrilateral sail added to the mainmast). Also the prison on board navy ships.

Bucko — any ship's officer who was prone to enforcing orders with fists, boots, or a belaying pin.

Bulkhead — partition forming the wall of a cabin or dividing the hold into watertight compartments.

Bulwark – the side of a ship above her gunwale that provides some protection to the crew from being washed overboard by boarding seas.

Bunt – the middle part of the sail. When furling the sail, the last task is to "roll the bunt," which is hauling the furled bunt on the top of the yard and tying it with gaskets.

Buntlines – small lines used to haul up the bottom of the sail prior to furling. There are usually four to eight buntlines across the foot of the sail. When a sail is to be furled, the buntlines and the clewlines are hauled, gathering up the sail. When the sail is supported by the buntlines and clewlines, the sail is said to be hanging in its gear.

Capstan – a vertical windlass used for raising yards, anchors and any other heavy object aboard ship. The capstan bars radiated out from a central barrel like spokes of a wheel, and the seamen gripped these, and walked them around. See **windlass**.

Chains – a position on planks extending out from the hull abreast of the foremast, from where a seaman swung the lead to determine the depth of the water.

Clew – the lower corners of a square sail or the lower aft corner of a fore and aft sail.

Clewlines – lines used to haul up the lower corners of a sail prior to furling. See also, buntlines.

Close-hauled – when a ship is sailing as close to the wind as it can. A square-rigged ship could usually sail no closer than five to seven points to the wind.

Companionway — a ladder or set of stairs leading down to accommodations from the deck.

Compass Points – the compass is divided into 32 points. Each point is 11.25 degrees.

Corvette — a flush-decked warship with a single tier of guns.

Course – In navigation, the course is a direction that the ship is sailing, often also called a compass course. In sails, a course is the lowest square sail on a mast. The main course is often called the main sail and the fore course is often referred to as the fore sail.

Cresset — a metal basket holding oil, which was hung in the rigging and lit at night.

Crosstrees – two horizontal struts at the upper ends of the topmasts used to anchor the shrouds from the topgallant mast.

Dogwatch – a work shift, between 1600 and 2000 (4pm and 8pm). This period is split into two, with the first dog watch from 1600 to 1800 (4pm to 6pm) and the second dog watch from 1800 to 2000 (6pm to 8pm). Each of these watches is half the length of a standard watch. Effect of the two half watches is to shift the watch schedule daily so that the sailors do not stand the same watch routine every day.

Douse — originally to put out a fire by throwing water on it, adapted to extinguishing a lantern, and, at sea, to taking in sail.

Downhaul – A line used to pull down a sail or yard

Dunnage — light material used to pack about casks in the hold, to prevent shifting. In seamen's slang, it describes a sailor's baggage. In the latter case, also known as **duds**.

Falls — ropes used to lower boats from their davits.

Fiddleboards — folding racks, made of sticks, which prevent dishes sliding off a ship's table in bad weather.

Fife rail – a rail at the base of a mast of a sailing vessel, fitted with pins for belaying running rigging. See **Pin rail.**

Fo'c'sle, or forecastle – the accommodation space for sailors. In many ships, it was inside the bows, reached by a ladder, and in whaleships and sealers it was furnished with double-tiered bunks.

Footropes – a rope or cable secured below a yard to a provide a place for a sailor to stand while tending sail.

Fore-reaching – a form of heaving-to in which the ship continues to slowly sail forward on a close reach rather than losing ground and drifting backward.

Foremast – the forward-most mast.

Foresail – the fore course, the lowest square sail on the foremast.

Forestay – stay supporting the foremast.

Freeboard – the amount of ship's hull above the water, the distance from the waterline to the deck edge.

Futtock shrouds – shrouds running from the outer edges of a top downwards and inwards to a point on the mast or lower shrouds, and carry the load of the shrouds that rise from the edge of the top. See **Shroud**.

Gaff – the spar that supports the head (top) of a quadrilateral fore-and-aft sail, the head of the sail being laced to the gaff. Unlike a **yard**, it pivots against the mast at its lower end.

Gam – originally a term for a group of whales, then adapted to a group of whaling vessels. Became a word describing visits between whaleships.

Gaskets – gaskets are lengths of rope or fabric used to hold a stowed sail in place, on yachts commonly called sail ties.

Gunwale – also gunnel, the upper deck edge of a ship or boat.

Halyards – a line used to raise a sail or a yard. Originally from "haul yard."

Hash – a stew made from minced salt beef, crushed ship's biscuit, and onions, often made into a sea pie by having pastry on top.

Hatch – an opening in the deck of a ship. The main deck hatches are the main access for loading and discharging ship's cargo.

Hatch coaming – A raised frame around a hatch; it forms a support for the hatch cover.

Hatch cover – planks usually held together by metal strapping which form a rectangular panel. These were supported over a hatch by hatch beams. The hatch covers were then made watertight by stretching a tarpaulin across the hatch which was held tight by wedges.

Hatch wedges – wedges used to secure the hatch tarpaulin.

Hawser – a thick cable or rope used in mooring or towing a ship.

Heave down – to careen a ship by rolling it onto its side, when it is described as "hove down." Resourceful seamen could heave down a ship by hauling or sailing it onto a shallow beach, and then tipping it over by taking (breaking) out everything heavy on one side.

Heave to, hove to – in extreme weather conditions, to heave to allows the ship to keep a controlled angle to the wind and seas by balancing the effects of reduced sail and and a lashed helm, to wait out the storm. The ship drifts backwards slowly, generally under control without the need for active sail-handling.

Jackstay – an iron rod, wooden bar or wire rope running along a yard to which the sails are fastened.

Jib – a triangular staysail that sets ahead of the foremast

Jib-boom – a spar used to extend the length of a bowsprit on sailing ships.

Knightheads — timbers projecting through the deck, one each side of the stem. The bowsprit extends from between them. Originally they were carved to represent knights' heads, hence the name.

Larboard – the vessel's lefthand side when looking forward, and anything on it, such as the larboard boat. The opposite of "starboard." Replaced by "port" (which was always used for helm orders) in most ships by the 1840s, but clung to by conservative whalemen.

Latitude – a measure of the north-south position on the Earth's surface. Lines of latitude, or parallels, run east–west as circles parallel to the equator. Latitude ranges from 0° at the Equator to 90° at the poles.

Leech — the after (sternward) edge of a fore-and-aft sail or the leeward edge of a square sail. Watched by the helmsman to check direction when the vessel is on the wind.

Leeward – the direction away from the wind.

Lee rail – The deck edge on the side of the ship away from the direction from which the wind is blowing. The **weather rail** is the on the other side of the ship.

Lieutenant — the most junior of the commissioned officers, who served as the captain's deputy. When there were two or more lieutenants on board, the officers were ranked as first, second, third, and so forth, the first lieutenant being the most senior. On merchant ships these officers were known as **mates**, and were numbered off as first, second, third and fourth mates.

Logbook – the official record of the voyage, listing crew signing on and off. A record is also kept of discipline, injuries, births or deaths that occur on the vessel. A sea-log is that kept at sea, in sea-time, which is twelve hours ahead of civil time, being reckoned from noon instead of midnight. Many logkeepers changed the time and date of their logbooks to keep to shore time when in port.

Longitude – a measurement of the east-west position on the Earth's surface, an angular measurement, usually expressed in degrees. Points with the same longitude lie in lines running from the North Pole to the South Pole. By convention, one of these, the Prime Meridian, which passes through the Royal Observatory, Greenwich, England, establishes the position of zero degrees longitude. The longitude of other places is measured as an angle east or west from the Prime Meridian, ranging from 0° at the Prime Meridian to +180° eastward and −180° westward.

Luff — the windward or weather edge of a sail. Also an order to the helmsman to bring the ship up into the wind.

Main mast – the middle mast on a three masted ship.

Main sail – the main course, the lowest square sail set on the main mast.

Mainstay – stay supporting the main mast leading forward on the centerline of the ship.

Marlinspike – a polished iron or steel spike tapered to a rounded or flattened point, usually 6 to 12 inches long, used in ropework for unlaying rope for splicing, for untying knots, opening or closing shackles and a variety of related tasks.

Martingale chains — chains at the bow for securing the jibboom in a vessel with a square-rigged foremast.

Mere — a Maori club, made of hardwood, whalebone, or stone, and with a sharpened cutting edge.

Midshipman — a non-commissioned officer ranked just below a lieutenant, who could be commissioned as a lieutenant once he had served two years and had passed his examinations at the Navy Yard.

Missing stays — if a ship, when tacking, runs up into the wind, but fails to bring her bow through the eye of the wind, and falls off onto the old course, she is said to have missed stays.

Mizzen - the aftermost mast and smallest mast, the third mast on a three masted ship.

Mooring lines - lines or hawsers used to hold the ship fast against a dock.

Oakum - old rope picked apart for caulking seams.

Outhaul - a line used to haul or stretch a sail on a yard or boom.

Pannikin - a small metal pan or cup.

Passed midshipman — a junior officer who has passed his lieutenant's examinations but has not yet been promoted to lieutenant.

Pierhead jumpers - the last sailors brought aboard a ship before she sails, often purchased from boarding house masters or crimps. Often, also, a refugee from the law.

Pin rail - a strong wooden rail or bar containing holes for pins to which the running rigging is belayed fastened on sailing vessels usually along the ship's rail.

Plum duff - the sailor's treat, a pudding made of flour, raisins, and sugar (or molasses), leavened with dripping, cream of tartar, and baking soda, mixed with water, formed into balls, and steamed for several hours. It was served with more molasses.

Poenamu — New Zealand greenstone, or jade, wrought into cherished ornaments, or into prestigious greenstone clubs, called **mere pounamu**.

Pod - or **gam**, a shoal of whales.

Point of sail - a sailing vessel's course in relation to the wind direction. When the wind is astern the ship is on a "run." When the the wind is coming across the side, the ship is on a "reach." When the wind is more from aft it is a "broad reach." When the wind is on the beam, it is a "beam reach" and when the wind is forward of the beam, it is a close reach. When a ship is sailing as course as close to the wind as possible it is "beating" or "going to weather."

Poop deck - the raised afterdeck, with the **afterquarters** underneath. The helm is aft on the poop deck.

Preventer stays — strong ropes lashed to masts or spars to prevent damage in foul weather.

Purser — officer on navy ships responsible for ship's accounts and for issuing provisions and clothing.

Ratlines – small lines secured horizontally to the shrouds of a ship every 15 or 16 inches forming rungs, allowing sailors to climb aloft.

Reach – a point of sail in which the wind is blowing across the side of the ship. When the wind is more from aft it is a "broad reach." When the wind is on the beam, it is a "beam reach" and when the wind is forward of the beam, it is a close reach.

Recruits — fresh provisions and supplies, also fresh water and firewood. To "recruit" a ship was to reprovision.

Reef sail – to reduce the wind-exposure of a sail by rolling or folding it up and securing it with short ropes called "reef-points."

Roaring Forties – the name given to strong westerly winds found in the Southern Hemisphere, generally between the latitudes of 40 and 50 degrees.

Rogue wave – a large and spontaneous ocean surface wave that occurs well out to sea, and is a threat even to large ships. Rogue waves over 100 feet in height have been recorded.

Run – the point of sail in which the wind is directly behind the ship. Also another name for the **lazarette.**

Running rigging – rigging used in the raising, lowering and trimming of sails and other gear aboard ship. Running rigging is intended to move, whereas standing rigging is not.

Sailor's palm, or sailmaker's palm – a tool of leather and metal which fits on a sailor's hand so that he can use his palm to push a heavy sewing needle through tough material such as rope, leather and canvas.

Salt horse – sailor slang for salted beef.

School — a **pod**, or **gam**, of whales. Also a shoal of fish.

Schooner – a fore-and-aft rigged vessel, originally with only two masts, but with more masts as time went on. A **topsail schooner** had a square sail rigged on the foremast. Could be very fast craft, so schooners were used for surveying, blockade running, and smuggling.

Scupper – opening in the side of a ship at deck level to allow water to run off.

Sextant – an instrument used to measure the angle between any two visible objects. When used to navigate at sea, the sextant is used primarily to determine the angle between a celestial object and the horizon.

Shanty or shantey– a sailor's working song used when handing sail, pumping or using the capstan.

Shantyman – a sailor who leads the singing of the shanty.

Sheet – a line used to control a sail, secured to the sail clew.

Shipkeeper – a man left to look after a ship while the others are away.

Ship-rigged – a vessel with at least three masts which is square-rigged on all masts.

Shroud – standing rigging supporting the mast from side to side.

Skids – planks on which anything is stowed or rolled.

Skipper – technically the captain of a fishing vessel or whaler, but applied to the master of many a merchant vessel.

Slop chest – store of clothing and personal goods carried on merchant ships for issue to the crew usually as a charge against their wages.

Sounding — finding the depth of water beneath the ship's keep by heaving a **leadline**.

Spanker – a gaff rigged fore-and-aft sail set from and aft of the aftermost mast.

Speak – to communicate with a ship at sea by slowing down (hauling aback) so that a conversation could be shouted with speaking trumpets. With whalemen, this was a very formal process, involving information about last port, the captain's name, and the amount of oil taken. Then, if circumstances allowed, it was followed by a **gam**.

Spring stay — the stay that extends from one masthead to another on a fore-and-aft rigged schooner.

Square sail – a sail, usually rectangular, secured to a yard and rigged square, or perpendicular, to the mast.

Square-rigged — a ship or mast with sails set on yards rigged square, or perpendicular to the centerline of the ship.

Standing rigging – the fixed rigging that supports the masts, yards and spars of a sailing ship. Standing rigging includes stays and shrouds, and unlike running rigging is not intended to move.

Starboard – the right side of a ship, nautical term for the right.

Stays – standing rigging used to support the masts along the centerline of the ship. Each mast has backstays and forestays.

Staysail – a fore and aft sail set on a stay, either between the masts or between the bowsprit and the foremast.

Stern all – to back a boat out of trouble, by dipping oars, and pushing the blades towards the bow.

Studding sail — an extra sail set outside a square sail, secured to a **studding boom**, and used to take full advantage of a fair wind.

Sun sight – the most common sight taken in celestial navigation. A ship's officer with a sextant can determine the ship's latitude by measuring the sun's altitude (height above the horizon) at Local Apparent Noon. With an accurate chronometer, the officer can also determine latitude observing the time of Local Apparent Noon as compared to the time in Greenwich, England.

Supernumerary — a person who is entered on the muster book, and receives rations, but is not part of the crew.

Tack — to alter the course of a ship by turning the bow so that the wind is blowing against the other side of the vessel. Also the lower forward corner of a fore-and-aft sail.

Taffrail – the rail across the stern of the ship.

Taiaha — a Maori weapon, a long wooden staff that was tapered at one end like a spear, and fashioned into a club at the other end, and was wielded two-handed, like a quarterstaff.

Tons, or tonnage — a flexible kind of measurement used to indicate the cargo capacity of a vessel. It has nothing to do with displacement or weight.

Top – a platform on each mast at the upper end of the lower mast section whose main purpose is to anchor the shrouds of the topmast that extends above it. The top is larger and lower on the masts but performs the same function as the cross trees.

Topgallant sails, the sails set above the topsails.

Top-hamper, or hamper – slang for the sails, masts and rigging of a ship. Can also refer to only the light upper sails and rigging.

Topsail – the sail above the course. After the 1850s most topsails were split into upper and lower topsails to make sail-handing easier. Windjammers tended to have upper and lower topsails.

Touch the pen — an illiterate sailor would sign the ship's **articles** by making a cross or by touching the pen as the shipping officer wrote his name for him.

Watches – regular periods of work duty aboard a ship. The watches kept on sailing ships usually consisted of 5 four-hour periods and 2 two-hour periods. On many merchant ships the watches were divided into the captain's and the mate's watch or starboard and port watches. The captain did not stand a watch so the Second Mate stood the watch in his stead. By tradition, the captain's watch stood the first watch on the sailing of the ship from its home port, while the mate's watch took the first watch on sailing on the return voyage. On whaleships, the watches were divided between the two, three, or four officers. The captain seldom commanded a watch, so he slept all night, unless the ship was in dangerous waters.

Weather Deck — the open deck.

Weather rail – on the side of the ship in the direction from which the wind is blowing. The lee rail is the on the other side of the ship.

Whaleboat — an open boat about twenty-five feet long, designed for chasing whales, pointed at both ends, with a six-man crew. The boatheader, or officer in charge of the boat, steers from the stern with a long steering oar, which he wields from a standing position.

Windward – the direction from which the wind is blowing.

Windbound – ship that is becalmed, incapable of moving due to lack of wind. Or a ship trapped in a reefbound lagoon by a wind blowing directly onshore.

Windlass — a mechanism for bringing up the anchor chain. Unlike the **capstan**, it is mounted horizontally. It is operated by heaving on hand brakes or handles hooked to ratchets on the windlass barrel.

Wing and wing — the sail-set of a two-masted schooner with the wind dead astern. The mainsail is broad on one side, and the foresail broad on the other.

288

Yard – a spar rigged horizontally, "square" to a ship's mast, used to set a square sail.

Yard Arm – the extreme outer end of the a yard.

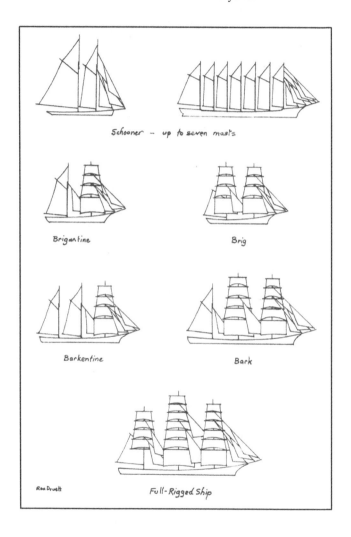

Schooner – up to seven masts

Brigantine

Brig

Barkentine

Bark

Ron Druett

Full-Rigged Ship

More great reading from Old Salt Press

**True-life castaway drama
from the author of *Island of the Lost***

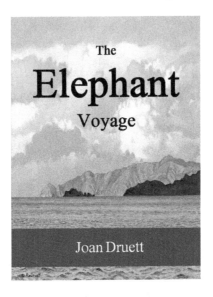

In the heady climate of the nineteenth century goldrushes, "going to see the elephant" was a saying that described an exciting, often dangerous, and usually profitless adventure. In the spirit of the bestselling *Island of the Lost*, the story is told of the "elephant voyage" of the crew of the Connecticut schooner *Sarah W. Hunt*. When their boats are blown out to sea, off one of the most icy and hostile islands in the sub-Antarctic ocean, twelve men are abandoned by their skipper. Six survive, to be carried to New Zealand, where the inquiry and courtcase that follow become an international controversy. ISBN 978-0-9922588-4-9

Thrilling yarn from the last days of the square-riggers

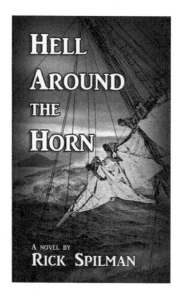

In 1905, a young ship's captain and his family set sail on the windjammer, Lady Rebecca, from Cardiff, Wales with a cargo of coal bound for Chile, by way of Cape Horn. Before they reach the Southern Ocean, the cargo catches fire, the mate threatens mutiny and one of the crew may be going mad. The greatest challenge, however, will prove to be surviving the vicious westerly winds and mountainous seas of the worst Cape Horn winter in memory. Told from the perspective of the Captain, his wife, a first year apprentice and an American sailor before the mast, *Hell Around the Horn* is a story of survival and the human spirit in the last days of the great age of sail. ISBN 978-0-9882360-1-1

Another gripping saga from the author of the Fighting Sail series

Newly appointed to the local revenue cutter, Commander Griffin is determined to make his mark, and defeat a major gang of smugglers. But the country is still at war with France and it is an unequal struggle; can he depend on support from the local community, or are they yet another enemy for him to fight? With dramatic action on land and at sea, *Turn a Blind Eye* exposes the private war against the treasury with gripping fact and fascinating detail. ISBN: 978-0-9882360-3-5

www.oldsaltpress.com

Old Salt Press is an independent press catering to those who love books about ships and the sea. We are an association of writers working together to produce the very best of nautical and maritime fiction and non-fiction. We invite you to join us as we go down to the sea in books.

Joan Druett is a maritime historian who is an expert on whaling history and women at sea, and who is also the author of the bestseller *Island of the Lost*. She lives in New Zealand. Her website is *www.joan.druett.gen.nz*

CPSIA information can be obtained at www.ICGtesting.com
Printed in the USA
LVOW01s0113240714

395707LV00019B/433/P